I0678307

Meet Me at The Melbourne

The Melbourne Community Cafe, Volume 1

Gemma Frances

Published by Gemma Frances, 2024.

Meet Me at The Melbourne

2nd Edition

Copyright © Gemma Frances, 2024

ISBN: 978-1-7635781-1-1 (paperback)

ISBN: 978-1-7635781-0-4 (e-book)

www.gemmafrances.com[1]

@gemma_frances

Cover design by Spencer J

Dedication:

For my children; my proudest achievements

♥ 1 ♥

The international airport terminal loomed behind them heralding the end of their time together, and the glare of the drop-off zone's harassed parking attendant lent a sense of urgency to the farewell they could do without. Winter rain slashed across the windscreen, lending greater intimacy to a moment that in any other circumstances would have been eagerly embraced by the young couple.

'Stay with me here in Australia,' James implored, his eyes beseeching as he reached across the car's gearstick to grip Eve's knee, the warmth of his hand penetrating through her jeans. 'Please? Stay...'

Eve's resolve wavered as she risked one final appeal. 'Come with me? It's not too late. I'm sure you could get a seat on my plane, and-'

But it was no use. James slowly shook his head. 'We both know I can't.'

Eve felt her heart shatter, and as she looked at James one last time, she was certain it could never be whole again. Those striking grey eyes, that tawny hair, the mouth that had kissed her so many times... She reached out and brushed his cheek with her palm, the hint of stubble beneath her fingers drawing her mind back to the shared intimacy of the night before – a night that marked the end of their years together. She wanted to imprint him on her mind forever. The memories they'd shared would be her only comfort from now on.

Her head pounded with the pressure of unshed tears as she leant across the handbrake to press her lips against his one last time, forehead to forehead. 'I love you, James,' she said, her voice catching in her throat.

'I love you too,' he murmured against her mouth.

With that, Eve dashed from the car as fast as she could to the loos of Melbourne airport, the accumulating puddles and her cumbersome suitcase containing all her worldly goods the only things to impede her momentum. Slamming herself into a cubicle, she promptly burst into tears. She hadn't stopped to look behind her. If she had, she would have heard James whisper into the silence she'd left behind: 'I always will,' before bending over his steering wheel where he sobbed unselfconsciously into the palm of his hands, rousing not an ounce of sympathy from the indignant parking attendant who waved him on his way.

If Eve hadn't have left when she did, she would never have been able to go at all, and somewhere deep inside she felt certain she was doing the right thing for both of them – and James knew it too, otherwise he couldn't have resisted the urge to chase after her.

There was a tentative knock upon the cubicle door. 'You alright in there, darl?' someone asked, as much from curiosity as concern.

'I'm fine,' Eve lied. But it was no use, and she slid onto the floor and cried until she really did have to pull herself together and get going, otherwise she'd miss her flight back home to England.

♥

MEET ME AT THE MELBOURNE

Eve brushed a stray tear from her cheek as she glanced absentmindedly from the aeroplane window across the dawn-streaked landscape of her home, already dotted here and there with the living room lights of Newcastle-upon-Tyne's earliest risers. If she was just visiting, this was usually the highlight of her arduous journey from Australia - tracing the familiar path of the River Tyne as it met the North Sea between the North and South Shields' piers, searching out landmarks such as the Tyne Bridge and St. Mary's Lighthouse, straining to see her parents' own coastal street as the plane banked sharply from land to sea and back again before lining up to make its landing.

But this time was different. Her excitement was engulfed by grief and loss, anxiety and fear, and the knowledge she would never again call Australia home. She'd worked hard as a nurse in a busy city hospital, made some amazing friends she would miss keenly, and rented a tiny apartment that had eventually endeared itself with its quirks and imperfections. She'd also fallen deeply in love with a man that no other could ever measure up to, but she had lost him, and at thirty years of age Eve now faced the prospect of a lonely, uncertain future of starting over again in a country she had yet to rediscover.

The plane glided low to land, skimming the fields leading up to the runway before making a skilled landing, braking hard, then turning sharply towards the terminal. She was glad of her jumper and scarf when she exited the airport into the biting morning air, even if she was by now bedraggled by the thirty-hour journey and in desperate need of a shower. She'd replayed her goodbye to James over and over in her mind during the flight and could scarcely believe it had been more than a day ago already – time and almost ten and a half thousand miles of distance pulling him further and further out of reach.

'Got the post-holiday blues, have yi, pet?' empathised the rather nosy taxi driver she'd hailed outside the airport. He had a thick Geordie accent, greying orange hair and prying eyes. He didn't bother to await a response. 'Been somewhere nice, have yi? Bet it was warmer than it's been here. Call this summer?' He gestured out of the window where they whizzed past paddocks grazed by a weak early morning sun. 'Pah!'

Eve wondered how British people would fill their time without the weather to complain about, when to her there was such beauty to be encountered in all weathers and in every season. The grass and trees were of a lush and vibrant green she'd rarely encountered in Australia, and the sky held the promise of a bright and cheery day. 'Australia,' she answered reluctantly. 'I've been living over there.'

As the taxi driver covered the familiar roads at a hair-raising pace, she recalled a trip home several years ago when she'd brought James to visit her family for the very first time. She'd been surprised to discover just how much he'd enjoyed the drive home from the airport; blooming meadows dotted with old cottages of stone, quaint villages and country pubs with names like The King's Head and The Rose and Crown. They'd shared a giggle at The Hairy Watermelon and The Ploughman's Trousers.

As they'd neared her parents' house, he had not expected to encounter such a pretty coastline in a country that was definitely not renowned for its beaches. He'd enjoyed it so much that one of the first things they did together was walk the ragged length of sand dunes at Seaton Sluice, stopping for tea and a wedge of Victoria sponge in a charming tearoom overlooking a small harbour dotted with colourful old sail boats. When her dad had pulled into the paved driveway of their nineteen-thirties semi they were not expecting James to find the unremarkable, tiny house so endearing. It was thrilling for her to see her home anew through his eyes and she'd been taken aback by how much she'd wanted it to please him.

'Australia!' The taxi driver whistled. 'By, that must've been a long flight. I've always wanted to gan te Australia me'sel – I've got relatives awa there, yi see. The Buchannan's – have you heard of them? Hail from Scotland, they do,' he added, with a hint of pride at this added layer of diversity to his heritage.

'No, sorry.' Eve suppressed an eye roll.

'Wife won't go though. She's an arachnophobe – thinks a huntsman spider will pick her up and run off with her. Sometimes I'm not sure I'd mind if it did. Still, I'd like to get there one day. Visiting family now are yi?'

'No, I've come back home for good.' Eve's voice was heavy with the implications of that seemingly innocuous declaration.

'You've moved back *here?*' The driver was aghast. 'What on earth for?'

Eve's cheeks flushed and her eyes brimmed. She was unable to speak for the lump in her throat.

'I see...' He looked at her astutely from his rearview mirror. 'He must've been a fool.' He otherwise couldn't think of a good enough reason to justify this young woman's return to miserable old Blighty. 'Cheer up, pet. A bonny lass like you won't be on the shelf for long, you mark my words.'

♥

Her parents were on the doorstep waving ecstatically as soon as the taxi pulled into view. They'd gotten up early specially, even though Eve had brushed off the offer of a lift to save them the trouble of getting out of bed at such an unearthly hour on a weekend morning. Despite the circumstances she couldn't wait to see them, and she wasn't going to spoil their excitement when she knew they were so pleased to have her home again.

'Well, look at you all dressed for Christmas,' her dad, Robert, joked as he smothered her into a giant bear hug. 'Thought it was always hot Down Under.'

Contrary to Eve, he was dressed with the typical optimism of a Brit in summer - in shorts, a polo shirt, and striped espadrilles, despite the threatening drizzle. She noticed he'd acquired an extra smattering of grey amongst his thick brown hair than the last time she'd seen him and felt a stab of guilt for her prolonged absence.

'Hello, bairn,' said Carol, her mam, whose pale blue eyes creased warmly at the corners as she smiled. No matter how old she got, Eve would always be her 'bairn.' 'How was your flight?'

'Oh, you know – long - but otherwise fine.'

'Did you get much sleep?'

'Nah.' She'd been too distraught to sleep.

'I love your hair,' Carol piped into the awkward silence. 'You suit it dark, and it's starting to get some length now. You look gorgeous, even if you are dressed for four-foot of snow - James was mad to let you go.' As she enveloped her daughter into a perfumed hug, complete with the comforting notes of vanilla and rose, Eve blinked away tears.

'You must be exhausted.' Robert wisely changed the subject. 'Come on, I'll take your suitcase up for you, and your mam will put the kettle on.' He dragged her bulging suitcase along the driveway, practically giving himself a hernia as he tried to lift it up the steps and over the threshold. 'Geez, what've you got in here, a kangaroo?'

'Just what remains of the last few years of my life, Dad.' Eve was unable to prevent the edge to her tone, and Carol shot him a warning look.

He threw a casual, 'Is that the kettle I hear?' over his shoulder as he disappeared up the stairs and the two women shared a wry smile.

Eve breathed in the familiar smell of home, finding comfort that little had changed since her last visit. She fished from her luggage offerings of Aussie favourites such as Tim Tam biscuits, Moccona coffee, and billy tea, and handed them to her mam to put away. Then she settled onto the battered old chesterfield with a steaming cup of tea and a selection of her favourite biscuits sitting untouched beside her. She was scrolling through her old posts – pictures of her and James' life together – when her phone rang. It was Emily, her closest friend. They'd grown up together, and Eve's heart lifted to hear her voice.

'Welcome back!' said Emily. 'What took you so long? You didn't need to go traipsing the globe to look for a nice man when there's plenty right here on our doorstep.'

'Huh.' Eve recalled several of her old boyfriends and the fact Newcastle was usually crawling with men out for a good time on their stag dos, and heartily disagreed. If it wasn't for one in particular, she'd never have gone travelling to begin with.

'Except for Whiny Wayne, of course,' Emily continued, with that uncanny knack old friends have of knowing what the other is thinking.

Eve shivered involuntarily. 'Yes, but let's not go there.' Unlike Emily, who had married very happily the previous year, Eve didn't have the best track record insofar as relationships were concerned – but James was different. Anyone could see how happy he'd made her.

'Anyway, enough of all that, I'm just glad you've returned to us at last. So, how are you feeling? Exhausted? Heartbroken?'

Eve sighed.

'For what it's worth, I think you've done the right thing.' Emily of all people understood why she'd made the decision she had. 'Have you heard from James at all since you came back?'

That's what Eve had been hoping for when she'd picked up her phone but there was nothing from him, and the sense of finality made her despondent. She realised a part of her still longed for him to pursue her, not to simply have let her go.

'I'm guessing that's a no. But it's a good thing - you said you weren't gonna text otherwise it'd only make your separation even harder. He's just sticking to what you agreed.'

'I know, but it's as if he's moved on already when I haven't even begun to.'

'Have you contacted him?'

'Of course not.'

'Well then he's probably crying into his can of Fosters right now thinking the exact same thing about you... Enough moping, what are you doing tomorrow?'

'Sleeping, obviously.'

'No, you're not - you're coming to Tynemouth to have lunch with me, and I won't take no for an answer. I have the day off and a little treat planned. You can mope and bore me silly about your lost love the entire time if you like, but I must warn you - I have some rather important news of my own...'

Eve was suitably intrigued, but Emily hung up before she had a chance to pry. Perhaps she was pregnant? Whilst she'd be overjoyed if that was the case, she had to suppress a pang of envy that her friends' lives all seemed to have a sense of direction that hers was currently lacking. Regardless she felt better for the call – the prospect of an afternoon with Emily was something to look forward to, and it might prove to be just the tonic.

♥ 2 ♥

When Eve had hung up, on Carol's nod Robert shifted uncomfortably in his armchair before making himself scarce, the prospect of any exposure to any female histrionics enough to banish him to his greenhouse for the rest of the morning.

'So, how are you feeling?' Carol ventured. She didn't want to upset Eve, but she didn't want them to ignore the elephant in the room either.

Eve recalled a night with James when it became apparent that he absolutely did not share her desire for them to live in the UK. They were cosied up on the couch on one of the rare occasions their shift schedules coincided, and after indulging in a takeaway and a bottle of wine they were watching a movie of James' choosing, from which Eve's concentration couldn't help but waver in favour of scrolling through her phone.

'Do you know that in the UK kids are entitled to up to thirty free hours a week of childcare from three years of age?' she'd remarked casually, in an opportunistic lull between special effects that seemed to be of more import than the storyline. 'Isn't that great for working parents?'

'Mmhmm.'

'And according to Google,' she'd continued, 'it looks as though your physiotherapy qualification is transferrable too. You could be up and running over there in no time - it might even be the perfect opportunity for you to move into sports physio instead of hospital physio like you'd hoped.'

'Is it?'

'Yes! And look at this house I found - it'd be an ideal first home together. It's quite small by Australian standards but it's actually pretty generous for the UK...'

Eve waved her phone enthusiastically under James' nose, but his gaze barely flickered from the TV screen.

'Call that a garden? Nature strip, more like.'

Eve fought back a wave of irritation. 'See? It's only got three bedrooms but they're all a good size, and housing is so much more affordable over there compared to what it is here. Look - it's walking distance to that beach you love, and close to my parents' place too, but not *too* close.'

James exhaled. 'Yep.'

'Don't look then.' Eve was hurt.

James dragged his gaze from the TV and turned to look at her. Wordlessly he took her phone and gave a cursory glance at the property's images. 'Nice,' he said, with a distinct lack of enthusiasm.

Her frustration bubbled over. 'You're the one who's been talking about putting down roots - *you* suggested we consider buying a house together! And you've been moaning about your job for ages.'

The tension between them was palpable. *'Here.'* James gestured to the general air about him, and Eve's eyes were drawn to the vista of identikit apartment blocks outside their apartment window. 'In Melbourne. I don't remember saying anything to you about moving overseas.'

'Well,' Eve stumbled, 'that's how I interpreted it. I'm always talking about moving back home, and you never said we couldn't at least think about it.'

'When did I say I'd think about moving to England?'

'When we first got together.'

He rolled his eyes. 'I have thought about it, and it's just not something I want to do.'

'But how do you know if you won't even try? Can't we go over there and see what it's like?'

'I've been. *Three* times.'

'Yes, for a handful of weeks. I'm talking about staying for a couple of years - then you could make an informed decision either way instead of just writing it off like this.'

In Eve's opinion, their condensed visits to the UK to stay with her parents weren't enough for James to base his decision on, and she couldn't get her head around his stubborn refusal to give it a go. How could they seriously consider putting down roots in Melbourne when his own family lived interstate, a two-hour flight away? Who would help with their children when they finally got around to having them? It made logical sense that they should go to the UK where housing, health and childcare were more affordable, they could both earn a good living in their respective careers, and Eve's parents who were semi-retired would be on hand and eager to help them out as much as possible.

But James wouldn't budge. 'It wouldn't change my mind. You're the one who chose to leave home and come out here, Eve. I've never chosen to travel or live overseas, and if I know myself well enough I never will. My home is here, and I love it.' As much as he enjoyed visiting the UK, the prospect of endless bleak winters, mindless football banter (soccer had nothing on the AFL) and stodgy national dishes were enough to put him off the idea of ever making it his permanent habitat.

'I didn't *choose* to live here though, James, did I?' Eve's voice rose a couple of notches. 'I can't help that I met and fell for you. I stayed in Australia far longer than I'd ever intended so we could be together because I thought that's what we both wanted. That's what love does - it makes you consider doing things for the sake of another person that you might not have been prepared to do otherwise.'

The pair eyed one another testily across the couch, their faces flushed red and the distance between them as uncomfortable as the conversation they were having. James' eyes were a turbulent shade of grey, and Eve's temper flared. She felt duped. She'd always got the impression that when it came to the crunch, James' feelings for her were strong enough that he would be prepared to at least give life in the UK a good try, but this was the first time she'd got the sense that just might not happen *ever.*

She'd given years of her life to be with him, years in which she'd battled homesickness and worked a job that had led her to burnout - all for the sake of their relationship because she'd thought what they shared was worth it. But clearly James didn't feel the same way otherwise he'd be prepared to do the same thing for her.

'Can't you think a little more about it - for us?'

But James wasn't listening. His focus had already returned to the TV, where he seemed determined to keep it.

For the very first time it dawned on Eve that she needed to figure out what she really wanted for her future, and fast. Should she fully commit to a life in Australia with James and all that entailed - raising a family thousands of miles from her home with little support in a situation that was certain to come with childcare and financial challenges - or return home to England where she'd always felt she belonged? It was a question that would gnaw at her mind and her sense of security more and more over the coming weeks.

'So, what do you think you'll do now?' Carol prodded, bringing Eve abruptly back to the present.

'Oh, I don't know... Quit nursing, open up a coffee shop, and swear off relationships for good, I think.' It didn't sound like such a bad idea - in fact, when things with her nursing job had been at their worst, she'd often thought of opening a coffee shop where she'd still be able to pursue her love of people, but in a far less emotive setting and without it being to the detriment of her own wellbeing. But her mind was too foggy and distracted to focus on that now, not when her separation from James was still so intense.

'How about you go up and get some rest after your long flight?' said Carol. 'Whilst we're thrilled to have you home again, we'll only ever be happy if you are - whether that turns out to be here or in Australia.'

♥

The hot water soothed Eve's aching muscles and racing thoughts. She wrapped her hair up in a towel and padded to her room. Her bedroom had always been a time-capsule of her teenage years - an excess of pink, glow-in-the-dark stars, and posters of her favourite popstars and celebrities - even an old lava lamp. She gasped when she entered and instead discovered instead a more suitable haven awaiting her.

There was a papered wall of tiny, trailing flowers, and the tired old carpet had finally been pulled up to reveal the underlying floorboards that had been richly stained, adding warmth to the large room, and pulling it all in cosily together. The cupboard slotting into the bay window had been repainted and topped with scatter cushions forming a cosy seat overlooking the garden where she could just imagine settling down with a steaming cup of tea and a good book. But best of all was that her old single bed that had reluctantly served her until adulthood had been replaced with a brand-new queen, plush with pin-tuck bedding, and the prospect of sinking her exhausted body into it was divine. She was extremely touched.

On the bedside table beside the lamp, she noticed a card addressed to '*The Bairn*' in her mam's near-illegible handwriting. Inside it said:

We are so very happy to have you home again. You can thank us for the room when you wake up - enjoy it for as long as you need. Love Mam and Dad x

'Thank you!' Eve yelled, before pulling off her crumpled clothing and climbing blissfully under the covers, enjoying the novelty of being able to starfish her body across the mattress after so many hours of sitting propped upright between her fellow passengers. She soon fell into a deep and dreamless sleep that brought with it a welcome reprieve from her constant thoughts of James.

♥

15

The next day, Eve awoke feeling groggy from jetlag and disorientated by her unfamiliar new surroundings. She'd automatically reached out to James upon waking before remembering all too late that he wasn't there. She heard her parents leave for work and took her sleeplessness as an opportunity to try out her new window-seat and watch the sun rise over the back garden. The horizon was tinted with thin streaks of peach casting all it encompassed in a buttermilk glow. She had forgotten how gentle the morning music of British birds was in comparison to that of their squawky Australian counterparts who'd been a lot tougher on the ears.

Before heading downstairs, she reflexively checked her phone, and to her surprise there was a message that read, *I know we agreed not to contact each other but I just wanted to be sure you arrived home safely. James.* Her heart momentarily lifted then sank at the brusque nature of the message. She responded with an equally inadequate, *I'm here safe and well thanks. Eve.* No kisses, no endearments, nothing but the maintenance of a polite distance that was wholly unfamiliar between them.

It felt alien to be exchanging such stilted communication with the same man who less than two days ago she'd been exchanging kisses passionate with grief and last-minute pleas for them to reconsider their situation so they could stay together. Even though she'd longed to go home for so long and felt certain she was doing the right thing, she hadn't anticipated how fraught and painful their parting would be or that it would make her question her resolve quite so strongly.

As the morning wore on, she grew restless. After so many hours spent travelling and sleeping her body was itching for activity, and she was relieved to locate her bike in its usual spot in the garage and hoped it didn't require any maintenance she wouldn't know how to provide. Her dad, and at one time her older brother Daniel who'd passed away when she was in her teens, had been the ones to keep an eye on those sorts of things for her.

She dressed casually in faded jeans and a vest, throwing on a pretty floral shirt for extra warmth. She tied her shoulder-length dark hair into a high ponytail before adding a slick of mascara to hazel eyes that were framed by a heavy blunt fringe, and a clear gloss to emphasize the full lips James had considered one of her most appealing features. She was careful to remember to take a spare set of house keys from the rack by the front door.

Taking the coastal route from Monkseaton to Tynemouth she cycled at the limit of her endurance. She barely took in the view; she was so focused on pushing her body out of its jet-lagged fog. The harder she rode the more her legs ached and the less she thought of James. It was exhilarating to feel the cool air rushing towards her face as she rode faster and faster, as refreshing as a splash of cold water.

On her approach into Tynemouth she rode at a more sedate pace, the natural beauty of the coastline proving an absorbing distraction. She soon found some sturdy iron railings to tie her bike to, before heading back up the steep hill into the picturesque little village above, perched on the clifftop to the backdrop of the old priory ruins. Today the priory's stone shone the colour of honey in the generous sunshine. Two rows of tall, handsome terraces formed Front Street, the main street of the village, separated in the middle by a busy parking strip that often struggled to accommodate the multitude of visitors.

There was a plethora of trendy bars, cafés, and restaurants to choose from; many seemed to have sprung up in her absence as the coffee culture that was already well established elsewhere had belatedly gripped the nation, insidiously replacing the age-old British penchant for afternoon tea and cake. She recalled how her social life in Melbourne had often revolved around meeting friends for late breakfasts of smashed avo' on toast, the bright orange yolk of perfectly poached eggs dripping in stark contrast to the green chunks of avocado. Breakfasts were complimented with either a fresh juice or smoothie, or an unbeatable Melbourne coffee - its froth cheerily emblazoned with an image of a heart or a leaf, a flower, or a smile.

Eve had tried so hard to avoid taking a job in nursing when she'd first arrived in Australia. She'd wanted to enjoy her time as a backpacker and had been looking for a role with minimum responsibility that made just enough money to support her travels and enable her to enjoy herself. She'd hoped to find work in one of the hundreds of coffee shops in Melbourne - it was the social aspect that had particularly appealed to her, the opportunity to meet and interact with lots of different people. But she'd underestimated how competitive the industry was, how sought after experienced 'baristas' were, and just how difficult it was to create a great cup of coffee of which the Melburnians were fiercely proud.

To be offered a job you would first have to pass a trial to prove your worth - like an acting audition but for baristas.

After handing out dozens of CVs from which she received no response, she'd paid for a barista course in the forlorn hope it might give her an upper hand amongst the competition. It didn't, and no trials were ever offered to her. It didn't help that despite the hours of training she was the only one in the group who hadn't been able to make a single drinkable cup of coffee. In the end she'd had no option but to either return to nursing or go home when her cash ran out. As it turned out, nursing was what enabled her to stay in Australia and provided her with a visa that allowed her to be with James. If she hadn't started working on the ward where he practiced as a physiotherapist, they'd never have met at all.

'Eve. Eve!'

She was initially startled to hear her name being called, but instantly recognised the voice and began searching for its owner. She could see a tanned hand waving in the distance, and sure enough, when the elderly couple in front turned off into a gift shop, Emily was revealed, grinning and waving at her. Eve picked up her pace, a huge smile on her face, and the two women met in a clash of handbags and long limbs that ended in a big hug.

'Steady on,' laughed her friend, patting her taut stomach. 'My baby might only be the size of a nectarine, but I still don't want it to get flattened.'

'Oh Emily, what wonderful news!' Eve felt she as though might burst with pride for her dear friend.

'You will be Aunt Evie of course. Now come along, I've got us a table booked. I want you to tell me all about your travels and your romantic trysts with hunky, long-haired surfer dudes with names like Brett and Trent. If you don't have any, you'd better make them up!' She tucked her arm into Eve's and led her to the new café across the road.

'Seriously,' said Eve, 'you've been watching way too much Home and Away.'

♥ 3 ♥

The Glass Slipper was a spectacle of chandeliers, distressed wooden furniture paired with transparent chairs, twisted branches knotted with ivy and fairy lights, and vintage wallpaper framed with dozens of monochrome portraits. Eve loved it – it was excessive and decadent. There were mothers and daughters sharing pots of tea and slices of cake, groups of women gossiping over glasses of sparkling wine, and grandmothers eating fluffy scones thick with jam and cream. A pianist played in the background.

Eve licked her lips in anticipation. 'Emily, this is perfect!' They were shown briskly to their table by a pouting young waitress.

'I know. *I* styled it - excess is all in this year.' Emily managed a flourishing interior design business. 'And for my pains I've been granted a lifetime of free treats, so I've ordered us the afternoon tea. All I'm craving these days is cake, but I suppose I'll just have to skip the champagne and celebrate the long-awaited return of my best friend with an Earl Grey instead.'

'What's it like being Mrs. Horton?' Eve asked. 'I haven't seen you since the wedding. And how many weeks pregnant are you now? When are you due? You look fantastic by the way - your hair is amazing.'

She admired the elfin platinum crop Emily was sporting. It made her high cheekbones and cobalt eyes pop.

'Well, being Mrs. Horton is pretty great, except for when I can't prise Mr. Horton from his console. I'm thirteen weeks gone, and the baby is due on Boxing Day. I hope she (I'm convinced she's a she) doesn't come early because I'd hate to miss out on my Christmas dinner - I doubt the hospital version will be up to scratch. But I don't want to talk about me - I want to hear all about your trip. Expedition, rather.'

'Oh,' Eve dismissed, 'living and working in Australia isn't so different to living or working here, except that in summer it's hotter and you can have more picnics. I nursed shifts just like I did here. It really wasn't as exciting as it seems.' There was an element of irritability to her tone - most of her UK friends incorrectly assumed she'd been living a life of idol luxury for the past few years. She blamed TV.

'You mean you didn't spend all your time lounging in a hammock by the beach, drinking Fosters and eating barbecued kangaroo steaks whilst wearing a corked hat and singing Waltzing Matilda?'

'Far from it.' Eve sighed. They'd lived miles away from the nearest beach.

'If I'm not mistaken, I think you might be missing a certain someone - is that why you're so tetchy today?'

Eve was saved from answering by the arrival of three tiers of pure, indulgent yumminess, though her appetite had suddenly taken a bit of a nosedive which was fine because Emily couldn't get enough of the cherry and coconut scones and chewy honey flapjack on offer. Eve fingered an egg and watercress sandwich, somewhat awed by her friend's newfound appetite.

'Evie...?'

'Ok, ok, I give in. I miss James like crazy and wonder if I've made the biggest mistake of my life by leaving him.

I'm thirty, unmarried and childless, with the beginnings of crow's feet. I have no job or prospects to speak of and still live with my parents.'

'What a catch!' Emily grinned into her crestfallen face. 'Don't worry, my brother still fancies you. And you flitting off to the other side of the world has only made the torch he's been carrying for you all these years shine brighter, even if you are a wrinkled, jobless bore. Said he's looking forward to seeing you some time soon, actually...'

Eve rolled her eyes at Emily's caustic humour, realising at the same time how much she'd strangely missed it. 'Thom? Nah, I can't look at your little brother like that – makes me feel like a perve. I still remember that time he wet the bed when you had a sleepover for your fourteenth birthday.' Eve grimaced. 'And *my* torch is still burning for James.'

'You'll have to extinguish that flame if you're to have any chance of happiness back here - either that or get on the first flight back to Australia and tell James you got it all wrong.'

If only it was so straightforward. That had been the trouble from the start - it was always just so complicated. 'How can it be that the powers above make everything converge to bring you to The One, only to throw so many obstacles in your path that you have to let him go?'

'Maybe the powers above have more in store to surprise you with. Perhaps James wasn't The One after all, and the real One is about to make himself known to you.'

Eve guffawed, tea spilling over onto her saucer in a most unladylike fashion. Emily was the second person to say something along those lines to her since she'd come home.

'Look, instead of pointing out all the things you haven't got going for you, let's look at the things you have. Or, if we can't think of any,' Emily grinned, 'we'll keep you so busy you don't have time to think about James, and before you know it, the pain will have passed, and you'll be ready to move on and live happily ever after with my brother instead. Then we really will be sisters.'

She sat back smugly, arms folded across her non-existent baby bump. They'd finished their lunch and were sharing a pot of Earl Grey, the pot's heat maintained by a sparkly tea cosy. Tendrils of perfumed steam curled the air. The charm of The Glass Slipper was as much in its attention to detail as it was in its delicious fare.

Sitting opposite a glowing and contented Emily, Eve realised she hadn't thought enough about what life would entail beyond her flight home from Australia, nor anticipated that in leaving James she'd end up left so far behind her peers. Could he be feeling the same way, she wondered? But men were different she supposed - less driven by their biological clock. If she'd stayed in Melbourne, married James, and they'd bought a house together perhaps she too would be cradling a bump right now, but at what cost? She was certain they each would have sacrificed as much as they'd gained, and she would have lived her life with a constant sense of dissatisfaction that she wasn't living it in the right place. Resentment would have crept in, insidious in its eventual destruction of all that was precious to them both. It was far better to have made a clean break - an expression that in no way did justice to the turmoil associated with the lived experience of it. It wasn't that she didn't want all those things - she did, but only in the right circumstances and with the right person to share it all with.

So, what should she do now? She was good at supporting people, but for the sake of her mental health she needed to find a different way of going about it than nursing - the oncology aspect triggered too many emotions associated with the loss of her brother. Nothing jumped out at her enough to make her want to go back to university and re-train as something else. All she knew for certain was that she didn't want to diminish the contribution she could make to the local community she lived in - helping others had always been very important to her.

'When I was in Melbourne,' she ventured, 'I did have this crazy idea of something I'd love to do - you know, if money was no object, and life was like a fairytale.' Eve fiddled self-consciously with her napkin, and Emily tried to look nonchalant lest she decided not to tell her what she had in mind. 'I'd like to open a café here in Newcastle - somewhere trendy and inexpensive with a good mix of students, professionals, and families. It would be an Australian-style café, subtle though – not a cork hat in sight. It'd have a Melbourne-themed menu, breakfasts mainly, and offer a real sense of community spirit.' She blushed. 'That's how I see it anyway.'

It would be based on the cafés she'd frequented in Melbourne - they had a massive coffee culture over there and she'd often found herself wondering what it would be like not just to work in one but to open her very own. It seemed like it would offer her just the sort of balance she was looking for, something she hadn't yet managed to find in nursing.

'But you can't offer community spirit, can you?' Emily challenged. 'It's not something you can simply buy from a menu.' She had as much an eye for potential as she did for pitfalls. 'People have to choose to invest in being part of something with others. That's what creates community, isn't it?'

To Eve, it would be a place where care would be taken to create an environment in which people from all walks of life were made welcome. A place where they could feel a sense of inclusion within their local community; somewhere to belong, make new friends, and share skills and interests - or simply a safe space to unwind. It wouldn't be impersonal, aloof, or excluding - she would make certain it was the opposite of those things.

She would provide a community program of activities where anyone; particularly those who might be at a higher risk of social isolation such as the elderly, speakers of other languages, and new or single parents; would have the opportunity to connect with one another. She would also provide a place where those in need could rely on gestures of generosity and care, even if it was something as simple as a hot drink on a cold night and a filling meal.

Eve had no idea if it would actually work or if people would even want to come, but she did know that the prospect stirred within her a deep sense of passion that had otherwise been sorely lacking for some time now.

'I think you should go for it!' Emily had visions of tucking into a 'roo burger at Eve's café with a bunch of other new mums, prams containing peacefully sleeping infants by their sides (it was only a vision after all). She was pleased to see her friend so enthused. 'But what about your real job?'

Eve sighed. She really didn't want to go back to nursing, but realistically she would have to, at least to begin with. 'I'm not sure - I'll have to do some casual shifts until I figure things out. I need to have some money coming in otherwise I won't be able to afford to move out or do fun stuff like this.' She gestured at the bustle about them. 'As much as I love the idea of running a café, it's still only a dream.'

'Look around you, Eve - there are stacks of cafés round here nowadays and they all took somebody with the nous to start them off. Why don't you take some time to really think about all this stuff? Life's too short to waste in a career that doesn't bring you joy or satisfaction. And you know what they say - where there's a will, there's a way...'

Was it really as simple as Emily made out, Eve wondered? She definitely had the will, but could she find a way? If there was ever a good time in her life to do something about it, it was probably now when she was at a crossroads. And if Emily could run a successful business, why couldn't she? But not everyone shared Emily's natural confidence.

'Anyway, we'd best get a move on because I need to get to my midwife appointment and that miserable waitress has been throwing us daggers for the last half an hour.'

Emily threw back some daggers of her own as she pulled on her blazer, waving Eve's hand away when she tried to put down cash for the bill that inadvertently included some sneaky Australian dollars. 'Whoa, that looks like Monopoly money.' She peered suspiciously at the bright purple plastic note. 'This is my treat - you can pay me back when I'm skint on maternity leave and you run your own café.'

When her back was turned, Eve slipped a generous tip onto the table in efforts to appease the angsty young waitress who now had a queue snaking all the way to the door. She exited *The Glass Slipper* with a new spring in her step and visions of a bustling café of her own fresh in her mind. It was a hope, a dream for the future, that if she was fortunate might just be enough to fill the hole in her heart that leaving James had left behind – and who knew what adventures she might invite into her life in the process?

♥ 4 ♥

Emily drew her friend into a hug. 'See you again soon, I hope.'

'Thank you so much for the lunch and encouragement.' Eve patted Emily's tiny tummy fondly. 'And good luck with the midwife today.'

She already felt so much better from the indulgent food and company. She waved as Emily disappeared around the corner, heads following appreciatively as they had a habit of doing so wherever she went, until she vanished leaving nothing behind but an enticing trail of perfume and a few sets of hungry eyes.

Outside, the sea air carried a chill, but the sky was promisingly bright, and the sun was still high. Wiley seagulls prowled the outdoor seating areas of the main street for leftovers, and their cawing provided a backdrop to the sounds of the village. It was relatively quiet in Tynemouth, but there was still the occasional old couple wandering hand in hand, visitors exploring the various boutiques, dog-walkers making for the beach, and locals enjoying a pub or café lunch.

As Eve cycled the coastal route home she mulled over their conversation and considered her options. One thing that had become clear during her time in Australia was that she'd made the wrong career choice with nursing. She'd been nursing since she'd left uni and had done so mostly because she wanted to help others, but also because it had been a degree that paid a bursary and would enable her to retain her savings for travel while achieving a qualification at the same time.

After her brother, Daniel, had passed away during her final year of school, she'd wanted to do all she could to support other people fighting a similar battle. She'd gravitated towards oncology nursing but had been totally unprepared for how emotionally drained it would make her feel. Looking back, she'd been too young, and it was too soon after Daniel's death. She'd struggled to remain professionally detached, and no matter how much she wanted to, she hadn't been able to single-handedly change the outcome of her patients' prognoses to save them from her brother's fate. It had broken her heart, especially when comforting grieving relatives, and she couldn't help but see her own and her parents' grief mirrored in their tears.

It was Daniel who had first inspired Eve to travel. Though they'd fought like any siblings when they were growing up, she'd always idolised him. He'd taken a gap year to travel between finishing college and starting university. Eve had missed him sorely but had thought him so brave and adventurous she couldn't wait until she was old enough to follow in his footsteps. She'd found his tales from overseas thrilling, and they'd inspired her with a longing to experience those things for herself one day – aside from that time he'd eaten a tarantula. She could live without that experience.

After qualifying as a nurse, Eve had gained some experience and saved hard before quitting to begin some overseas adventures of her own. She'd initially been reluctant to go in case the reality of the absence of both their children hit her parents too hard, but they'd supported her all the way and had even bailed her out financially when she couldn't find work. She'd taken the typical backpacker route - starting out in the States before making stops in Fiji and New Zealand, finally arriving in Australia to celebrate the New Year at Sydney Harbour Bridge watching the spectacular fireworks display she and Daniel had marvelled at on TV as children.

She'd been attracted to Melbourne because several friends she'd made were heading there, and it offered less of the more dangerous types of creepy crawly and more distinct seasons - even a cool winter – which would help her feel more at home. As luck would have it, one of her closest friends, Bex, an Aussie she'd met on the very first night of her travels at a hostel in New York, was looking for a housemate in an apartment she'd found to rent there. The apartment was conveniently close to the hospital where Eve would later end up working, and Bex had kindly let her stay at mate's rates until she'd found her feet. She hadn't realised it at the time, but things had fallen into place almost as if they were meant to be - and then James had appeared in her life, and it had felt as though their meeting was meant to be too.

♥

When Eve arrived home, after storing her bike in the garage she perched on the window-seat in her bedroom to try to relax with a good book. It sat unread and untouched however, as her mind was racing between thoughts of James tangled amongst her thoughts of Daniel, nursing, and the café idea she'd toyed with during her time in Australia. She checked her phone but there were still no messages from James. She knew she should resist but couldn't, so on Facebook she sent him a simple, *'Missing you,'* and waited to see what might happen. With the time difference it would be one-AM in Melbourne, and though James had an early start at work, if he felt anything like she did, he could still be awake.

Impatient with awaiting a response she made a call to a local nursing agency to distract herself. Due to police checks it would be a while before she could start working again, but at least she had some money put aside from her savings that was originally to be used for a home deposit with James. Though the cost of living in Australia had been extremely high, her wages had been higher too and she often seemed to have more disposable cash than when she'd worked in the UK – she was reluctant to delve too deeply into this reserve, because who knew what it might come in useful for?

Eve heard the front door.

'Eve, are you in? I thought with all this time on your hands you might've had my dinner ready for me coming home.' It was her mam.

She could hear her soft tread on the stairs, then her door burst open, and Carol poked her head round, grinning. 'Only joking – I've got us a takeaway. Dad's working late tonight so I thought we might have a girls' night in. I've got Leo!'

She waved The Wolf of Wall Street DVD in the air. Eve had been unable to resist anything Leo-related when she was a teenager, and he was at the height of his boyish good looks and post-Titanic fame.

'Mam,' Eve laughed. 'Do you have any idea what that's about? Much as I appreciate the thought, I think it's more suited to a boys' night in than a girls' one.'

Carol was crestfallen.

'But,' she reached up onto the top shelf of her wardrobe, 'we do have Catch Me If You Can – that'll spare our blushes. And I have some nail polish here too. I'll give you a manicure if you like.'

'Throw in a pedicure and you've got yourself a deal.'

Carol smiled, glad to have her daughter home and eager to make the most of it before she inevitably spread her wings again. She couldn't live with her parents forever and she wouldn't want that for her either. She had her own life to live. 'Perfect. I'll go make dinner then you can tell me all about your afternoon with Emily and her,' she tapped the side of her nose, '*big news.*'

'And I'll go hide The Wolf of Wall Street from Dad.'

As Carol's footsteps receded down the stairs, Eve risked a final glance at her phone before joining her. *'Missing you too, my Beautiful Pom,'* read the unexpected response from James. *'So much so that I can't sleep without you in our bed beside me. Wish you were here...'*

His message tugged at her heart – Eve wished she was there with him, nestled in the warm crook of his arm.

'Get some sleep,' she replied, *'you've got work in a couple of hours. Just remember how much of the bed I used to take up and you'll be fine.'* The messaging wouldn't make their

separation any easier, but she couldn't help herself. *'P.S. Wish you were here too.'* She sighed. More than he could ever know.

♥

Several hours later, neatly manicured of fingers and toes with bellies full to bursting from a good dinner and a family-sized bar of chocolate, Eve and Carol decided to call it a night. She said goodnight to her parents and waited patiently for their muffled chatter to transition into unfortunately rather less muffled snoring, then reached under her bed and slowly pulled out her suitcase from underneath inch by inch, careful not to make too much noise. She crept onto the wooden floor, wincing when it gave a creak here and there, and stopping sharply to await the reassuring drone of her parents' snores before continuing again. She knelt over the case and unzipped it carefully, the contents she had so painstakingly packed in Melbourne now bursting out untidily.

As she unpacked, the blue corner of her Australian passport peeped out from beneath her clothes. She'd received it a few months ago after finally becoming an Australian citizen – she had acquired citizenship to keep her options open with James when she hadn't been sure where things were heading between them. She fingered the kangaroo and emu emblem of the Australian coat of arms emblazoned on the cover, flicking through the blank pages, and wondering what those years had been for. Had it all been for nothing? She put the passport in a safe place out of sight amongst a folder of other important documents, doubtful she'd be needing to use it again any time soon.

Lastly, she reached under her clothing, feeling around for what she knew she would find safely hidden inside a sock-stuffed shoe in the depths of her suitcase. At last, her fingers caught upon the cool metal. She tugged gently and pulled out the elegant white-gold engagement ring, its solitaire diamond reflecting the light of the crystal chandelier above. She studied the tiny crystals studding the loop of the ring, marvelling at James' implicit understanding of her taste. She slipped it onto her ring finger but took it off again immediately. It still didn't feel right to be wearing it, and a familiar sense of anxiety swept over her that had crept in from the very moment of his proposal.

It was then that she'd known for sure she couldn't go through with it. It was sunset on an ocean beach near where they were staying for a romantic getaway on the Mornington Peninsula, and they had indulged in a small feast as James had plied her with champagne late into the summer evening until the deep blue of the sky began to glow with streaks of yellow and peach; the sun a huge, luminous disc lighting a rosy path across the ocean that looked almost as if they could walk across it to explore the very ends of the earth. Their chatter stilled as they were caught up in the beauty of the moment. Just as the sun burst red before disappearing out of sight for the night, James reached into his pocket, dropped to one knee in the sand, and presented her with the ring.

Given their bleak conversation a few weeks prior, it had been wholly unexpected, and Eve had said yes without thinking and allowed him to slip the ring onto her finger, discovering in the process how a featherlight piece of metal could suddenly feel like a heavy weight on her heart. Though James was presenting her in near-perfect circumstances with almost everything she'd ever wanted, when it came to it, she had realised instinctively that *almost* wasn't enough. She'd wondered what on earth she was going to do about it before it was too late.

She looked at the ring sadly before putting it away at the bottom of her jewellery box with a heavy heart. The proposal would remain her secret.

Overwhelmed by the emotional wrenches of the last few days and feeling torn between two worlds that had so stubbornly refused to reconcile for her and James, she climbed back into bed and sobbed herself to sleep, reaching a longing arm across the empty space beside her.

♥ 5 ♥

Several weeks passed, and summer was at its peak. Eve made a decision that was of utmost importance to her future in England - to enjoy and appreciate every small thing that had lost her James but brought her home. She was certain that an inability to make peace with her decision would lead to a life clouded by regret and an unceasing turmoil of the *what ifs* and *if onlys* that had plagued her final years in Australia, causing her to feel torn and displaced. In the absence of any viable option to bring her two worlds together, the only option left was to embrace the path she'd chosen rather than continuing to mourn the one she had left behind.

It started with the small things - Marmite on toast for breakfast each morning, dunking her favourite biscuits in her tea, Yorkshire puddings and lashings of gravy on hot Sunday roasts, bike rides and brisk walks by the seaside, immersing herself in the season, and absorbing the abundance of culture and history that was all around her. Most importantly of all, she made time for the family and friends who had drawn her home.

She didn't message James once, not even in her weakest moments, and in turn he stopped messaging her too. She slowly began to make peace with her decision and to even start enjoying herself again. That was all well and good however, until the nursing shift from hell threatened to undo each small gain she had made.

There was nothing unusual about it to begin with – she'd worked several shifts at the emergency department by now and had earned a reputation as a reliable and hard worker. She was even getting to know some of the regular staff. When she'd left home that Sunday afternoon and caught the metro into work, quickly changing into her uniform before dashing into Emergency to make her three-thirty-PM start, there'd been no hint of what was about to unfold.

Within an hour of her shift beginning, a twenty-two-year-old man was rushed into hospital by ambulance, arriving unconscious and in a critical condition, his distraught mother on the offensive and demanding answers to questions they were not yet in a position to provide. Eve, as it turned out, was in the wrong place at the wrong time, and when the young man - Nick was his name - once stabilised unexpectedly entered cardiac arrest a short time later, it was she who happened to be in the closest position to attempt to resuscitate him.

Despite the best efforts and sheer will of all involved, it was no use, and Nick passed away that summer's afternoon, the season's unashamed beauty mocking the tragedy of a young life lost. It had been a complication of his late-stage cancer, she'd later learned, an aggressive but highly treatable cancer more commonly affecting young people that had gone undetected for some time. His symptoms had been misattributed one too many times, and by the time he was eventually accurately diagnosed his prognosis had been poor. The tale echoed all too familiarly with that of Eve's own brother - he even looked a little like him with the same wavy, dark hair - and her composure began to crack. She couldn't get beyond the thought that he simply shouldn't have passed, and she was angry with herself and with the world that had failed him.

'Eve, I need you to go with Doctor Searle to speak with his mother please,' directed the Sister, her voice a mixture of compassion and defeat. 'We'll sort things out here then she can join him in a few moments.' She gestured to Nick's lifeless form surrounded by the equipment and machinery that had failed to revive him.

Recognising that her colleagues were each occupied with a task of their own and aware this was neither the time nor the place to assert her own needs, she resisted a quell of panic at what was to come, blinked away the tears that had risen to her eyes, and swallowed the painful lump in her throat. She nodded, her dread intensifying at the devastating news she and the doctor would have to impart to a woman they were strangers to, a bereft mother to whom she knew they could offer no comfort.

Mrs Cox had been directed to the family room earlier to enable the staff to focus on Nick's immediate medical needs without the emotional distraction of her presence. She was anxiously mid-phone call when Doctor Searle knocked softly on the door and entered, Eve taking a deep breath before following in behind him. Fortunately, the small room was empty save for Mrs Cox, and Eve observed how starkly minimal it was in its comforts at such a time. Mrs Cox quickly terminated the call, her hopeful look diminishing to one of despair at the sight of the pair whose faces clearly conveyed without the use of words that the worst had already happened. That it was too late.

'No... No! He... He can't go. Let me see him!' She pushed past them, their protests futile as they tried but failed to encourage her to wait a few more moments for the nurses to get her son ready to be seen.

'Mrs Cox!' Eve raised her voice slightly, but the woman was already out of the room leaving them no option but to follow helplessly behind.

Mrs Cox tore open the door to Nick's bay, startling the nurses who were still working around him.

'Nick!' she cried, and her body began to shake. 'Not my son. My darling boy...' She touched his cool brow and held his hand, pressing her head against his arm as she wept loud, wracking sobs. Eve saw her own parents' grief reflected in this woman's sorrow.

The Sister threw her a look of irritation as though to imply that the situation had obviously not been managed properly. Eve shrugged then turned to leave, walking straight out of the bay, out of the ward, out of the emergency department, and out of the hospital altogether; the haunting and grief-stricken wails of Nick's mother ringing in her ears with each footstep as she marched desperately to reach fresh air, faster and faster, hot tears of her own stinging her eyes as she struggled to catch her breath.

I can't do this anymore, she realised as she gulped lungfuls of warm air, conspicuous in her uniform yet ignoring the curious glances of those coming and going from the hospital and the embarrassed looks of the paramedics who were waiting by the parking bays for their next job. She knew she could get sacked, but the thought did not unsettle her half so much as the prospect of encountering even just one more shift like this.

Her mind made up, she quickly went back inside to collect her belongings from the locker room, discarding her uniform in the laundry hamper. Afterwards, she wiped her eyes and walked straight across the carpark, out of the hospital grounds, and away from her career without so much as a backwards glance.

♥

The sky darkened during the train journey home. Eve replayed the afternoon in her mind repeatedly. Nick, like Daniel, had had his whole life ahead of him. It wasn't supposed to end like that, cruelly snatched away when it was just beginning, his mother and the rest of his family left to pick up shattered pieces and wondering how they could ever adjust to a world without him in it. Life was reduced to an overwhelming succession of griefs and losses, troubles, and heartaches - no sooner had a person overcome one hurdle than another would be thrown in their way at random. It was all terribly unfair.

Just as she neared her parents' cobbled driveway a rumble of thunder rattled overheard followed by a piercing crack of lightning after which the first drops of rain began to fall, gently at first, then pounding hard by the time she'd put her key into the front door.

'What are you doing home already?' asked a puzzled Robert, who had come into the hallway when he'd heard the key in the lock. He glanced at the hallway clock, noting that

Eve had returned home from work a few hours early looking very distressed. Carol appeared, and a look of mutual concern passed between the pair as they took in her rain-spattered clothes, puffy eyes, and smudged mascara.

'What's wrong, love? Are you sick?' Carol asked.

Eve nodded mutely before making straight for the stairs leading up to her bedroom. She needed to be alone. Carol made to follow but Robert waved her aside.

'I'll go,' he whispered. 'Best give her a bit of time to herself first, though.'

Just then the phone rang, and Carol went to answer it.

'Don't answer that!' Eve yelled, but it was too late because she already had.

A short while later there was a knock on her door. Eve knew it was her dad because she could distinguish the heavier sound of his footfall coming up the stairs. He let himself in then came over to her where she sat with knees pulled up to her chest, jumper stretched over the top of them down to her ankles just as she'd done with her nightie when she was a child. Robert kissed the crown of her head and pulled her into a cuddle. His hug was like a balm, the familiar scent and strength of him having a soothing effect on her frayed nerves and raw emotions.

'I know what happened, love. Your mam spoke to the Sister when she called earlier. Seems you caused quite a stir - they were all worried about you.'

Really? thought Eve. All they cared about was getting the job done, not the emotional toll of that work on their staff. 'What did she say?'

'Your mam explained... You know...' Robert sighed awkwardly. 'About Daniel.' He looked sad as he spoke his son's name aloud. They didn't talk about him very often anymore though they remembered him often enough in their hearts. 'She seemed to understand - says you're welcome to come in and have a chat with her about it if you want to. She'll put in a good word with the agency, she says, though I'm guessing perhaps Emergency might not be the best option for you for a little while.' He blundered through the last bit, not quite as skilled as his wife at putting such matters delicately.

In other words, thought Eve, they thought she was too much of a loose cannon to risk having her back in Emergency upsetting the patients' families again. She nodded. 'It doesn't matter, Dad. I'm not going back there anyway.'

'Aha.' He sat quietly for a few moments, unsure what to say next.

'I was thinking,' Eve ventured carefully, unsure of how he might react, 'of opening up a café...' She was surprised that in the grand scheme of things opening a café no longer seeming as unattainable or unrealistic an idea as she'd originally thought. 'I could use the money I saved up when I was nursing in Australia - it should be enough to cover the rent of a place, for a while at least.'

Robert frowned. 'A café, eh?' He couldn't mask his concern that she might throw away her savings and a secure career to chase what sounded suspiciously like a pipedream. He'd worked for the same company since he left high school, and he was sure that what Eve needed at this time was stability and certainty to which to anchor herself whilst everything else in her life seemed so... messy. There must be something else she could use her nursing qualification for - despite the circumstances, not to use it seemed like such a waste of all her experience and abilities.

Eve was irritated by the lack of enthusiasm in his response. 'Emily thinks I could do it.'

'Aye, I'm sure you could.' He patted her on the shoulder, clearly unconvinced. 'I'll leave you be, pet. Your mam'll bring you up a nice cup of tea.' It was his answer to everything.

He got up slowly with a groan, massaging the base of his spine as he did so, and Eve glared at his retreating back. He'd become the target of her rage about living in an unjust world. Robert didn't realise it, but what she perceived as his lack of support for her café idea appealed to her determined nature and only served to instil in her a strong desire to prove him wrong. Besides, she didn't really have a whole lot of other options to choose from, and wasn't it her responsibility to embrace life and to really live it when unlike so many others she was fortunate enough to still be able to do so?

To Eve, life was a powerfully precious gift, scary in its fragility and yet beautiful in its strength and resilience. She knew too well that it could be taken away from her at any time, so she wasn't going to sit back and allow hers to simply pass her by.

♥

Before heading to bed that night she checked her phone one last time, and she was glad she did, because waiting for her was an exciting email from Emily:

Eve,

Remember our conversation at The Glass Slipper about how you'd like to open your very own café? Well, you wouldn't believe this, but...

An old colleague of mine once did the interior of an Italian restaurant in Heaton, just off Chillingham Road, a few years ago. She stayed in touch with the owner (reading between the lines I think she fancied the pants off him, if you ask me), and anyway - he's leaving. He was renting the place but now he wants to move the restaurant into larger premises, so... THE LEASE IS UP FOR GRABS! It's got a coffee machine and kitchen gear and everything, the whole shebang. So, what do you say we go check it out sometime next week? I've got Wednesday afternoon off because I'm going for my 20-week scan, where we'll hopefully be able to confirm that she is indeed a she (fingers and toes crossed). She's the size of an artichoke now by the way, though I must admit we had to go out and buy one from the supermarket because we had no idea how big that is, hehe.

Anyway, let me know as soon as you can if you fancy heading there for an early dinner and a bit of a nose around that evening. Hope all is well with you, and that you're still being disciplined as far as James is concerned.

Hugs, from Emily and bump xxx

Eve typed an eager reply before tucking herself into bed, amazed that another door had opened so soon after she'd closed the last one behind her – and in Heaton, no less, an increasingly trendy suburb only a short metro ride from the city-centre, and with the diverse community she'd hoped for. It served as a reassurance that she was choosing the right path. It was probably just a fancy, but perhaps it was Daniel watching over her.

♥ 6 ♥

The following Wednesday evening, Eve blustered along rain-dampened Victoria Terrace to meet Emily for dinner at La Terrazza restaurant in Heaton slightly later than planned. She was running late as she'd gotten stuck in peak traffic and the usual roadworks on the Coast Road, then she couldn't find a parking space close by - a matter which didn't concern her too much, since the prospect of ever actually running her own café still seemed far out of reach. That didn't stop her from shaking out her umbrella and pausing when she reached the restaurant however, to assess its facade with a shrewd eye.

The drizzle coupled with the heat from the restaurant's kitchens had caused its windows to become opaque with condensation, muting the lighting and blurring the outline of its customers. She could just make out the low hum of chatter emanating from inside. She noticed that the restaurant itself took up the entire ground floor of one of the terraced red-brick houses of the area. Unlike the other buildings it was larger and double-fronted, with a cobbled alley dividing it from the back yards of the more commercial properties on Chillingham Road, which could best be described as the main high street and thoroughfare of Heaton.

The restaurant's position at the end of the row of terraces meant it benefitted from a sense of removal from the rest of the street which she was sure the other residents appreciated, though she did wonder how whoever occupied the floor above faired with all that bustle and chatter. Its proximity to Chilli' Road meant that it would also benefit from a level of visibility and footfall that would be unlikely if it was any further removed. The property boasted bay windows and, she surmised, a small, concrete back yard typical of the time-period where in decades past outdoor 'lavvies' would have been before its slow gentrification began.

The facade was only slightly removed from the pavement by a low brick wall topped with pointy black railings, an intricate gate, and a narrow concrete yard. The current leaseholders appeared to have done little to distinguish the restaurant from the rest of the properties on the street, so it remained unobtrusive with only a neat wooden sign set above the door announcing its presence, and a printed menu patterned subtly with trailing ivy that was mounted on the wall by the gate. The only decoration Eve could see came in the form of a couple of hanging baskets on either side of the front door, and the door itself was painted a traditional racing green.

If this was her café, in fine weather she would slot a couple of tiny tables and chairs out the front to allow extra seating for her customers. She would surround the tables with colourful pots of herbs and flowers and string up lanterns to make a feature of her café's entrance, while also utilising some of her own small produce to flavour their dishes. She would even make use of the little window overlooking the alley to trial a takeaway coffee service for busy morning commuters like they did in Melbourne. *She would...*

She was snapped abruptly out of her reverie by the rat-a-tat-tat of Emily tapping impatiently on one of the restaurant's bay windows with her long, freshly manicured nails. Eve dashed inside, oblivious to the lingering gaze of the attractive Italian waiter who seated her.

♥

Emily was a stickler for punctuality (she'd sacked several employees for less). 'What time do you call this, slacker?' She drummed her fingers on the table. 'It's not as though you have a job to go to anymore – not like the rest of us.'

'Thanks for reminding me.' Eve rolled her eyes. 'Whoa, Emily, you've ballooned overnight!'

Emily heaved herself up to give Eve a hug, revealing a tidy bump that had only just begun to properly show. Emily had always favoured a figure-hugging wardrobe, and pregnancy had done little to alter that fact. Today her bump was emphasised by a clingy jersey dress she'd teamed with a pair of flats.

'I'm so happy to finally have a bump to flaunt. Before, I just looked bloated!' Emily retreated into her seat. 'I'm at the halfway mark, and now all that ghastly morning sickness has passed I can focus on just enjoying my pregnancy - before I become the size of a house and have to stop enjoying it all over again.'

'So... Is she a she?'

Emily's smile lit up her whole face, and Eve knew that even if she'd wanted to keep the news to herself, the secret was out now anyway.

'Congratulations!'

'*I know*!'

Emily beamed, fishing out her scan picture and pointing out some indistinct part of the grainy image apparently demonstrating that she was indeed a she. Eve nodded as though it was obvious to her too. 'I'll finally have an ally to gang up against Mark with when he hogs the TV remote - someone to play Barbies with when it all gets too much.'

'How does Mark feel about that?'

'Chuffed! He's way more laid back about this sort of thing than I am. And now I know we're having a girl, I can make a start on the nursery - I never thought I'd say this, but an excess of pink is an absolute must.'

Eve raised an eyebrow - motherhood was already changing her friend. 'This calls for a celebratory, erm, glass of juice? Sparkling water?'

'Sparkling water will have to do.' Emily was momentarily glum. 'Then cake. Lots of it. Tell me, what do you think of this place? I mean, it's perfect! Look at those parquet floors - you'd hardly have to change a thing! The pizza oven might have to go, and it's a shame they've blocked in the fireplace, but still - this could all be yours very soon...'

Eve glanced around. Despite the extra space afforded by the property's double front, a supporting wall unfortunately cut right through the two seating areas. This had been somewhat overcome by the addition of wide arches on either side of the entrance hall, which maintained an impression of flow of space without compromising the sense of intimacy. She counted a total of eighteen seats in the former 'living room' she and Emily were sitting in, and supposed the room opposite would accommodate roughly the same – perhaps a few more given it didn't have the counter that took up so much space. It seemed a manageable number, though in reality she knew nothing about catering for so many.

'I love it - it's exactly what I'd be looking for if I were to open a café!'

'What do you mean *if*? I'm not going to let you not do this, Eve.' And with that, Emily raised a hand and waved across to the passing waiter who appeared in a jiffy. She had always had a gift for commanding immediate attention.

'Madams, you are finished with the menu? Ees not often I have the pleasure of taking the order of two such beautiful ladies.'

He simpered at and flattered the pair as though it was an art form of which he was master, and the two women shared a giggle. He was indeed incredibly attractive with dark curly hair, tanned skin, lean muscle emphasised by a crisp white shirt, dark eyes that narrowed as he studied the women unapologetically, and a full mouth that twisted into a flirtatious grin. His attentions were enjoyable to them both, though it was clear he had a habit of sharing them with any girl who caught his interest. Emily thought it might not be a terrible thing for her friend to have some fun.

'Yes, we'd like to order, but first my friend has a few questions about the lease of the restaurant.' Emily gestured at Eve. 'My colleague told me about it - she did the interior here some time ago. We wondered who it would be best to talk to?'

'Oh, I understand. Very good. So, you want to run a restaurant?' he asked, his eyes confidently meeting and holding Eve's, who wished the ground would open and swallow her whole.

She glared at Emily. 'Erm... Well, no, a café actually.' Her face flushed.

'A café? Very good, very impressive. This would make a fine café - it *was* a café before we arrived. This ees my father's business. We have been happy here, but we will be moving somewhere larger in a few weeks. I will be glad to give you his contact details when you are finished your meal - he is the chef here, so he cannot be disturbed tonight.'

A few weeks? That didn't leave much time at all. 'Thank you, yes, if you will that would be great,' Eve stuttered, feeling silly. She hated being put on the spot, and wondered how to get out of her predicament now the waiter obviously thought she was seriously interested in taking over the place.

'Very good. Now, what would you lovely ladies like to order?'

'Are you on the menu?' Emily grinned.

'That,' he replied, 'can always be arranged.'

♥

The ladies enjoyed a delicious dinner - Eve had the gnocchi topped with asparagus, chargrilled chicken, and lashings of parmesan; and Emily feasted on herb bread followed by a huge vegetarian pizza, unable during her pregnancy to partake of her favourite fettuccine marinara. Their waiter, Paolo, was inordinately attentive, and as nice as it was to be flattered (and as much as Emily encouraged it), the unexpected male attention only served to remind Eve of how much better her life had been when James was still a part of it.

There'd been no contact between them for weeks now - she had hoped this would be the relationship equivalent of ripping off a plaster as opposed to peeling it off slowly, but in reality, the reverse was true. She wondered what James was doing right now without her - if he felt her absence in his life as strongly as she felt his in hers. If only he would come to her and stay...

But it was no use. They'd circulated the same argument for years, each time arriving at the same impasse. She was home now and committed to staying. After a shaky start, she'd just have to move on and make the best of it. As much as she missed Australia, she didn't miss it enough to want to make her life there. She needed to forge a life for herself here, and one that certainly did not include a return to nursing. If she was to pursue her café idea, she'd be able to bring some of what she missed of Melbourne home to Newcastle, and that might be enough to sustain her. Insofar as relationships were concerned though, she realised she'd eventually need to bring herself round to the possibility of starting afresh with someone new.

It was with that thought in mind that as the two women fought over the last bites of their complimentary tiramisu, Eve didn't reject Paolo when with a wink and a smile he slipped his number into her hand along with the promised contact details for his father.

'Call me,' he whispered in her ear as they left the warmth of the restaurant and stepped out into the dusky night, his breath hot on her neck.

'Phwoarrr, half your luck!' Emily exclaimed when they were no longer in earshot. 'That accent! If only I was still single and didn't have a bun in the oven.'

They linked arms as they walked to their respective cars under a rosy sky. The drizzle had cleared, and the streets were dry.

'Nice car! How on earth did you afford that?'

'It's my dad's,' said Eve. 'He's letting me borrow it 'til I can buy my own.'

'That's good of him, but he'd have kittens if he saw the way you've parked.'

Eve knew that was true.

'Get yourself away, then. You have phone calls to make and a café to open. Have you thought about what you're gonna call it?'

Eve grinned. 'Yes, actually - The Melbourne. The Melbourne Community Café.'

'Looks like you'll soon be bringing a slice of Australia to The Toon. I'm so excited for you! Let me know what Paolo's dad says about the lease - six weeks doesn't leave us much time to get organised, but you know I'll help you out with the interior. Thom's been doing most of the heavier work for me lately, and I'm sure he'll have no qualms about helping me help *you*.'

'That would be great.' Eve ignored the insinuation about Thom and was grateful for Emily's use of the word *us*. 'Let's not get ahead of ourselves just yet though - I'll have to wait and see what Paolo's dad has to say first.'

'Well, he's not going to say anything if we stay standing here, is he?'

'Ok, ok, I'm going!'

Emily blew her a kiss, and Eve crossed her fingers before very carefully attempting to steer her dad's precious Golf out of its predicament, her stomach churning with anticipation as what had started out as a dream looked increasingly set to become a reality.

♥ 7 ♥

Eve knew next to nothing about opening a café, so the next six weeks were a crash course of research, phone calls, emails, legalities, licensing, estimates, guesstimates, negotiations, and calculations that were almost too scary to contemplate - a great way, she discovered, of taking her mind off James. She'd saved a lot during her time in Australia and had only dented the sum marginally thanks to her nursing shifts, living with her parents, and not yet having bought her own car. Most of the advice she'd read online indicated that she'd need at least twenty grand to begin with, so she was keen to make as many small savings as she could without compromising on what was most important - great coffee.

With a good word put into La Terrazza's landlord by Paolo's father, Gianni, she was able to negotiate a twelve-month lease at a discount if she agreed to pay the first six months up front. It was a gamble, but one that would give her some peace of mind initially, as her biggest expense would already be dealt with. She planned to put the rest of the money aside in the hopes it would remain relatively untouched until the next payment was due - minus the costs of decor, stock, and staffing.

Eve couldn't envisage when she might afford to take a wage for herself - a prospect that made her shudder with anxiety though she tried to push it to the back of her mind. Fortunately, the space came furnished with the necessary kitchen equipment she would need, as well as with air-conditioning, display cabinets, sound and security systems, and a till. To save money she'd decided to rent the existing espresso machine from Gianni, determined not to purchase one herself unless her venture proved successful. Everything she'd read had warned against making such an expensive purchase to begin with.

By her calculations she should have just enough to get started and push through the first few months - she'd just have to hope the café itself would get her through to the end of her lease. If she failed, she shouldn't fare too badly after only one year - she was prepared to risk her savings, but she wasn't prepared to get herself into debt. If The Melbourne died on its feet, she would cut her losses and run. To what or to whom she didn't wish to contemplate, so she devoured advice as though it were one of her own dishes she might serve, keen to avoid as many of the potholes and pitfalls that would inevitably crop up for the uninitiated - which is where Paolo came in.

Eve had seen no reason to keep Paolo's number once she'd sorted everything out with his father. That's why when she'd encountered him unexpectedly at La Terrazza one late-summer's afternoon, she'd looked at him sheepishly as he'd invited her inside and politely informed her that Gianni was busy running errands and had asked him to be there to hand over the restaurant keys on his behalf. She couldn't help noticing how different Paolo looked dressed casually in faded blue jeans, black thongs (she could no longer bring herself to call them flip-flops), and a simple white shirt pulled taught across the muscular bulk of his chest and arms, his mop of dark curls unruly above his brow. She could see the hint of his waistband and politely averted her gaze, but not before Paolo caught the look and grinned, his eyes glinting with mischief as she blushed furiously.

'I'm here to collect the keys,' she said, automatically clearing her throat when her voice came out as a croak.

'Of course, give me a moment and I will try to find where my father put them. He is a great chef, but ees not so great at the housekeeping.'

That accent. He rifled through drawers and the few remaining packed boxes that littered the floorboards. 'Excuse me for one moment and I will check the kitchen. Ees the least obvious place, and therefore the most probable!'

Eve watched his retreating back and heard Paolo sigh as he clattered about the kitchen in pursuit of those elusive keys. She stood self-consciously near the counter. She fluffed up her thick, shoulder-length hair and reapplied a slick of lipstick, swapping her weight from foot to foot, trying to appear nonchalant. Then she checked herself and wondered what on earth she was doing. She wasn't interested in him in that way, and she was certain she was just a bit of sport as far as he was concerned. No doubt there was a lengthy list of women he'd already conquered, and she wasn't going to succumb and add herself to it, even if those around her did keep hinting that perhaps it was time she put James behind her and had some 'fun.' She didn't think a fling would be much fun at all, in fact, it still felt as though it would be something of a betrayal. After experiencing what it was like to be so loved by someone, nothing as superficial could satisfy her again. Could it?

She distracted herself by studying the space around her, still astounded that in the three months since she'd returned home from Australia this was the direction her life had taken - one she could never have anticipated. La Terrazza looked vastly different stripped bare of its character – of its very essence. It was unnaturally silent in the absence of conversation and the clatter of dishes and without the tempting smells of garlic and rosemary permeating the air. Now the space was a blank canvas, and it was easier to imagine it as it would be as a café. *Her* café. She found herself eager to bring it to life once again.

She was so preoccupied with working out the seating arrangements that she didn't realise Paolo had re-entered the room until she heard the jingling of keys.

'Found them,' he said, holding out the keys, well aware that in order to get them she would first have to cover the distance between them.

Gingerly, Eve took the keys from his grasp and slipped them into her handbag, trying to minimise the inevitable moment when their fingers would meet. Paolo was happy to linger, a smirk playing upon his lips at the frisson of electricity that passed between them with only the briefest of contact.

'They were in the cellar, of all places.' He tutted. 'Papà must've left them down there during our final clear-out this morning. When I say clear-out, knowing him he most likely cleared-out the cellar by *drinking* the wine, rather than by packing it up.'

'There's a cellar here too?' Eve was surprised. Gianni hadn't mentioned it.

'Ees more of a hole in the ground, really. We use it for storage - like a larder. You access it from the back of the kitchen. Ees also useful you will find, for hiding difficult customers – and small children.'

Eve laughed a nervous laugh. 'Well, I'm not planning on having many of those – difficult customers, I mean.' And she was looking forward to welcoming families with their children.

'Oh, there will always be plenty of those. Trust me. But you must be particularly wary of the ones who do not call you back when you give them your number.' Paolo arched a sculpted eyebrow.

'Actually, I think the lesson is that one should not give out one's personal number out to one's customers in the first place,' Eve quipped.

'And where ees the fun in that?'

She didn't have an answer.

'I wonder,' Paolo ventured carefully. 'Would you care to join me for a final glass of wine at La Terrazza? Papà must have missed a bottle when he cleared out the cellar this morning - ees a very fine red made in my hometown.' He brandished the bottle with a mixture of pride and pizazz. 'Perhaps we could drink to new beginnings - to the last of many celebrations here for me, and to the first of many for you.'

'Oh!' Eve was taken off guard. 'I'm not sure that would be such a good idea. I'm driving, and I still have so much left to do for the cafe - I had no idea how much work would be involved just in starting out.' It was the truth.

'Well then, I think ees time to consider taking a small break, don't you? Please allow me to do what I can to help you. Perhaps my years of experience as a restaurateur could help? At worst, you might learn what not to do.' His expression was cajoling, his eyes amused. 'Besides, I cannot stay for much longer. My father will return soon to collect the last of the boxes, then this place will be well and truly yours. I promise to overlook the fact I will be sharing my wine with a very beautiful woman.' He openly appraised her face and the soft fullness of her figure.

Against her better judgment, Eve decided that one glass of wine with Paolo couldn't hurt, especially if it would soon be curtailed by Gianni's return. She felt like a duck out of water as far as the prospect of running her own business was concerned, so she reasoned that it couldn't hurt to pick Paolo's brain over some of the processes she was still unsure about - it was a lovely day, after all, and she certainly could do with a little rest.

Paolo knew instinctively that she had made up her mind in his favour, and before she could change it again, he deftly produced two glasses from a box over by the bay window, then uncorked the wine with a flourish and poured out the ruby liquid, his dark eyes holding hers as he did so.

'Salute.'

'Salute,' Eve repeated, the word unfamiliar on her tongue as they clinked.

Paolo laughed, and she allowed herself a tight giggle. After a single sip of the rich, creamy liquid he gestured for her to follow him into the back yard where they sat side by side on the low concrete step in the sunshine as he regaled her with tales from his days back in Italy as a youngster, before his parents' messy divorce.

Eve felt her shoulders begin to relax for the first time in weeks, the tension dissipating as one glass of wine soon turned into two. The sunlight warmed her bare shoulders and kissed her cheeks, and Paolo worked hard to make her laugh. She hadn't realised how uptight she'd been lately, and she finally gave herself permission to enjoy herself once again in male company. After a while, they spread themselves out upon the dry concrete that had been gently warmed by the sun.

♥

'Did you get the keys?' It was a text message from Emily.

'Got more than I bargained for,' was Eve's cryptic reply.

'Intrigued...'

'Embarrassed...' Blushing emoticon.

'Collecting keys is not usually a cause for embarrassment.'

'May have kissed Paolo. Or to be more precise, fended off his attempts at kissing me.'

Open-mouthed emoji. *'I wouldn't fend him off with a ten-foot pole! Oh, to have been in your shoes...'*

'You're welcome to him. We shared some amazing wine though, and he gave me some sound business advice. Before he pounced. Fancy taking advantage of me in my delicate condition!'

'I'm the one who's in a delicate condition, and he can take advantage of me any time. Now, back to work - you don't have time to flirt with sexy, single Italian men. I expect a Melbourne mood-board by Monday. It's high time we got started on that interior!'

Eve rolled her eyes, and her cheeks burned as she recalled Paolo's almost kiss. They'd easily polished off a full bottle of wine between them before lounging back in the sun, conversation flowing surprisingly easily as a gentle breeze played at Eve's hair. Paolo was a natural entertainer and an animated storyteller. His childhood in southern Italy sounded idyllic to Eve, and she thought it sad that his father had chosen to leave that existence behind him soon after he had separated from his wife. Several years later, Paolo, who had inherited his father's passion for cooking, chose to join Gianni in England where he planned to establish a new family business after he had lost their original restaurant in Italy during the divorce proceedings. Thanks to previous experience, their ventures had all proved moderately successful, but Paolo said he'd found it difficult to settle into his new life in the chilly northeast of England and would sometimes find himself pining for home.

Eve shared little about herself other than for glossing over the circumstances of her recent return home from Australia - she appreciated the distraction from her own worries and was happy just to listen and enjoy the moment. Paolo filled the silence almost as though he were simply thinking out loud, and he offered some valuable advice she was very grateful for that could never be matched by her online research alone. He answered her many questions but eventually they both fell silent, the only sounds those of the birds overhead, a neighbour hanging out their washing in the yard next door, and the ever-present rumble of traffic on Chillingham Road.

'Would you ever consider going back home?' she asked him after a pause. She'd been lying on her back watching the clouds rolling slowly by, but now she turned onto her side to face Paolo, genuinely interested in what he had to say. A drive to return to her roots was something she could really relate to.

'Home? Nah. Home is here, and it is there – ees wherever you are and wherever you choose to make it. Perhaps one day I will go back, some-time in the future - it has been my dream to open my very own seafood restaurant by the coast. But for now, my father needs me here, and this work suits me while I have no family to concern myself with.'

Eve nodded before rolling back again and gazing upward at the sky. Paolo covered the small distance between them, reaching out a hand to gently brush her hair back from her cheek whilst simultaneously bringing his torso and then his mouth over hers, his eyes ardent as his face blotting out the sun.

'Dio, sei cosi bella,' he murmured. 'My, you are so beautiful. And quelle labra - those lips...' He pressed his lips onto hers, and Eve could taste the creamy remnants of the pinot upon them.

'Whoa - Paolo!'

Eve pushed his hand away and recoiled backwards tugging her cardigan tightly around her chest, but in the confined space between back yard and kitchen there wasn't anywhere for her to go. A second kiss just missed her mouth and landed awkwardly on her chin, warm and with a hint of moisture. From the look on Paolo's face, he was clearly unaccustomed to having his advances so rebuffed.

'Paolo? Paolo! Dove sei? Where are you?' It was Gianni, his father, his voice made hoarse from decades of cigarettes and barking orders to his underlings.

'Sono qui, Papà!' Paolo shouted, leaping away from Eve, and smoothing out his clothing. He ran one hand through his tangled hair then swept up the wine bottle and glasses in one fluid motion. 'Outside.'

Eve followed suit, unsure what to do next. In ordinary circumstances she would leave, but this was now her café, and she was unable to go anywhere before Paolo and Gianni did, as she would need to lock up behind them.

'What on earth are you still doing here?' Gianni tutted as he poked his head round the door. 'This is no time for you to sit on your ass. Veloce - hurry! The van is parked outside, and you must carry the last of the boxes out for me. I am exhausted.' He wheezed. 'Ah, hello Miss Eve, I did not see you there.'

As Gianni took in the empty wine bottle, stained glasses, and Eve's flushed cheeks he politely averted his gaze. Paolo appeared uncharacteristically ruffled, a smudge of lipstick marring the corner of his mouth, and the older man allowed himself a slight grin at his son's expense.

'I see my son has given you more than just the keys,' Gianni smirked, gesturing at the wine bottle. 'Consider it a welcome gift. We will get out of your hair now. I wish you all the best in your new café, and I sincerely hope you enjoy the level of success that we ourselves have experienced here.'

'Thank you.' Eve didn't know what else to say. 'I wish you well too, in your new premises.' She stood there awkwardly, clutching her cardigan about her, and hardly daring to look in Paolo's direction. This had the unfortunate effect of making it look as though more had happened than actually had.

Paolo grinned, now totally unphased, and she couldn't help but wonder how many compromising positions he'd been caught in over the years. Thank goodness she hadn't given in to him. Within moments he'd packed up the rest of the boxes and he and Gianni were gone, leaving Eve almost a stranger in the empty hallway of her new café.

When she heard the rumble of the van's engine retreating into the distance, she decided she'd best stay put until she was no longer over the limit. She ran a finger along the smooth, freshly-polished counter – Paolo and Gianni had kindly left the place in pristine condition for her - and smiled wistfully at the till before bursting into a fit of the giggles. It was all very real now, and perhaps it was the wine, but she was suddenly excited about all that lay ahead. If only there were a few more drops left in that wine bottle to help celebrate her special moment.

♥ 8 ♥

It was the first week of October and autumn was only just beginning to make itself known. Eve had always considered it one of the country's most beautiful seasons, where the land would display its glorious colours with pride like a peacock parading its open tail. Spring and autumn in Melbourne though lovely tended to be on the short side, so she relished the opportunity to bask in the distinct beauty that was unique to and openly exposed by each passing season back home.

She had allowed herself a whole month to furnish her café and get it looking how she wanted it. She planned to open at the beginning of November, but with the run up to Christmas she wasn't convinced that was the best move, and wondered if she should regard those couple of months as a trial-run before starting properly in the New Year. In the meantime, she would become established and get a feel for what worked and what things didn't. It might turn out useful if things were a little quiet to begin with, then she could make any changes and improvements that were necessary. Her customers might even be able to offer some suggestions – she understood how important it was to create a good first impression if she wanted people to continue coming back.

She'd received some exciting news from her closest Aussie friend, Bex, who had decided following the end of another failed relationship to finally get round to the travelling she had been putting off for years by heading over to the UK for a working holiday. In her younger days, Bex had worked as a barista at a Brunswick café and her coffee-making skills far-outweighed Eve's, so Eve was delighted when Bex offered to visit Newcastle and teach her how to make Melbourne-style coffee. Properly. She was expecting her arrival the week before opening day, and she hoped Bex could be persuaded to stay on a little while longer to help her get things off the ground.

Eve had allowed Emily full reign over the interior - not that she'd had much choice in the matter - and the manual labour was overseen by her younger brother Thom, whom Eve was still studiously trying to avoid. That had been easy so far - Emily wouldn't allow her to set foot inside The Melbourne until it was complete as she wanted it to be a surprise. The only thing Eve knew for sure was that she was allowed to purchase crockery and other decorative items to the colour-theme she'd hinted at on her mood-board, sparking one of the most enjoyable parts of the process so far - shopping.

Though Eve had always had Emily's full support to realise her dream, what she hadn't counted on was the reaction of her parents. When she'd committed herself to the café's lease her dad had been gobsmacked at the risk she'd taken with her career and her savings, and he'd retreated into his newspapers hopeful that his wife would find a way to bring his headstrong daughter back to her senses.

Much to Robert's surprise though Carol shared his concerns about what might happen should things not go Eve's way, she was really excited about the café and felt this could be Eve's way of finally putting down roots, or of testing the soil at least. It was something different for Carol to focus on too, outside of the confines of her unsatisfying administration job and pairing her husband's socks. She'd always wanted a hobby, and if grandchildren weren't on the cards just yet then maybe this could be it. Which is why, tanned and refreshed upon her return from a holiday in Nice, she'd embraced the shopping aspect of the café's preparations almost as eagerly as Eve did.

'You mustn't mind your dad, love,' said Carol as they pored over Eve's lengthy shopping list one afternoon over a coffee, ticking off each of the items they'd acquired that were now safely bubble-wrapped in shopping bags and packages cluttered untidily about their feet. 'He's just worried about you, that's all.'

'He doesn't have to be,' Eve huffed. 'I'm an adult, and parents are supposed to believe in their kids, aren't they? Even when they're grown up.'

'He does believe in you! He's just thinking about the money and what might happen if the café doesn't make enough of it to support you and return what you've put into it. Then you'll have lost all the savings you've worked so hard for. Those are legitimate concerns. He wants what's best for you - we both do - and as you're well aware, ventures like this involve risk.'

'So much of what there is to be gained in life involves a level of risk. I've had enough to deal with lately - I just want Dad to be pleased for me like everybody else.'

'I'm sure he'll come round; he usually does. Let's not let it spoil our afternoon, eh? And I love having you home again, even if it does mean bickering over crockery instead of clothes.'

Eve conceded the point, albeit reluctantly so as not to ruin their day, and together the pair followed their shopping expedition up with a trip to the supermarket which marked another enjoyable stage of the preparations - menu tasting, or to be more precise, menu concocting.

♥

'Oh, David, this is divine!' Carol enthused. 'Can I call you David? Abbreviations are so vulgar.'

Dave nodded. Eve felt like reminding her mother they were Made in Newcastle, not Made in Chelsea, and that she was happy enough to abbreviate her dad's name when it suited her.

'This is exactly what I was aiming for,' said Eve.

'Mmm,' Carol licked the runny yolk of a perfectly poached egg from her lips. 'You're a genius. And that bacon - so crispy.'

Dave shrugged as though to say, *'What did you expect?'* He nonchalantly wiped invisible dust from the shoulder of his pristine white tunic and puffed out his chest, clasping his hands behind his back. He was tall and powerfully built, but his form had a softness about the edges that exposed the importance he placed on regularly 'tasting' his fare. His manner was brusque and abrupt, his voice gruff. He seemed as though he would be very comfortable barking out instructions at others. His hands, however, were incongruously deft and artful. 'Care to try my mixed-quinoa porridge?'

Carol grinned. Eve felt like a judge a cooking show, but whilst Dave was having no difficulty in hitting tens, his manner was more of a six at best. Fortunately, she wasn't hiring him for his personality, and he'd be largely tucked away in the kitchen. He was a creative and well-referenced chef, but most importantly he had a great understanding of the menu she was aiming for.

'Aside from adding the yoghurt mousse for smoothness,' he said, 'I took the liberty of adding some crumbed pistachio and pomegranate seeds to balance the textures.'

'Fantastic!' said Eve. 'It looks delicious. I'm very keen for you to express your creativity in the kitchen so long as we stay true to the Aussie theme.'

Dave had been a real find. He was a particular recommendation of Gianni's - he'd worked for him a few years prior, then left to chase a promotion to sous chef at a popular bistro in the city. Now he was ready to branch out on his own as head chef, so Eve's job offer was perfect timing. Dave was no stranger to demanding work, and though working at an unknown café would be a bit of a gamble (not to mention a step down), it was a chance to demonstrate his skills and explore his creativity as a vital cog in a completely new venture. It might not earn him any Michelin stars, but it was a step in the right direction.

'Yum.' Carol had spooned the bowl clean. 'Sweet, crunchy, and soft... A perfect harmony of flavour and texture.'

'Been watching MasterChef again, have you, Mam?'

Carol sniffed. 'Jamie Oliver, actually. He's a dish in himself.'

'Is there anything you think we might be missing?' Dave proffered the draft menu they'd put together to help keep them on task, and Eve gave it a thorough appraisal. They'd agreed to keep things simple initially, starting with their all-day brunch.

'Let me see... We've got the pancakes, French toast, Bircher, The Vego, The Big Aussie, The Smashed Avo, The Feta and Field Mushroom Sourdough, the zucchini fritters... What about a BLAT?'

'What on earth's a BLAT?' Carol grimaced. 'It sounds terribly uncouth.'

'I didn't think anything was uncouth to a Geordie,' said Dave. He'd grown up south of the Tyne.

'Like a BLT - but with avocado,' Eve explained. 'Very popular. We could serve it with our halloumi fries. Though on second thoughts that might not be the best flavour combination.'

'We can try it. If it doesn't work, we can always offer the fries as a side dish. How about a pumpkin soup? If I remember rightly, that was always on the menu over there - we could serve it with cream and a side of damper bread.'

Dave had worked in Australia himself a few years back - another reason Eve hadn't hesitated to hire him. 'Great idea!' She grinned at Carol as though unable to believe her luck.

'Looks like that's all sorted then,' said Carol. 'Now, I think it's time David here had a breather so we can sample some of *your* creations.'

She patted the seat next to hers at the shiny new breakfast bar - one of Robert's proudest DIY ventures - and Dave allowed himself to relax into it, red faced from the heat of the oven. He discarded his chef's hat on the bench-top revealing wispy tufts of light brown hair that pointed in all directions and made him look older than his years.

Eve had been looking forward to this. As much as she thoroughly enjoyed cooking herself, she was more interested in getting to know her customers and overseeing the café's community program than she was in spending her days confined to the kitchen. Dave on the other hand, seemed as though he'd be perfectly content with keeping out of people's way. Eve loved to bake, so they'd agreed that every other day she'd prepare a batch of Aussie-themed sweet treats. She'd decided upon a small selection of lamingtons, ANZAC biscuits, banana bread, yo-yos, honey joys for the little ones (a cornflake cake made with honey instead of chocolate), and a selection of sweet and savoury muffins - all the typical things she'd so often seen displayed in giant jars set upon Melbourne café counter-tops everywhere.

'Just a sec,' she said, as she prised open an airtight container stuffed with samples of each treat she'd spent a few hours perfecting the previous evening and placed it on the bench before Dave and her mam along with a plate and a couple of forks. Carol's eyes widened. She'd been on a diet for as long as Eve could remember.

'Oh, this isn't fair.'

Eve handed her a yo-yo. 'Life's too short.'

'Lamingtons.' Dave risked a rare smile that softened his pale blue eyes. 'I haven't had one of these for years.' He tucked in eagerly, skewering a fluffy lump of white sponge-cake coated with a thin layer of chocolate sauce dusted with desiccated coconut before lifting it up to his mouth. 'Mmm,' he said, swiping away a couple of cheeky strands of coconut that clung onto his upper lip. Eve made a mental note that the way to this man's heart was clearly through his sweet tooth.

'I'll go for the banana bread,' said Carol. 'It's got fruit in it and no cake in the title so it must be healthy.'

'Not quite as healthy as the vegetable muffin, though,' said Dave.

'We'll save that for my husband - he could do with losing a few pounds.'

'Did someone say my name?'

Robert appeared at the most opportune time - Eve was sure she'd inherited her own sweet tooth from him, and she cursed him for it.

'Been cooking up a storm, have we? Don't mind if I do.' He grabbed a yo-yo from the box and tried but failed to stuff it into his mouth in one go.

'Dad! I had my eye on that.'

Robert feigned indifference. 'Did you? Well, they're for tasting, aren't they? I thought you might need an objective opinion.' He brushed some crumbs from his tash before shoving in the last mouthful of jam and cream-filled biscuit then peering mournfully into his empty palm. 'Very nice - tastes like a giant, jammy custard cream.'

'Come round to the café idea now, have you?'

'I wouldn't go that far.' He grabbed a honey joy for the road.

'What's the verdict then?' Eve asked when he was gone.

'Oh, I would give you an eight out of ten,' said Carol.

Praise wasn't really Dave's thing. He checked his watch. 'I'd better get going, it's late.'

Eve shook his hand. 'We should both try to get some rest before the big day.'

'Ha, not likely. This is your last chance for rest - trust me.'

Eve saw him to the door and thanked him for all his help, basking in the satisfaction of yet another task completed - the menu. It was dark outside, but clear and starry with a chill in the air that hinted at the coming winter. Gratefully she retreated into the warmth inside - how she had missed central heating during Melbourne's colder months.

After completing the mammoth task of clearing up the kitchen she said goodnight to her parents then went upstairs to her room, relieved to have found someone so capable to work with. It was all feeling very real now and much less impossible than it had seemed in the beginning. All she had left to do was master the art of making a drinkable cup of coffee. Thank goodness Bex would be arriving soon.

♥ 9 ♥

Newcastle Central Station was bustling. The station itself was an impressive feat of Victorian-style engineering. There were commuters exiting east-coast trains in smart suits and shiny shoes, carrying briefcases and talking importantly into their mobile phones; rowdy colleagues celebrating an early finish at the former first-class waiting area that was now a popular bar; and well wrapped-up travellers warming their hands on hot takeaway cups as they pulled neat little wheelie cases across the bridge spanning the platforms, anxious not to miss their train to whichever destination they'd decided to spend their weekend. And there were several who, like Eve, were waiting patiently beneath the arrivals board, one eye on the clock and eager to greet their loved ones.

Eve hugged her coat tighter to her body and stuffed her hands deep into its pockets, reminded as she did so that in defiance of the laws of meteorology, the beautiful arched station had always been freezing inside regardless of what the temperature was outside, which was brisk with an early setting sun. She peered up at the mammoth screens to find out what platform to expect Bex' train from London Kings Cross to arrive at. She didn't have long to wait before she glimpsed bright pink hair and an ill-fitting camel coat bobbing cheerfully amongst the crowd who'd just alighted the fifteen-forty-two and were now crossing the bridge in a synchronised huddle towards the exit barriers.

Eve recognised Bex immediately, even though last time they'd seen each another she'd been sporting a severe red bob. She waved, an unexpected mixture of emotions pooling in her chest. She missed Australia, she acknowledged for the first time in months, and aside from the pain of leaving James she also missed the good friends she'd made over there. It was bitter-sweet to be home again and yet continue to have her heart divided across the two countries, with people she loved and cared about on both sides. No matter how much she wanted to, she was never able to hold everyone close all at the same time - while in one country she was left with only the memories of the other to carry in her heart.

'Bex!'

'Eve, how are ya?' Bex discarded her over-stuffed backpack to better hug her friend, and Eve clung on tightly, tears clouding her eyes as memories of their many shared experiences in Australia together flashed into mind.

Eve knew by now that the 'how are ya?' was less a question than it was a greeting.

'Bex! It's so good to see you! How was London?' She plucked at a strand of Bex' hair. 'Pink?'

'I know – a bit girly but it's the only colour I haven't been yet. I'm thinking of going metallic next. London was bloody cold, though I've been warned to expect worse Up North and it looks as though they weren't kidding...' She shivered.

'Don't worry,' said Eve, 'you'll warm up once we get out of the station - it's always freezing in here. Do you fancy a look around the city? You can drop your backpack in the boot.'

'That'd be awesome.' As they walked to the car, Bex' hair and unique style attracted the odd glance to which she seemed oblivious. 'I'm dying to hear all about your café though, how's it going?'

Eve grinned at the familiar tones of Bex' prolonged and slightly nasal vowels. 'We open on Tuesday! My friend, Emily - you'll meet her at La Terrazza tonight - is doing the interior for me with her brother. Mate's rates and all that. We'll get to see it for the first time tomorrow. By the way, I'm so grateful to you for taking time out from your travels to help me out.'

'Are you kidding? You were always harping on about how nowhere's got a thing on Newcastle - this is your chance to prove it lives up to the hype. And no offense, but you need to learn how to make a decent cup of coffee *so* badly.'

Eve knew this was true. 'Thank goodness you're here – my success is entirely in your hands.'

'No pressure or anything.'

♥

Together they shared the first leisurely couple of hours Eve had experienced in weeks. She was jubilant showing Bex around her beautiful town - it was a crisp yet clear early evening and she could tell her friend was impressed with the thousand year old ruins of the 'new' castle that was the city's namesake, and with the contrast between the seven bridges spanning the Tyne, one of which had borrowed the design of the Sydney Harbour Bridge - albeit a much smaller version in green instead of black.

They scaled the art centre's glass elevator where they enjoyed a panoramic view of the river where the cities of Newcastle and Gateshead converged, the lights of the Millennium bridge alternating from colour to colour. Bex was rather less interested in the expanse of late-night shopping that was on offer, preferring instead to dress ever-practically in her ethically sloganned shirts, jeans, and sensible walking shoes.

Back home, Carol treated their guest to a buffet of ham and pease pudding sandwiches – a local delicacy of which the Geordies were extremely proud - served on chewy stottie bread with sides of coleslaw, scotch eggs, and salad. As a confirmed vegan, Bex picked around the things she couldn't eat, careful not to cause offence, and marvelled not for the first time as she listened to Eve and her parents chatter at how different the Poms were to the Aussies in many respects. She'd never before been anywhere so cold or where people drank so much tea and ate so many biscuits; or where people seemed in such a hurry to escape the dreary weather yet if you dared criticise it would become fiercely patriotic and defensive all at the same time. Her time in London had shown there was certainly some truth to term 'Whinging Poms' that the Aussie's had ascribed to the Brits.

Bex was quite taken with Eve's parents' homely little house and was looking forward to a break from hostel living even if she did only have a sofa-bed to sleep on in what had once been Daniel's bedroom. The pair enjoyed a quick cuppa with Robert and Carol, the former of whom made Bex laugh in his attempts to mimic her accent; the latter of whom couldn't stop thinking how lovely Bex might look if only her hair wasn't such a ghastly shade of pink; then the two friends dashed upstairs to get ready in time for Emily's expected arrival at eight. It was opening night at La Terrazza's new premises, and Gianni had insisted Eve and her friends should be there as his special guests.

When the doorbell rang, Carol welcomed Emily inside, patting her baby-bump and dishing out outdated parenting advice.

'Special delivery for Miss Winters,' said Emily, thrusting a ceramic pot of flourishing garden rosemary at Eve. 'I found it standing on the doorstep of your café this morning and I think I have a pretty good idea who sent it - a certain Italian stallion, perhaps. It put Thom's nose out of joint, that's for sure.'

Bex, intrigued by the news of another man in Eve's life, stepped forward to touch the tips, the herb leaving a trace of its distinct aroma upon her fingertips.

'Bex, Emily; Emily, Bex.'

Emily regarded Bex with an irrational touch of territorialism and stared disapprovingly at her colourful hair.

Bex broke the silence. 'G'day! It's great to meet you. Eve told me so much about you back when we were in Oz. Love your dress.' Bex didn't care much for dresses, and it was a bit too short and clingy for her taste.

'Time to get going if I'm dropping you off in town.' Robert chivvied them. 'There's a match on tonight and I don't intend on missing it.'

Eve set the pot of rosemary aside. 'We're ready.'

'Paolo also left this,' Emily gave her a small envelope that looked suspiciously as though it'd already been opened. Eve raised an eyebrow.

'What? A married, pregnant woman has gotta get her kicks from somewhere, and there should be no secrets between friends.'

Just as Robert ushered them out of the door, Eve quickly scanned the note:

Bella Eve, please accept my sincere apologies for the kiss. I thought it fitting to offer you a piece of Italy to bring to The Melbourne both as an apology and as a nod to your café's heritage. Buona fortuna. You'll be fine! Paolo x

♥

La Terrazza's opening night had been delayed by the impromptu departure of Paolo back to Italy to visit his mother for the first time since he and his father had moved to England – a trip apparently inspired by his recent conversation with Eve.

Bex was more than happy to accompany Eve and Emily to the event, hopeful for her first taste of the northern nightlife she'd heard so much about. She had visions of Geordie Shore-esque fake-tanned, false-lashed, big haired, big heeled and big chested women who left little to the imagination whatever the weather; and from what she'd observed so far from the window of Robert's Golf as they'd pulled into the city centre, she wouldn't be disappointed. Her mouth agape, she had to stifle the urge to leap out and smuggle them all into a big winter coat. She certainly wouldn't be parting with hers tonight, even if it did make her stand out like a sore thumb – they were only eight-hundred miles away from the Arctic Circle after all.

During the journey, Emily had taken immense pleasure in bringing Bex up to speed on Eve's rather limited post-James love-life. Fortunately, despite a lot of prodding on the subject, Bex said she had no gossip to pain Eve with regarding James insofar as romance was concerned, and Eve was secretly relieved – if she'd heard otherwise, it could have ruined her night.

Robert dropped the women off outside the ivy-entwined pillars of the entrance to La Terrazza, the breeze from the River Tyne ruffling their hair in a manner they found most irritating. Bex felt like a fish out of water in her borrowed skinny jeans, sandals, and strappy vest - she didn't really do dressing up having spent most of her adult life frequenting the grungier parts of Melbourne where she'd always blended in seamlessly. Together the three women made for the steps and a formal waiter held the door open for them with a flourish.

'Oh, it's lovely,' said Eve as she absorbed their surroundings.

The walls of La Terrazza were painted a warm shade of cream and the floor was tiled in terracotta. Faux columns lined the walkways, twisted with reams of ivy and fairy lights. A mural dominated the far wall, depicting a vista of lush hills dotted with citrus groves set against a backdrop of cobalt ocean. It was an image of Paolo's home, and the overall effect was of a sun-drenched terrace in Italy overlooking the sea. Candlesticks flickered upon pristine tablecloths, and the air was heavy with the scents of buttered garlic and herbs.

'Ah, Miss Eve.' Gianni greeted Eve with a kiss on each cheek. His portly frame was dressed in a black suit and tie, and he was clearly in his element to find his opening night was such a success.

'I'm glad you're having a night off from the kitchen!' Eve handed him the most expensive bottle of Prosecco she'd been able to find.

Gianni grinned. 'Thank you - you shouldn't have! I will save it for best. How pleased we are to have the pleasure of your company on our most special evening. It must be your special day coming up soon too?'

'Yes - Tuesday. I'm so nervous.'

'I remember that feeling back when I first started out as a young man. You will be fine. Ees a lot of hard work but is worth it. I will find my son - no doubt he will be pleased you have come.'

Eve spotted Paolo before Gianni did, and she pointed him out to Bex. He was serving espresso to a young woman whom to Bex embodied the look she had perhaps unfairly began to associate with many of the women of the area. Not surprisingly, Paolo's level of attentiveness appeared unequal to the task required.

'That's him?'

'That's him,' Eve confirmed.

'The one who's all over that half-naked girl over there with the massive knockers?'

'Yep.'

'Who at this very moment appears to be slipping something into her hand?'

'Uh-huh.'

'Just like Emily said he did when he met you?'

Bex regarded Eve, unsure as to how she might react to the situation after her disappointment with James. 'Maybe it wasn't his phone number - maybe she had just, uhm, spilled some pasta sauce or something and he was helping her clean it up.'

'Seriously,' said Emily, 'what on earth did Eve expect brushing him off like she did? She should have just gone for it. *I* would have done in her position. A man like Paolo isn't going to hang around.'

Bex raised an eyebrow. Her own take on how to help a friend overcome the ending of her relationship James was clearly vastly different from Emily's.

'I *am* actually here, you know,' said Eve. 'Oh no, he's coming over. Quick! Act normal.' She lowered her eyes to the floor, and when she raised them again, Paolo was standing in front of her. Now it was *his* turn to look sheepish.

'Eve!' He cleared his throat. 'How wonderful it is to see you again. I know you've been very busy lately - I was not sure you would make it here tonight.'

'Evidently.'

Emily smirked.

Paolo pretended not to have heard her. 'I trust you are well and that you received my letter and your gift?'

'I did, thank you,' said Eve. 'It was very kind. Did the rosemary really come all the way from Italy?'

'From my mother's very own garden.'

Though his lusty behaviour did take the shine off the gesture somewhat, perhaps that was as sincere as Paolo got. 'You didn't have to. How was your trip?'

'Great! It had been such a long time - Mamma was very pleased to see me. I have you to thank for that.'

Eve was happy for him. 'You seem to be having a good opening night. Great turnout...' She gestured around her at the full tables, inadvertently catching a loaded stare from the blonde, who pushed her shoulders back to enhance certain attributes of hers as though to remind Paolo of what was on offer, though Eve doubted he had forgotten.

Paolo followed her gaze, and his cheeks had the grace to colour slightly. 'Ahem... Yes, very good. Now,' he recovered swiftly, 'I have taken the liberty of reserving you the best seat in the house, just in case. If you and your friends would like to follow me?'

'*Course* he has,' Emily whispered.

He led them to the only remaining booth, upholstered in plush velvet, before procuring a bottle of sparkling rosé from the bar that he declared was on the house and leaving them to peruse the menu. They saw him wipe his brow as he walked away.

'Was that *lipstick* on his collar?' said Emily after she had let the others squish in before her, clearing the way for the innumerable bathroom visits she'd no doubt need to make.

Bex poured out two wines and a glass of water for Emily. 'I think he smelled of perfume.'

'*Cheap* perfume.' Emily sniggered.

'Well, if nothing else,' said Eve, 'I think we can be assured of good service tonight.'

'To good service,' Bex raised a glass.

'To great friends,' said Eve.

'And to The Melbourne!' Emily laughed as they clinked glasses.

♥ 10 ♥

The next morning, Eve awoke unseemingly early following a sleepless night of willing away the hours until the moment arrived when she was finally permitted to visit her newly decorated café. She'd barely been able to contain her excitement all morning, much to the amusement of her parents and Bex, and in efforts to pass the interminable waiting time she'd drank three cups of instant coffee and munched her way through an entire packet of custard creams. She pestered Emily like a child on Christmas morning, repeatedly texting to find out when she could come around, but the visit was postponed several times until everything was exactly right. The caffeine jitters combined with the heightened anticipation of these small delays and setbacks almost sent Eve into a tizz.

'We can go now!' she yelled, holding up her phone triumphantly when it finally beeped with the go ahead.

A nonplussed Robert glanced up at her over his newspaper.

'Quick!' She was exasperated.

'That's my cue to get my shoes on, I suppose,' he muttered, putting down his newspaper and kicking off his slippers.

Carol reached for her handbag and Bex grabbed her little backpack from upstairs, both equally excited. Together they made their way to the car, the last of the browned autumn leaves banked up by the side of the road crunching under their feet as they walked.

'I can't wait to see the place,' said Bex.

'Me too,' said Carol. 'Always was a creative thing, Emily.'

Eve nibbled at her nails and willed her dad to take the most direct route, just this once.

♥

To protect his precious Golf, Robert refused to park within what felt like a square mile of the café, afraid that some hoon - to borrow a turn of phrase from Bex that had tickled him - would ride roughshod between the double-parked cars of the narrow streets off Chillingham Road in which Eve's café was located, potentially dislocating a wing mirror or worse.

'Hurry up.' Eve chided him.

Her parents were of a similar mind – *please let this work out for our daughter*. Though Robert remained privately worried and slightly sceptical about the whole thing, he was under strict instructions from his wife not to show it.

Bex was thinking how charming the little identical rows of red brick terraces were - she'd never before seen such uniformity amongst residential housing - another British quirk. Perhaps they lacked imagination?

Eve stopped in her tracks outside the double-fronted property tucked right at the end of Victoria Terrace, its side parallel with the alley running behind Chilli' Road, and together the four regarded the façade of her new café.

'Surprise!' An ever-increasing baby bump burst out of the racing green front door, followed closely by Emily herself who had been awaiting their arrival from the window.

'Emily it's, it's...' Eve was overcome with emotion, her voice thick and her eyes filling with tears. 'Thank you, it's wonderful!' She hugged her friend tight. Even Robert was impressed by the finish.

'I know.' Emily was nothing if not confident. 'And you haven't even seen the inside yet. Come on, rabble.'

Eve hung back as the others went ahead without her, her eyes locked on the sign above the front door where 'The Melbourne Community Café' was painted neatly against a dove-grey background. Paolo's rosemary and other herbs tumbled from the hanging baskets that still remained as a nod to the building's history, and Thom had fitted a couple of heat lamps above each bay window to enable Eve's customers to use the little outdoor tables they'd managed to cram in on cooler days like they did in Melbourne.

Inside, Emily had salvaged a huge wooden worktop that could easily sit twelve people, and which took up about half of the café's seating area. This, she explained, was where the community program could take place – it was slightly removed from the rest of the café to limit noise and afford its participants a little privacy. The wall behind it was a chalkboard divided into a timetable where the program's activities would be displayed.

The outer walls of each of the two seating areas had been stripped to bare brick, creating a stark look that wasn't to Eve's personal taste but was in keeping with what she'd seen in countless Melbourne cafés. Mirrors of all shapes and sizes were hung, softening the bare walls, and infinitely reflecting and bouncing light within the café's interior. Taking into account her overall use of colour and texture, Emily had masterfully managed to create an aura of rustic warmth, which was exactly what Eve had been hoping for.

'Bonzer!' Bex grinned, and the others couldn't help but laugh.

'Oh, Ems, it's perfect – better than anything I could've hoped for.'

Pendant lights illuminated the counter and tumbling plants spilled from every shelf and surface. A cushioned bench dominated the far side of the activities table, and each of the bay windows had been converted into tiny nooks for two. The window overlooking the alley was now a hatch where coffee would be served during the morning rush hour, and the crockery and glassware Eve and Carol had bought were stacked and ready to be put to good use. Robert had donated a pile of old board games from the attic, and a bookcase had been crammed with the contributions of family and friends. A children's play area was sectioned off by a miniature picket fence complete with its own table and stools.

'They don't pay me the big bucks for nothing,' said Emily. 'But it's Thom you should thank. He did all the manual labour - I just brought the vision.'

'Is that a polite way of saying you bossed him about the whole time?' Carol grinned. 'I'm pleased to see you haven't lost your sense of modesty.'

'Did somebody want me?' A deep voice reverberated from somewhere near the kitchen then a strapping figure emerged, silhouetted by the light from the window behind him.

There was an audible intake of breath from Bex. '*I* want you!' she breathed, but Thom didn't seem to notice. His eyes were on Eve, slowly taking in the changes to her appearance since their last encounter. She was even more lovely in person than his memories had done justice.

Eve felt something happen to her insides as she returned his look - something she hadn't felt for a long time and tried hard to quell. She struggled to equate the bespectacled little nuisance from her youth with the paint-splattered Adonis before her. Though they'd both attended Emily's wedding, Eve hadn't paid him the slightest bit of attention as her heart had belonged firmly to James. As far as she recalled, Thom had been involved with someone back then too.

'Thom.' She extended a hand to his. 'It's been such a long time. I'm so grateful for all the work you've put in here - I honestly can't thank you both enough.'

Thom shrugged. 'Pleasure! Work tends to slow down for me in the run up to Christmas anyway, and I wanted to help Emily out.'

'This must have come in over budget, surely.' Robert frowned, and Carol gave him a nudge.

'It's *who* you know,' said Emily. 'I have my contacts.'

'Do you have any plans for the back yard yet?' Thom asked Eve. He was all sandy blond hair and defined bone structure, with the same cobalt-blue eyes as his sister's. The resemblance between them was slightly disconcerting and it took her a moment to gather her thoughts.

'I'll have to leave it for the time being. I know it's a bit of project-'

'Total eyesore,' Emily agreed.

'But it'll be winter soon and I'll have to see how things go with the café before another big spend.'

'She's working to a strict budget.' Robert knew he was risking the wrath of his wife by speaking up, but he couldn't resist.

'If she doesn't learn how to make a decent cup of coffee soon, she'll be closed by spring anyway,' said Bex. 'Barista-ing isn't exactly her forte.'

'If you like,' said Thom, 'I have some ideas if you're ever thinking of extending outdoors for the warmer weather. I think you'll be surprised what we could achieve on a budget.'

The prospect of warmer weather still seemed a long way off. Emily glanced from Eve to her brother, amused at the exchange between them and secretly hopeful. He wasn't usually so persistent.

'I'll keep that in mind, thanks.'

'Landscaper too now, eh? Man of many skills,' Robert mumbled.

'Well, I'd best be heading off. I'm quoting someone for a job this afternoon. I'll just grab my gear from the back.'

Eve gaped at his retreating form. It was solid, sturdy, and strong.

'We're going to head off now too,' said Carol. 'Your dad and I are going for a walk to find somewhere nice for lunch. Soon we'll just be able to drop in here! Thank you for everything you've done, Emily, we couldn't be more grateful.'

'I'll drop by next week,' said Thom as he pulled on his jacket. 'Your worktop needs sanding. You're not in a hurry for it, are you? I'd come sooner but I've got a job on.'

'No rush.' Eve blushed at the prospect of seeing him again so soon. 'Call in whenever suits.'

When he'd gone, Bex determined it might be a bit rude at this precarious stage of her acquaintance with Emily to discuss her brother's absolute hotness right in front of her. 'So,' she said instead, 'coffee, anyone?'

Emily disappeared behind the counter to fiddle with some buttons and music filled the air. 'Looks like I've finally got the sound system figured out.' She settled into a chair, propping herself up with the cushions.

'Oh, and before we get started, I almost forgot - I have something for you.' Bex reached inside her backpack and handed Eve a bulky package wrapped in brown paper tied with twine. 'Careful, it's fragile! Hopefully, it's survived the journey.'

Eve unwrapped the gift, and inside were two long strings of fairy lights, with each light slotted into a mini glass jam-jar. 'How thoughtful! Thank you. No Melbourne-themed café would be complete without a jam-jar light feature! I know just the spot for them too. I'll run them from either side of the front door to the gate posts. They'll look lovely and welcoming, especially on these dark, chilly nights.'

'Yes,' said Emily, 'and you can decapitate your customers in the process as they try to access the outdoor tables.'

Eve conceded that she may have a point and pondered a way around it. Thom would know.

'Hey, I just had a thought - isn't this Victoria Terrace? As in *Victoria,* Australia?' said Bex.

'Oh yeah, you're right! I hadn't thought of that.' Victoria was the Australian state Eve had lived in for the past few years. 'Maybe this was meant to be?'

'Maybe it's Daniel looking out for you,' said Emily. 'He would have been so proud.'

'Come on,' Bex chided. 'We haven't got all day – with coffee-making skills like yours we'll need Daniel to give us a miracle if you're going to learn by Tuesday.'

She tipped a batch of coffee beans into the grinder, reaching for a carton of milk from the well-stocked fridge under the counter and pouring out a generous measure into a metal jug. Whilst she made it look easy, Eve knew otherwise and sighed.

'Make mine a decaf!' said Emily, savouring the nutty aroma.

Eve begrudgingly took the jug, listening intently for that elusive sound the milk apparently made the moment it was ready. Unfortunately, it remained elusive, and within moments foaming milk frothed upwards and out of the jug like an erupting volcano. It was going to be a long afternoon.

♥

Late on Monday evening, Eve was weary of both body and mind after an intensely busy weekend of getting everything in The Melbourne just right - scrubbing out the kitchens, collecting deliveries, adding the finishing touches to their menu and agreeing on pricing, and baking up a selection of Aussie sweet treats ready for their opening day. Hardest of all however, was learning how to make a decent cup of coffee upon which her future success sorely depended.

She was eventually able to collapse into bed, the anticipation of the day to come almost, but not quite, preventing her from getting a good night's sleep before sheer exhaustion took over. Despite all that had happened over the course of the past few months and the continued heartache of losing James that never quite left her, she slept soundly in the knowledge of how lucky she was to be able to pursue something, if not someone, she was sure to love.

♥ 11 ♥

Eve couldn't quite believe today was the day. She groaned when her alarm pierced her dreams at six-AM, thinking how crazy she was to choose a career where she would have to kiss the promise of a lie-in goodbye indefinitely, and where she was sure to turn into a pumpkin if she went to bed any later than nine o'clock. She showered quickly before tying her thick, dark hair into a messy bun, leaving out a brush of blunt fringe. She applied mascara and a slick of bright red lipstick, its colour contrasting nicely with her plain uniform of black skinny jeans, flats, and a fitted white top.

She wasn't at all sure what to expect that brisk early morning where the sun was yet to make its appearance over the little red brick terraces and only the thinnest streaks of pink and yellow tinted the sky. Dave arrived on the dot, just as a cheerful Bex brought the coffee machine to life to bring them each a caffeine hit, and Eve fussed over how to most appealingly display the treats she'd stayed up late baking the night before. She'd decided to start small, relieved to have Dave's experience to rely upon with regards to how much stock she would require among other nitty gritty she would just have to learn as she went along.

'It's almost eight!' said Bex as she spooned the chocolatey foam of her cappuccino into her mouth.

Eve chewed the skin at the side of her nails, a nervous habit she'd developed in her teenage years that her mam had often berated her for. She was anxious. What if no-one came? Was an Australian-style café really suited to the

Geordie palate? And what if no-one attended her community program's activities? That was the part of the café she felt most passionate about, and whilst she really hoped her customers would embrace it, people were always so busy these days, weren't they?

She paced back and forth between the café's two seating areas. Was the temperature ok? Did the music she'd chosen create the right atmosphere? Was it too loud for whoever was living upstairs, and would they file a noise complaint and try to get her closed down? At a loose end, she decided to inspect the kitchen.

'Is everything going ok in there, Dave?' she asked. 'Do you need a hand with anything?'

As he competently sliced through fresh vegetables at a rate she found alarming, he peered at her through narrowed eyes. He was clearly affronted by the implication he might not have everything well and truly under control, and Eve made a mental note to leave him be in future. Chastened, she backed out of the room.

When at last the clock struck eight, the two women quickly donned their burlap aprons. Bex ran outside to put up the wooden street sign that would alert passers-by to the presence of the café and direct them towards The Hatch where they could purchase their rush-hour takeaway coffee before they opened up proper. Eve pushed up the shutters and they waited. And waited some more.

When the clock reached eight twenty-five, it felt as though a lifetime had passed. Was no-one going to come?

'Don't worry,' said Bex. 'I's our first day - hardly anyone knows we're here! And stop chewing your fingers or you'll put people off! No-one wants one of those in their latte.'

Based on Paolo's advice, Eve had deliberately avoided advertising the café as open for the first week or so, anxious not to bite off more than she could chew when she was only just finding her feet and getting a feel for footfall and turnover, or whatever jargon was best applied to these circumstances. She was seriously beginning to question whether that had been the best way to go when a cheery good morning caught her attention. She peered down from the hatch.

'Brr, it's bloody freezing. I'm Tony - I live in the flat upstairs.' He was dressed in a smart black business suit and carrying a shiny briefcase. He looked about forty, with a distinguished demeanour and salt and pepper hair.

'G'day, how are ya?' said Bex.

Tony took in her pink hair and massive nose ring - Eve had had a hard time that morning convincing Bex to stick with the requisite black and white uniform she'd decided upon - and in retribution she hadn't been able to resist sticking in the most attention-drawing piece of jewellery she owned ('I *am* here voluntarily you know,' she'd argued). Eve was sure it must be against health and safety regulations.

'What can we get you?'

'An espresso please, two sugars.'

'Coming right up.' Bex quickly prepared his drink.

'I'm Eve.' She leaned out of the hatch to shake Tony's chilly hand. 'Our music isn't too loud for you, is it?'

'Nah. I'm usually up for work through the week anyway, and on weekends I'll most likely be here in your café. I'm looking forward to it, though I must admit I'll miss Gianni's pizza - he makes a mean pepperoni. As it is, I'm glad to have somewhere so convenient to grab a caffeine hit on my way to work.'

'Here you go.' Bex handed him his coffee and he took a sip.

'Mmm... I could get used to this. How much do I owe you?'

'This one's on the house,' said Eve as she stamped a loyalty card and passed it down to Tony. 'You're our first customer!'

'The first of many, with coffee like that.' He put the card straight into his wallet, grimaced at his watch, then dashed off to catch his train.

'He doesn't look like someone who would live in a little flat above a café,' Eve remarked.

'And what should someone who lives in a little flat above a café look like?' Bex thought nothing of it, she didn't think it would be all that unusual in Melbourne.

Eve shrugged.

'Is anyone there?'

It was a harried looking young mother, hair scraped into a bun revealing a couple of inches of dark roots. She was pushing a plump toddler, and a little girl dressed in a navy school uniform was clutching one of the pushchair's handles whilst rocking from foot to foot with a finger in her mouth smiling shyly up at them. It was the first day of school after the half-term holidays apparently, and the family were struggling to get back into their usual routine.

'This place is *such* a lifesaver. I'm in desperate need of caffeine. Strong, hot, long black please - no sugar,' said the woman.

Eve thought it best to let Bex prepare her drink, worried she might put people off if she did so herself, but Bex persuaded her to do it instead. It was the only way she'd learn, after all. The woman took a sip and Eve held her breath.

'Mmm, delicious, thanks.' And off she went after being handed a loyalty card and a complimentary honey joy slipped in a paper bag for the little girl to enjoy later.

'By Jove, she's finally got it!' Bex grinned.

'Oh, look - it's just gone nine.'

It was gratifying after weeks of stress, hard work, and painstaking preparations to at last unlock the café's front door ready for business for the very first time. Eve turned the sign from Closed to Open.

♥

Aside from a string of customers from the local businesses on Chilli' Road, things at the café remained relatively quiet until lunch time. One couple popped in expecting to find La Terrazza still in its usual location. They weren't intending to stay until Eve managed to convince them otherwise, the promise of some hot pumpkin soup on a chilly day winning them over. The pair were closely followed by a group of men and women in smart dress who appeared to be holding a meeting of some sort, bolstered by the premise of coffee and a hearty lunch. Things generally slowed down again after that; the presence of the new café still largely unknown except to Paolo and Gianni, Tony who lived upstairs, and the other inhabitants of Victoria Terrace to whom curiosity had gotten the better of them.

Dave peeked his flushed face out of the kitchen from time to time to see how his food was going down with the locals, keen to make as good an impression as possible so they would want to return or at least put in a good word with their friends and family. He was a perfectionist at heart, and Bex impressed everyone with her fantastic coffee and her creative use of coffee art topping a delicate layer of creamy foam.

'When will you teach me how to do that?' Eve was envious of her skill with the milk jug as she watched Bex pour out yet another pretty leaf, a nod to the autumn season.

'When you're ready,' she responded, cryptically. 'So never! Haha.'

Emily paid them a surprise visit with her husband Mark in the afternoon, baby bump resplendent in a woollen jumper dress, thick tights, and a pair of gravity-defying ankle boots.

'What are you two doing here?' Eve was thrilled to see them, and she felt a surge of pride as the pair regarded the café with its few customers dotted here and there whose clean plates showed they had clearly enjoyed their fresh Aussie take on food.

'We're on our lunch break, but we thought we'd drop by on your first day to make you look busy and popular. I'll have the mixed quinoa porridge, and Mark will have-'

'The Big Aussie.'

'I was going to say the Bircher. Mark, I thought you were watching your weight?' Emily patted his stomach. 'All that video-gaming you've been doing lately.'

'I'm growing a sympathy belly for you. Anyway, now we're married I thought I had your permission to let myself go.' In reality, he looked as trim as ever.

'Well in that case,' Emily relented, 'you won't mind if I treat myself to a lamington then, will you? Eating for two and all that.'

'You won't be able to get away with that one for much longer,' Bex joked.

Emily gave her a stony look. 'I didn't think people working in the food industry were supposed to wear nose-jewellery. Aren't you supposed to have a big blue plaster covering it up?'

'You're starting an Avid Gamers group?' Mark pointed at the community program over on the chalkboard.

'Oh, Eve, can you wipe that one off? As if he needs any more encouragement. Mark, we are having a *baby* next month. You can play with her instead. There won't be any time for video games for at least five more years.'

Later that afternoon when things had slowed right down, an elderly couple wandered in hand in hand. The man was wearing a tweed cap upon wisps of white hair, which he removed after holding the door open for his wife, gripping her elbow gently to help her up the little step inside.

'We're gannin' on a cruise te Australia after Christmas,' the man said proudly in a strong Geordie accent Bex could barely comprehend. His name was Stanley. 'We only live 'roond the corner - thought we'd try out the food before we gan awa there, yi kna? Get a bit of a taste for it. Have yi any kangaroo?'

'No,' Eve laughed, gesturing to them to a comfortable seat side by side in one of the bay windows, 'but you might find something else to try.'

'We'll be going to Melbourne too,' the old lady said. Her name was Betty. 'My sister moved there forty years ago, and I haven't seen her since. We write to one another, but it's not the same, is it? I've always wanted to visit but we could never afford it 'til now. Have you been there?'

'I used to live there,' said Eve, 'which is why I've opened this place. I'm sure you'll have a wonderful time. My friend Bex who works here is Australian - I'll get her to come over and give you some travel tips.'

The couple beamed as they eased themselves slowly into their seats. 'Thank you, that's very kind,' said Betty. 'And well done, the place looks lovely.'

♥

Towards the end of the day when the food service had finished and Dave was busy clearing up and making his preparations for the next morning, Eve's parents made an appearance to see how they were all getting on. Robert had left work early specially and was relieved to find the day had been declared a success. He headed straight for the sweet's cabinet.

It was with a sigh of relief that at five o'clock Eve turned the sign on the front door to 'Closed' and together they cracked open a bottle of complimentary wine (she made a mental note to stop making so many things complimentary if her café was to have any hope of survival) to celebrate a first day that had gone without any disasters save for one complaint that someone's bacon wasn't crispy enough (which was soon rectified by Dave, who accused them of having an unrefined palate), and another that someone's flat white apparently wasn't flat enough (which was not well received by Bex, who complained that the Brits can't spot a good coffee when they get one). Eve accepted that you couldn't please everyone and there was no accounting for taste.

'So, how did it go?' Carol asked, as Robert tucked into a slice of toasted banana bread spread thickly with butter. She beamed with pride that despite what she'd gone through, her daughter still had the guts and motivation to make her dream a reality - a chip off the old block.

'Not bad at all, but I couldn't have done it without you two,' she gestured at Dave and Bex. 'Thank you *so* much.'

Dave had enjoyed the flexibility Eve had provided him with and relished the opportunity to call all the shots in his own kitchen. Bex gently reminded her that whilst she was more than happy to help for a few weeks, she couldn't stay in Newcastle forever and intended to continue her travels in the New Year. Eve didn't begrudge her that for a moment, and they were a tipsy party as Dave said his goodbyes and

Robert drove the women home, Eve and Bex waving at their new neighbour with the salt and pepper hair who was just approaching his flat.

'Don't go getting any ideas ladies - women aren't his thing,' Dave whispered as he eyed Tony hungrily from head to toe. 'More's the better.'

Eve looked at her chef in surprise - she hadn't picked it.

'He *can't* be!' Bex swatted Dave on the arm. 'I had designs.'

'Thought so. I have a finely attuned gaydar, which is more than I can say for some.'

Eve supposed he had a point, but she still couldn't quite believe it on either count. 'Oh well, I don't mind what side he's on so long as he continues to visit our café and doesn't complain to the council about all the noise! See you tomorrow – bright and early.'

Later that evening Eve crawled gratefully into bed exhausted from a late night, early start, and a long day spent on her feet. Despite the months that had passed since her return home, her last thought before she was lost to the enveloping fog of sleep was: *if only James was here to share in this new beginning with me.*

♥ 12 ♥

In her hurt Eve was livid, but she tried to keep her voice down so as not to attract the attention of her customers who were languidly sipping their coffees, flipping through newspapers, or otherwise pleasantly passing a wet Sunday afternoon.

'*You* have some explaining to do!' she said to Bex.

'What? What have I done?' Bex' face was almost as pink as her hair as she busied herself with polishing the already immaculate countertop, and Eve realised Bex knew exactly what she was talking about.

'You said there was nothing you had to tell me about James and his... his... post-me love life.' She spat out the words.

'You saw it, didn't you?'

'Yes, I bloody did.'

'Oh.' Bex steeled herself for the inevitable inquisition, all the while cursing James for having been too slow to un-tag himself from *that* picture.

'How long has it been going on?'

'I don't know.'

Eve tutted.

'Honestly! And I didn't think it was anything serious.'

'So, you *did* know.'

Bex explained that just before she'd left Australia, she'd heard from a mutual friend that James had started dating a new physiotherapist who had begun working with him at the hospital. She was sure it was nothing serious - everyone who'd ever seen him and Eve together knew how distraught they'd been by the loss of one another - but they'd made it clear it was over, so Bex suspected that his friends were as much behind his involvement with Isabelle, as Emily was in pushing Eve towards Paolo. In all honesty, Bex had been too preoccupied with the breakdown of her own relationship and travel plans to give it too much thought, and she'd worried that a blow of this kind was the last thing Eve friend needed when she had her café to attend to.

'How old is she? She looks young. Do you think she's prettier than me? Do you know if they've slept together?'

Bex could see that Eve was in danger of creating a bit of a stir. A fat tear had already slid down her cheek, and she didn't care who saw. 'No and no,' she answered quickly, grabbing a tissue, and urging her to take five minutes out the back whilst she saw to everything. 'We can talk more about this later - but not here.' She gestured about the café, which was enjoying its busiest day since they'd first opened.

The fight left Eve as quickly as it had arrived, and she stalked through the kitchen and out into the back yard, grabbing her coat and ignoring Dave's quizzical look as she stomped past him.

♥

The rain had stopped but the concrete yard was still saturated, and Eve could hear the drip-dripping of water as it dispersed from the building via an old, haphazard guttering system. Eve knew what she'd seen that morning wasn't Bex' fault and already regretted how she'd spoken to her, and that she had stupidly done so in such proximity to the customers upon whom her livelihood now depended. She cursed herself for having checked her phone during a quiet moment, otherwise she would still be in blissful ignorance and enjoying her café's busiest afternoon so far.

A glutton for punishment, she felt inside her coat pocket for her phone and opened her newsfeed, but the picture had gone. For the first time in several months, she allowed herself to enter James' profile, but she didn't find it there either. It wasn't on his wall or buried amongst his other pictures. Like her, since their separation he'd barely posted a thing - his last posts were birthday wishes from his friends months ago. *But where was she?* Eve needed to see her again to see how they compared, and whether the image would shed some light onto the nature of her relationship with James. The only explanation for its absence was that he must have untagged himself, but why? To avoid hurting her when he was involved with someone else, even though he'd told her so many times that no other could ever live up to her? Well, it was a bit too late for that now.

She opened his profile picture - he'd used the same one for a couple of years now. It was a candid snap she'd taken during a picnic at their favourite spot on the ocean beach they would drive over an hour to on the rare occasion their rostered days off collided. The same beach where he'd proposed shortly before they'd agreed to separate. She still thought he looked gorgeous, even though he'd always been inclined to disagree. The picture showcased his striking eyes and defined cheekbones, but what struck her most about him was his ready smile and the open warmth his face projected, which this particular image captured perfectly. Never in her life had she met such a beautiful-hearted man, a man whose heart was written on his face.

It was devastating to see the arms of this man she had felt sure she would always love wrapped around the shoulders of another woman. In the picture they had been smiling happily into the camera, sitting in a long row of ex-colleagues Eve recognised enjoying a staff night out. She looked so at ease nestled in the nook of James' arm, which Eve still couldn't help but feel should only accommodate her. It was even worse knowing that the girl now occupying *her* space looked at least five years her junior and had a bronzed frame offset with dark tresses, fan-like lashes, and dimpled cheeks. It made Eve feel about a hundred years old and redundant, and not for the first time she bemoaned her porcelain complexion.

Most of all though, her heart still ached for James. She had stifled her feelings for him for so long, throwing herself into one thing after another in efforts to numb the pain, but finally she allowed herself to admit that the loss of him still burned within her. She cried hot tears alone in the back yard that grey, miserable day where the thick cloud seemed as though it would never lift.

'Meaow.'

Eve was initially too distressed to notice that she had company.

'Meaooow.' The cat tiptoed closer. 'Meaooooow?'

It circled her feet, nudging its damp sides against her legs. Startled, Eve looked down upon the creature. She smiled through her tears, dabbed at her nose with a tissue, then crouched down and reached out a cupped palm towards it. The cat approached her outstretched hand, sniffing at her fingers before, seemingly satisfied with its investigations, deciding to give one of them a surreptitious lick then nudging its head against the side of her hand. Aware that the cat seemed to have decided she didn't pose a threat, she reached out her other hand and tentatively stroked its smooth fur. Cat and Eve regarded one another, hazel eyes meeting startling green.

'What a lovely little cat you are,' she said gently as she took in its slim frame, sleek grey coat, and white socks. 'I wonder who you belong to?'

There was no collar. In response to her attention the cat meaowed a little louder then began to purr as she tickled under its chin and behind its ears.

'You must be cold, you poor thing. And hungry too?'

She entered the kitchen, returning with a tiny saucer of water Dave had reluctantly offered, only after noticing how upset she'd been. 'You do realise we'll never get rid of it now. Vermin!' he yelled.

But Eve ignored him. It was obvious he was neither a cat nor a people person.

Eve was gratified to watch the little cat lapping at the water she'd placed on the step - there was something restorative about caring for another living creature. She gave it one last pet, and after taking a deep breath and checking her face was back in order, re-entered her café.

♥

'Oh, thank goodness you're back,' said Bex. 'It's been hectic in here. You ok?'

Bex was trying to make a succession of coffees at once, but there were orders still to be taken and food yet to be served. As cafés went it wasn't manic, but for an unpublicised venue with only three members of staff, they were spread pretty thinly. It was as though the whole street had turned out to have a nose at their local new venue.

Eve nodded, scared to speak over the lump in her throat in case the tears came again. She needed to get some control over her emotions *and* her business, fast. 'Ok, I'll take over on the coffee machine, if you wouldn't mind taking orders and completing service?'

'Sure.'

Eve knew they were going to need an extra pair of hands; she just didn't know where the money was going to come from to pay for it. She absorbed herself in making coffee after coffee, and though the methodical act took her mind off other things, she was still all fingers and thumbs. She tried in vain to keep track of who wanted skinny milk, who wanted full cream, who wanted none at all, and any other request that tailored the humble coffee bean to one's personal preferences and cursed the variety her own menu allowed.

'Hey there! I'll have an extra hot, super-skinny, super-sized, three-sugared, half-caff, tall, flat, long black please. With extra foam, chocolate sprinkles, hold the whipped cream... and a partridge in a pear tree.'

Eve was so flustered she didn't quite take in what was being said, but she did notice that the voice that had said it was warm, deep and teasing. She looked up in search of its owner, burning a stray finger on the hot milk spout when she realised it belonged to Thom. He'd brought his sander, she noticed.

'Ouch!' She ran her finger under the cold tap.

'Mind if I set to work?'

His cobalt eyes were merry, and Eve wondered if he was pleased to see her. She gathered her faculties, which was somehow no easy task around Thom. 'We're a bit busy at the moment. Would you mind having a seat until it quietens down? I'll bring you a cuppa. What would you like? A latte? Cappuccino? You look more like an espresso man to me.'

'Do I? And what does an espresso man look like, exactly?'

Eve blushed beneath his penetrative gaze, which held a hint of flirtation she was in no mood for. She felt flustered and unsure of how to respond in a way that didn't encourage him further. She wasn't ready to contemplate anything romantic with someone new.

'Don't you know anything about tradies? We're surprisingly straightforward. Tea please - milk and two sugars. Actually, I think I'll put my feet up and read the paper – it's been a hectic day.'

'A tradie who takes tea with milk and two. How original.'

Thom grinned.

When she had a spare moment, Eve set about preparing Thom's tea and tried not to gawp as he took a seat near the counter, carelessly throwing one long leg atop another before clearing his throat and spreading a newspaper across his lap. Tony from upstairs had no such censure. He'd been indulging in a leisurely brunch over the Sunday papers, and his eyebrows rose appreciatively as Thom sat down. It seemed her chef was right about him after all.

'Phwoar!' said Bex an hour or so later when the afternoon rush had receded, and things had become steadier. There still the odd couple dotted here and there, including the elderly pair from the café's opening day - Stanley and Betty. Betty had kindly offered her services to run the Christmas Crafts activity over the festive period and was due to start soon.

Thom set to work sanding down the table. He wasn't used to sitting around, and infuriatingly he seemed to have become quite an attraction for their customers, old and young alike.

Eve ignored Bex. Her heart belonged to James. Didn't it?

Later that night, when a long first week of working at the café gave way to a much needed and precious Monday off, Bex and Eve met up with Emily at one of very few quiet bars in Jesmond, where they picked over and shared an occasional giggle at the handful of comments cards their customers had filled out for them. To their relief, the overarching feedback was generally positive aside from highlighting their need for an extra pair of hands on the weekends, but otherwise the girls unanimously declared The Melbourne's first week a success.

'Listen to this one,' Bex giggled. Feigning a posh English accent, she read aloud: *'I must admit I took quite a fancy to the pierced, pink-haired barista who made my first ever genuinely great cup of coffee.'*

'I wonder who wrote it? If only it was Tony, he's pretty sexy for an oldie.'

'And camp as Christmas, according to Dave.'

'Well, I don't know either of them,' said Emily, 'but by the sounds of it, Dave has already set his sights on Tony for himself.'

Bex groaned. 'Why is it so hard to find a decent, straight guy these days? I thought there'd be more of them on this hemisphere.'

'I thought you were sworn off men for good? Perhaps if you considered a more neutral hair colour and didn't dress as though you'd just fallen out of bed?'

'Play nice,' said Eve.

'Sorry, sorry. It's just that I'm bloated and uncomfortable and I've barely had a wink of sleep for about a month.'

'It won't be long now 'til baby's earthside, then you won't get any sleep for months. When my sister had one, she didn't sleep again for *years*.'

Emily sighed. 'It's so unfair.'

'Perhaps you should've thought of that before you got yourself up the duff.'

'*Bex!*' said Eve. 'I love you both equally, you know.'

'But I'm the one who's about to make you an Aunty.'

'And *I'm* the one helping run your bloody café when I'm supposed to be travelling.'

'*I* designed it.'

'Enough!' Eve sighed. 'I am quite obviously indebted to both of you, like, forever. So can we please stop bitching and have a good night?'

Emily blinked. 'There's no such thing as a good night when you're pregnant.'

Bex was suitably appeased when Eve promised to use one of their days off to drive her up to Edinburgh, so then at least she could say she had travelled to *two* countries and feel as though she was making a more constructive use of her time abroad; and Emily was happy when they suggested holding a baby shower in her honour and together they begam brainstorming ideas which made for an enjoyable change of focus from The Melbourne.

♥

Whilst waiting in the cold for the metro home, warmed from within by their excessive alcohol consumption, Bex and Eve huddled together on the blustery platform.

'I'm sorry I didn't tell you about James,' said Bex. 'I didn't think there was anything newsworthy going on between them and I was scared of upsetting you when you've had enough to deal with over here.'

'It's not your fault... But do you know anything about her? Do you know her name?'

'You really want to know?'

'Yeah'

'Isabelle.'

'Oh.' Eve had always liked that name, until now. Why couldn't it be something really awful, like Winifred? Gertrude, even?

'*You* left *him*, remember.'

Eve was crestfallen and Bex immediately wished the words unsaid, cursing the amount of prosecco she'd consumed. 'Whoops, sorry.'

'No, you're right. I still think it was the right thing to do though. We would've resented each other eventually, and probably ended up divorced, with kids thrown into the mix. It would've been complicated and awful.'

'Don't you think then,' Bex risked, 'that it's time you moved on, with someone new?'

'Mmm.' If James had moved on, Eve supposed it was time she at least considered it. 'I just can't imagine anyone ever taking his place.'

'Let them create their own place. Thom seems nice, and he's obviously crazy about you, even though you seem to be of the treat 'em mean, keep 'em keen school of thought. He's a spunk.'

'Oh, don't you start as well. Anyway, what about *you* and love?'

'Gaah, don't utter that swear word to me. I don't know - I think I've given up. Or at least put it on hold for a while. Wes really hurt me, the serial-cheating bast-'

'I know.' Eve bit her lip. 'What are we like? A pair of old maids. If I end up in my mid-forties and eaten by Alsatians, it'll be comforting to know that I'm not alone.'

'Speak for yourself - I'm two years younger than you so not quite as desperate.'

MEET ME AT THE MELBOURNE

A blur of yellow and black indicated the arrival of the metro that came to a screeching halt before them, and together the pair hopped gratefully out of the cold into a near-empty carriage and made their way home, each lost in thought about their respective romantic futures.

♥ 13 ♥

Harry was cold and hungry. He'd had nothing to eat since the previous evening at a public kitchen in town. The kitchen wouldn't open again for days - he'd have to bite down his hunger until then. It was late afternoon already it was getting dark. The sun was setting earlier every evening, and the nights were becoming bitterly cold and unbearably long. He shuddered at the prospect of another uncomfortable, tedious night wandering the streets alone and with an empty belly, the vast darkness and tormenting thoughts his only company. Not for the first time he cursed the coming winter, then he cursed himself and his own stupidity that had brought him to this.

His lonely wanderings had brought him from the outskirts of Newcastle city centre across Armstrong Bridge and through Jesmond Dene that sprawled into Heaton Park, then onwards into Heaton itself. The streets were quieting now as people drifted off into warm homes for hearty dinners. He had passed couples walking hand in hand; some elderly, others middle aged, still others who looked youthful and in love. Some were walking dogs; others were pushing prams containing rosy-cheeked infants. Some were being outrun by their sprightly offspring, excitedly racing fallen leaves that dropped into the Ouseburn stream, and others carried plump toddlers on their hips, pointing out the animals in Pet's Corner.

Mostly Harry kept to the sidelines, a sorrowful figure barely camouflaged by the stripped landscape. He knew that for some his presence was something to fear, whilst for others it was something to simply ignore. Many pretended they hadn't seen him, turning a blind eye to the reminder of an existence they hoped never to experience for themselves whilst at the same time pricked by some sense of guilt. They would avert their gaze, worried he might ask them to give him something, or worse, take something from them for himself. Others didn't notice him at all - he never strayed beyond the periphery of their lives. He didn't know which was worse, but still, he didn't blame them.

Harry didn't have a destination in mind as he meandered slowly through the red brick terraces, streetlamps and living room lights flicking on as the daylight faded. The sweeping darkness represented another day survived, and poignantly marked another day he had managed to stay clean, though he took little comfort from the fact. His mind now free from what he had taken to numb it only served to resurface the memories he'd used them to subdue, before dependency kicked in and the substance itself became the all-encompassing need. Now his thoughts were ever-present, gnawing like the hunger in the pit of his stomach.

He found that the constant movement kept him warm, the changing scenery adding an element of focus and interest to his day that would otherwise have been absent, and generally this combined to provide him with a welcome level of distraction, something else on which to focus his chaotic mind. It was a lonely existence, but it was better than the destructive one he had been living before. The loneliness was as painful as it was necessary. He needed to keep his distance from those who would tempt him back into trouble – they say misery loves company - and he didn't want to go down that path again.

♥

'Did you see that?' Bex asked, brushing her by now faded pink fringe back from her face to get a better view.

'What?'

Eve was preoccupied with wiping down the tabletops. It had been a busy day, and they were in a rush to get to Emily's house in time to attend her baby shower that evening. The downside of running a café she'd discovered, was that it left very little time in her life for anything else. Not that she was complaining - the ability to work for herself as a community presence doing what she loved and believed in was reward enough. Every day was satisfying, and she knew not many people could say that about their jobs, but sometimes she felt bone weary from such early starts and long days on her feet - the pace was exhausting.

'That guy over there - he looks rough. He keeps glancing over here.'

'Does he?'

Eve stopped what she was doing and walked over to the bay window, still holding the damp cloth in her hand, and following the direction of Bex' pointed finger she peered out into the twilight. Sure enough, there was a man standing across the street facing the café. It was difficult to make out much more than a dark, bearded figure with his hands stuffed deep into his pockets.

'Maybe he's lost or something - or it could just be your peculiar English fashions.'

'No, I think you're right.' Eve had encountered enough people like this guy during her shifts in Emergency. 'Go and ask Dave to rustle up whatever he has left from today before he throws it out. Quickly!'

Eve peered outside, and the stranger looked up and caught her eye. She held up a hand to gesture for him to come inside, then turned away briefly towards the kitchen to see what progress was being made, but when she turned back, he'd gone. *Bugger!* Just then Bex came dashing out of the kitchen clutching a container full of food. Eve shook her head. 'He's already gone.'

'Oh.'

'He – and people like him - are part of the reason we're here.'

'Maybe he'll come back...'

Eve nodded, but they both doubted it.

'What's this I hear about you giving away my grub?' Dave was flushed in the face from scrubbing the kitchen, and without his hat his hair was all skewwhiff.

'There was a man across the street looking into the café,' Bex supplied. 'He looked cold and hungry,'

'Huh. Some dodgy guy peeps through the window at two pretty young women and you want to put yourselves at risk by giving him *my* dinner? He could have been a flasher or anything!'

'If he was that bad, how come he left when we tried to help him?' said Eve.

'Because he was worried about getting caught.'

'Well, *we* think he looked like he needed help. And if he ever comes back that's what we'll give him. If he lets us.'

'First that darned cat and now a peeping Tom.' Dave tutted. 'That cat, by the way, has been stalking the back yard every day since you befriended it, you know. Thinks it's going to get fed.'

Eve was delighted. She'd always wanted a cat, but James hadn't been keen.

'Not much of a cat person, are you, Dave?' said Bex.

'It doesn't stop at cats - why else do you think I choose to slave away over a hot stove all day? So I don't have to deal with people - or animals, come to that. If that bloke comes round here again you can give him something if you must, but make sure I'm around when you do, and it had better not be *my* dinner.' He glanced at the clock. 'Don't you two have somewhere to be tonight?'

'Bugger!' said Eve.

After prising his dinner from Bex' hands, Dave headed back into the kitchen clutching it tight.

'He's a great big softy, really,' said Bex.

'You think?' Eve wasn't so sure.

Dave left by bicycle followed closely by the two women who locked up behind them. Eve had borrowed her dad's car for the night, and Bex eased herself in before taking hold of a box of pink cupcakes and resting it on her knee. The drive to Emily and Mark's house was short, but it being a weekend leading up to Christmas there was still quite a lot of traffic. At last, they pulled up outside the grand, three-storey terraced house that Eve had always openly envied, even though the streets surrounding it were always precariously double parked and the area seemed to predominantly house posh young students.

Though it was bitterly cold outside, lights glowed invitingly from within, and Eve spared a thought for the man they'd seen that evening and for others like him, sending up a quick prayer for their safety and comfort at a time of year that for some could feel more isolating than ever. Several friends of Emily's were arriving too – they were easy to spot by their baby paraphernalia - pink and white helium balloons, teddy bears, and a giant bunny rabbit with lopsided ears.

'Late again!' Emily was unimpressed. She and her bump looked lovely in a wine-coloured wrap dress, ribbed tights, and heels. She was wearing huge dangly earrings that sprung out from beneath her platinum crop and tugged dangerously upon her earlobes.

Eve gave her a smug hug. 'When you see what we've got you, all will be forgiven.'

'It had better be good. Come into my humble mansion and try some non-alcoholic mulled wine - my friend Julia made it in sympathy for me.' She grimaced. 'I'll do the rounds then join you in a little while.'

Eve and Bex grabbed a drink from the state-of-the-art kitchen that was purely for show - everybody who knew Emily and Mark knew they hated cooking and subsisted on some sort of posh, skinny version of meals on wheels. The bench was festooned with pink pompoms and bunting, and

Eve stacked up the little pearl-encrusted cupcakes she had baked to create something of a feature of them on the tiered cake stand.

They mingled with Emily's other guests, the more pretentious of whom Eve avoided as far as could not be deemed impolite. Bex oohed and ahhed over the period features of Emily's stunning home, though one or two of her interior designer friends seemed rather put out by their competitor's natural flair for colour and style.

There were games including, to the discomfort of the more conservative among them who considered it vulgar, a blindfolded game of 'Pin the Sperm on the Egg' which Bex thought was hilarious and to which she applied herself with great zeal. After gorging on copious amounts of food and drink they all sat to watch Emily open her gifts.

Mark had wisely made himself scarce - his idea of a baby shower involved a trip to the local pub with his brother-in-law where they would talk footy and drink a lot, making an obligatory toast to the baby's health if they were still coherent enough to do so.

Emily, unlike her usual pragmatic self, became increasingly emotional with each gift she opened - and there were a lot - until eventually she was almost balling.

'Thank you. Oh, thank you, you're all so thoughtful. I love you,' she sniffed.

'Are you sure you didn't get stuck into the alcoholic mulled wine by mistake?' Bex handed her a gift.

'Oh Bex. It's lovely. Lovely!' It was a voucher for Emily to treat herself to a pregnancy massage and a pedicure to help her feel more like herself. 'I haven't seen my toes for weeks and my entire skeleton aches.'

Eve gave her a handmade frame holding copies of Emily's scan pictures and a spot to put a photo of the baby when it was born.

'Eve. Aunty Eve. This is beautiful, thank you!' Emily hugged her friend as closely as her bump would allow. 'It's going straight up on the nursery wall.'

'There's something else as well...' Eve handed over an envelope, inside of which was a voucher for their first family photo shoot, including a make-over for the mother, some bubbles, and a few prints. 'And we'll babysit for you any time.'

'*We?*' Bex frowned.

When it became apparent that Emily was about to burst into tears again, Eve suggested she show them all the nursery. Emily pushed open the door to reveal a riot of clashing shades of pink - baby pink, rose pink, blush, cerise, cherry and champagne. The colour-scheme couldn't be less like Emily, but what was more surprising was that it somehow worked.

The far wall was papered in vintage paper she'd carefully sourced to be in keeping with the era in which the house was built. It was white with a print of tiny trailing pink roses, and she'd also had the pattern blown up and printed on the heavy drapes that made a feature of their sash windows. Swathes of pink fabric billowed from the ceiling and tumbled over the cot before gathering in folds at the floor, and the cot itself was perched on a plush pink rug over whitewashed floorboards. It should have looked too bright and busy, but instead the overall effect was tranquil and tempered by soft, touchable fabrics. A mini projector cast lights and shadows onto the ceiling above, ready to entrance their little one to sleep.

'Wow!' Eve gasped. 'It's beautiful.'

There were murmurs of agreement from the others.

'I should've brought my sunnies!' said Bex, shielding her eyes. 'Don't think your baby will be doing much sleeping in here – it'll be way too stimulated.' She couldn't resist the opportunity to pull Emily off her high horse occasionally, and a cheeky titter from one or two of the other guests suggested she wasn't the only one who felt that way. 'I hope they got the gender right at the scan.'

Emily was unphased. 'Boy, girl, or sea creature - we will love it equally.'

♥

Emily's guests had long since left, except for Eve and Bex who had their feet up on pouffes nursing hot cups of tea and picking over the evening's events.

'Oooarghh garrumph!'

'What was that?'

'That'll be the boy's home. It's about time!' Emily heaved herself up from the chaise longue and waddled over to the front door, letting in an unwelcome waft of frigid air. 'Forgotten your keys again have you, drunkard? What time do you call this?' It was close to midnight.

'Oh Ems, don't be like that.' Mark leaned in unsteadily for a kiss, blowing a toxic combination of smoke, beer, and cheesy chips into his wife's disapproving face. 'How was the baby shower?'

'*Smoking*? You've been smoking again when you promised you wouldn't. Where's your sense of responsibility? You're about to become a father. You know how bad it is for the baby, not to mention that I'm the one who has to bloody kiss you!'

Eve and Bex shared a look - it was time they were heading home. They grabbed their coats but were distracted by the commotion coming from outside. There was the incomprehensible, out of key rendition of an eighties hit which stopped abruptly when Thom tripped up the doorstep on his way into the house.

'Oof!'

Emily glared daggers at him.

'Sis!' He reached out his arms, apparently more to steady himself than to greet her. 'Don't be like that. I tried to stop him, but he's so bloody determined – I don't know how you put up with him.'

Another waft of smoky breath hit Emily square in the face. 'You too? Yuck, get away from me - you're both disgusting!'

She turned to face her husband, who was trying to put his arm around her. She shrugged him off. 'Get upstairs and brush your teeth. You're not breathing stale smoke into my face all night. It's late and we're going straight to bed.'

'It was just a cigar,' Mark muttered.

Emily faced Thom. 'One task. You had one task! Don't get him drunk, and don't let him smoke.'

'That's two tasks!' Mark's voice echoed down the stairs.

'I know,' said Thom. 'I'm sorry. I can still stay tonight though, can't I? I've missed the last train home.' He gave her a pleading look that would've melted most hearts, just not Emily's.

'You should've thought of that earlier. Eve will drop you off on her way home - *if* she feels like it.'

Eve and Thom caught one another's eye. They both knew better than to argue with Emily, especially a hormonal Emily.

♥

They travelled silently, Bex drowsy in the back seat and Eve and Thom feeling awkward to find themselves in such close proximity to one another for the first time in their adult life. Eve felt very conscious of the man beside her, especially when her hand brushed the side of his leg whenever she changed gear.

'You really shouldn't smoke, you know. Not only is it bad for you, but it's very off-putting to women – I mean, I can smell you from here! You must've missed all those campaign thingies, and didn't you see the gory image on the back of the pack?' The nurse in her couldn't help but point out what he already knew, and the Eve in her couldn't help but fill the silence.

Thom glanced over with those beguiling blue eyes that were barely discernible in the darkness. 'There's only one woman whose opinion I would value on this, if she'd give me half a chance. Three actually, if you include my mam and sister.'

'Oh?'

'Eve, you must realise...'

Emboldened by his alcohol consumption, Thom reached out a hand and placed it over Eve's knee, its warmth penetrating her thin black work-trousers. Her instant reaction to this unexpected touch from another man was to recoil, even though her skin beneath tingled. Thom retracted his hand as though burnt, and Eve's face flamed with the realisation that she must have hurt his feelings.

'Thom, I'm sorry, I can't... I...'

'It's ok, it's ok. I understand. I'll always just be Emily's brother to you. It doesn't matter... My street is the next on the left.'

Silence resumed, and Thom stared resolutely straight ahead, a myriad of thoughts playing on his mind. Eve's head was spinning - she could feel the tension of too many things left unsaid. She thought about saying something, but she wasn't sure how she felt about Thom nor about dating again, loving again, or pursuing anything with a man who wasn't James.

Thom retreated into himself, and when Eve dropped him outside his flat, he said a sober thank you before walking to his front door without a backwards glance.

'That was intense.'

'Bex, you perve!' Eve was mortified. 'You were supposed to be sleeping.'

'And you were supposed to be driving - not starting some torrid affair with your best friend's sexy brother. Now, slow down so I can hop in the front seat. Bloody tiny British cars, how's anyone supposed to fit in one of these?'

With that, Bex clamoured in front and pushed the passenger seat as far back as it would go and was snoring within moments, leaving Eve with only her flaming cheeks and discontented thoughts for company.

♥ 14 ♥

It was thanks to the creativity of the Christmas Crafts group that the café was looking so homely and festive one blustery December's day. Eve had heeded Emily's advice and strung up the strings of jam-jar fairy lights Bex had made to criss-cross between the café's two seating areas rather than hanging them outside as she'd originally intended, and they had also sprayed a light dusting of fake snow around the bay windows and lit them prettily from within, casting an inviting glow into the street outside that made it hard for people to resist popping in to warm themselves up with a hot coffee. Christmas cards were displayed on the wall behind the counter, and space was made in which to cram a slim Christmas tree festooned with miniature crackers and tiny parcels stuffed with sweets that were gifted to the children each day.

Betty and her group had created a game of Stick the Red Nose on Rudolph using Velcro – the humble pin was now a potential liability, apparently. The game took pride of place in the children's corner where it was well received by their littler guests. There was also a beautifully illustrated advent calendar revealing traditional scenes behind each door – though more than one disappointed child had declared it pointless because it didn't house any chocolates. It had been better received by the Golden Oldies.

They were developing a loyal following of local customers sooner than anticipated, and Stanley and Betty were among the most frequent to present there as the café became a focal point for their social lives.

'Say, "Sod this for a game o' soldias, am gannin' inte toon for a pint,"' insisted Stanley to Bex, who sighed then gave in. This had been going on all morning.

'Sod this for a game of soulchaz,' she said, 'am gawin' into toon for a point.'

'By, you can take the Aussie oot o' Austraylia, but yi cannit take Austraylia oot o' the Aussie! It's not "gawin" it's GANNIN'. And it's not "point" it's PINT!'

'Seriously Stanley, I do have work to do, you know.'

'Well, ne'one's ganna understand yi pet, if yi divven't try an' larn the local lingo. I should be chargin' for this.'

'I've managed pretty well so far, thank you very much, and no-one's gotten a wrong order from me yet.'

Stanley tutted. 'They're just humourin' yi is why.'

'I'll bring your tea over for you in a moment.'

'Brew, not tea.'

Bex sighed in exasperation, then disappeared to lay low behind the counter for a while. Stanley grinned, his rheumy eyes bright with mischief, before returning to a heated discussion on bowling techniques with his friend Edward who was sat beside him.

'Yi should de it like this next time, Ed...' Stanley demonstrated a move with an imaginary ball.

'WHAT?' Edward twiddled with the volume of his hearing aid. Bex wouldn't blame him if he was deliberately turning it down.

'Streuth, those bloody Golden Oldies. Rude, Grouchy Oldies more like,' she moaned as she prepared them fresh pots of tea.

Alongside Christmas Crafts, the Golden Oldies group had fast become one of the most popular on the community program's timetable. Other activities were a little slower in their uptake, which Eve had expected at this early stage and given the busy time of year. She'd originally been unsure whether to start the program before Christmas, but she needn't have worried as something about the spirit of the season brought with it a collective desire for connection and togetherness. The advert she'd placed in the local newspaper and on social media had helped generate almost as much awareness and interest as word of mouth, and Eve hoped that those who may have been feeling isolated would soon find a family of friends at her café.

She wasn't short of volunteers to get the community program off the ground - her mam had thrown herself into running the book club on her days off with surprising fervour, inviting a couple of friends along to help get it established. She'd started off with A Christmas Carol by Charles Dickens, which was a big hit, and the book club itself turned out to be the hobby she hadn't known she'd been searching for. She even lent a helping hand in the café on busier days, whereas Robert's contribution involved stalking the sweet counter for leftovers, thus counteracting the positive effects of his daily activity.

Eve was thrilled with the café's progress and how the local community seemed to have embraced it. Most of the people attending the activities were willingly contributing the requested donation that would pay for a menu item for someone in need, but she intended for most of the money to be donated to charity - she just wasn't yet sure which one.

'Why don't you give the money to a cancer charity?' Carol had suggested when she'd discussed it with her. 'That way it would feel like our Daniel was a part of what you're trying to achieve here.' Carol was immensely proud of Eve and all she had achieved in the short time since her return to England, and relieved that her break-up with James now seemed to be spurring her forwards rather than holding her back.

'You could hold some sort of fundraiser here,' Bex suggested. 'You could provide lunch and hold a raffle or something, with the cost of a ticket going to charity. The event could serve as the café's launch too – it'd be a shame not to mark the occasion in some way.'

Keen not to be outdone, when Eve later told Emily of the idea her two-pence was that this should take the form of a barbecue in the café's back yard just before Christmas, so that she could be part of it before her baby made its appearance. Eve agreed and lost no time in putting Betty and the Christmas Crafts group in charge of making the event as Aussie-themed as possible. But what on earth could be done to improve the drab and neglected back yard in such a short space of time?

'You do realise,' said Bex, 'that you'll need to swallow your pride and enlist Thom to do something with the back yard in time for the barbie, don't you? We'll never fit everyone inside.'

'There's no way he'll do anything for me now - why should he?' Eve was keen to forget that awkward car journey they had taken together. Not surprisingly she hadn't seen or heard from him since, and even Emily had stopped going on about setting them up.

'Because you'd be paying him to? He shouldn't have offered if he didn't mean it.'

'Paying him what? I barely have enough money to pay you and Dave. Unless he'll accept payment in lamingtons, we're stuffed.'

'I'm sure he'll accept payment of another kind...'

Eve blushed at the idea of being intimate with Thom.

Bex' salary at this stage was pretty much pocket money given her room and most of her meals were provided for, but Dave's level of experience commanded a more realistic sum, then of course there were the ongoing costs associated with the purchase of stock, insurance, and the impending winter utility bills that didn't bear thinking about. Eve was taking a pittance for herself, but she was hopeful of that increasing when things became more established. She was mostly either at work or asleep anyway, so she needed very little disposable income for the time being. Soon enough though she'd need to find a place of her own to live. She wasn't really in a position to outlay on the back yard for the sake of a single event at such a precarious stage.

'He'll do it for mate's rates, I'm sure. And his feelings for you aside, he'll probably be glad of any work he can get this close to Christmas. It's not like it needs much doing - just a lick of paint and some seating.'

'Ok, ok. I'll ask.'

There was no way around it. They hoped to sell sixty tickets, and if they came close, they'd never fit everyone indoors. Eve grabbed her mobile phone and steeled herself to make the embarrassing phone call in privacy outside. The little street cat was back again, she noticed, its presence calming and the soft grey of its fur echoing the cloudy skies above.

'Hello?' The voice that answered was distracted, the background busy.

'Hi, Thom, it's Eve.'

Silence. Then, 'Yeh...?'

'I wondered if I could book you in to do some work for me in the backyard? The trouble is, I need it rather urgently. It wouldn't take much, just a lick of paint or whatever you think will make it less of the eyesore than it is now. I realise it's short notice, but I'd be so grateful if you have the time. I know you'd do a great job.'

She knew she was babbling, so to stop her runaway mouth she chewed on her nails, wary of his response. It was a while in coming, and she was painfully embarrassed to have to ask a favour of the man she had slighted.

'I don't think I can fit you in before Christmas, I'm afraid. I'm snowed under here.' There wasn't a trace of his previous warmth and humour.

'Oh, that's a shame.' Eve felt a stab of disappointment. 'It was just for this charity event I have coming up. But that's ok, we'll make do. I'm sure it can't be that hard to paint a wall.' Though Eve feared her DIY skills were even worse than her barista ones. Bugger, they really couldn't make do.

'See you then.' Thom rang off abruptly.

'Bye.'

Well, that had gone well. Bex looked at her quizzically when she re-entered the café. Eve shook her head.

'Bummer. What are we gonna do, then?'

'Just make do, I suppose. I can't afford to get anyone else in to do it.'

'Did you tell Thom it was for charity?'

'I may have mentioned it, but it's not as though I'm really in a position to guilt-trip him.'

'Some things are worth guilt-tripping others over. Let's hope you've poked at his conscience a little bit, if not his heart.'

♥

Late that afternoon, Harry's attention was arrested by the woman with the bright pink hair and nose-ring who had noticed him last time he'd stood outside The Melbourne Community Café. He liked her pretty, bare face and quirky style, and there was something appealing in the strong set of her shoulders that hinted at her assertive nature. Like her colleague she was wearing a plain white t-shirt covered by a burlap apron; but her shirt had 'MAKE LOVE NOT WAR' stamped in block capital letters across its back. This amused him. He wondered what it would be like to go out with someone like that, but his heart sank with the realisation that at this point in his life he had nothing to offer anyone. He needed to sort himself out, but how could he with so many bridges burnt, a terrible credit rating, no home to go to, no family or friends to speak of, and work being so difficult to come by for someone with his record? What was the point of even trying when every road just led to another dead end?

Harry felt enraged. He was furious - furious with the twisted path of his childhood that had deprived him of love and normality and wrought him a lonely and crooked adulthood; furious with the so-called friends who'd exploited and derailed him; furious with the many professionals and systems that had failed him time and again and which continued to hold him tightly between a rock and a hard place; furious with the ex-girlfriend to whom many of his hopes for the future had been pinned then dashed to pieces by her betrayal; but most of all, he was furious with himself. He felt weak and worthless, crushed with guilt and shame and despair. For all the times he had been wronged in his life, he could not forget that he had wronged others too.

His ex-girlfriend had just announced her pregnancy and he was feeling overwhelmed. What did he have to offer a child? How could he give someone so vulnerable and dependent everything they needed, when as a grown man he could barely take care of himself? To make matters worse he was not entirely convinced the child was even his - though Stacey had of course insisted it was and the dates certainly did line up - but something about it was niggling at him.

Stacey could be very persuasive when she wanted to be - that had always been the problem. Despite his better judgment he'd felt less alone when she was around, even though she was like a poisoned apple - tempting until you discovered the rot inside. He had thought he could rid himself of her and start afresh - he'd been offered a bedsit only that afternoon in fact - but he'd lost it because he would now be bound to her forever just as she wanted, and his blood froze at the very thought.

Whether this was his child or not, he knew Stacey would be in no position to nurture it, and Heaven forbid any of her 'friends' should be allowed to try in his place. Having spent his teenage years in foster care following his mother's accidental overdose, he knew too well what could lie ahead for the child. He steeled himself to do the right thing, even if it did cost him the fresh start he had dreamed of that now could never be.

He was trapped, and his heart broke right there on the rain-dampened pavement just opposite The Melbourne Community Café, as he stood in the shadows and watched the woman with the pink hair through hopeless eyes blurred by tears.

♥

Bex peered out of the window into the night, attempting to judge how much left she had of her shift by how quickly it had gotten dark, and gasped. 'Look, Eve! It's that man! I just saw him across the street. Don't look - we don't want to scare him off again.'

'What should we do?' Eve was flustered, but Bex was already pulling on her hoodie and twisting a scarf about her neck.

'If I come out the front way, he'll run, so I'll go round the outside through the alleyway instead. He won't be expecting that.'

Eve nodded. They were just closing up, and the café was empty save for the two of them and their chef. 'Be careful.'

Bex gulped when she opened the door to the back yard and a powerful gust of wind blew her hood right off. It pounded her face, thrust the gate into the brick wall behind her, and blew into the kitchen tousling the salad Dave was putting away for tomorrow. He cursed profusely - he had already guessed and highly disapproved of her purpose. A cold, belting rain chose to descend right at that moment, soaking through her thin work trousers in moments. Bloody British weather, she thought, irritably.

She gasped again when she rounded the corner from the alley onto Victoria Terrace and encountered the sorrowful figure of a man crouched against the low wall of the property behind him, one arm shielding his face as his howling cries were tossed away on the wind as though worthless. Tentatively, she reached out a hand and rested it gently on his arm. He was startled, revealing eyes that were surprisingly youthful but pained, his clothing and beard from a distance having added years to him that clearly were not due.

Instinctively, though he flinched and let out a low moan of disagreement, Bex wrapped one arm about his shoulder and walked him inside out of the cold. Like a small child Harry allowed himself to be led.

♥ 15 ♥

'What the hell does she think she's doing, bringing someone like that in here when we don't know him from Adam? Quick, hide your handbags and stow away the cash!'

Dave's concern for the girls sharpened his voice as he wagged his finger at the till. He was temperamental at the best of times and a mass of contradictions - skilful and deft in the kitchen despite the awkward bulk of his frame; moody and gruff yet unbeknownst to the girls he would often put out a bowl of milk or water for the little grey cat that continued to frequent the café's back yard; fiercely independent and private yet he *loved* to be brought up to date with café gossip each evening; and his uncontrollable wispy hair and relative youth belied the extent of his professionalism and expertise. His manner was outwardly brittle, yet he was marshmallow inside, or so his colleagues chose to believe.

Eve rolled her eyes then dashed to the kitchen to open the door for the bedraggled pair. 'Go make him something hot to eat while I put the kettle on.' Her tone brooked no argument. Dave reluctantly obeyed, casting a narrowed eye at the muddy puddle on the floor as rainwater mingled with dirt from the man's clothing and boots in Dave's usually pristine domain.

'Hello there,' Eve said to the man, whose cries had subsided to plaintive sobs and who hunched his face down into the neck of his coat as though ashamed to be seen. All that was visible was his mop of russet hair and tufts of red beard. Eve's old bedside manner kicked in. 'Best be off with your jacket, love, it's soaked! Then we'll sit you down on that comfy chair over there,' she gestured across to the bay window, 'and Bex will find you some tissues and keep you company while I put the kettle on.'

Bex rested a hand on his arm and his sobs subsided, but he remained silent and averted his eyes, which were almost grey and clear as water. Eve had no idea how he liked his tea, so she made him a pot of English breakfast with milk and sugar on the side. She hoped the sugar would pep him up a little if he hadn't eaten for a while. Just as she set it down on the table, Dave presented him with a steaming bowl of spiced pumpkin soup served with lashings of sour cream and thick slices of buttered damper bread. He eyed the man warily before retreating into the kitchen.

'I'd better get paid overtime for this,' he muttered.

'There now,' said Eve, 'this is for you. And don't mind us - you just take your time while we finish cleaning up.' She gave Bex a pointed look, indicating for her to pick up where she had left off with the closing up of the café.

Without the girls' eyes on him the man threw himself into his meal, slightly reserved at first then with increasing fervour. When Dave poked his head round to make sure everything was ok, Eve gestured for a refill, and he rolled his eyes then disappeared back into the kitchen. After he had eaten his fill, they sat down beside him.

'Thank you,' he whispered. 'I'm sorry, I...' his voice cracked a little, then trailed off.

'It's ok, don't worry about it. What's your name?'

'Harry.'

'I'm Eve.' Eve reached a hand across to shake his. Harry seemed unsure but then he offered a hand that was chapped from the cold yet surprisingly clean with his nails trimmed short. Eve had heard there were places people could go to wash, and she was relieved he could retain that one small dignity.

'Bex.' Bex pumped his hand enthusiastically.

Harry smiled a little. 'Bex,' he said in a soft, thoughtful voice.

'What were you doing outside? We've seen you here before.' It was Dave bearing a fresh helping of soup, his voice conveying his suspicion and Eve glared at him.

'I- I don't know. I just... I walk. Everywhere. It keeps me warm and helps pass the time, and I happened to... pass by.'

'Twice?'

Harry nodded. 'I didn't mean any harm. It... Well, it always looks nice in here and I wondered what it might be like to be part of it, you know?'

'Is there anything we can do to help?' Bex asked when Dave was out of earshot.

Harry's features crumpled and he wondered briefly why for human beings, being shown kindness and care at moments such as these could more easily induce tears than quell them. Out it came, the story of his ex-girlfriend's pregnancy, which he felt was more likely to be a result of her recent fling with his ex-best mate than it was from their relationship, though she denied it. He remained unsure and was not prepared to leave the care of what might well turn out to be his child to chance.

'Jamie doesn't sound like much of a mate to me,' Bex was outraged, 'if he's gone and done all that with your girlfriend, and he's the one who got you into drugs in the first place.'

Jamie was older and had seemed so cool to an impressionable young Harry, though looking back as an adult he could see that Jamie had always had the upper hand and was basically just using him to do his dirty work. Jamie had used Stacey too, encouraging her to sell herself for his own gain until Harry stepped in to protect her and Jamie didn't argue - he just turned his sights to some other girl. At the time, Harry had assumed this was because he'd earned his respect, but he could see now that Jamie had just wanted someone younger and more naïve to use. That's why Harry couldn't get his head around what Stacey was thinking, going off with him like that after all that had happened between them.

'What will you do now?'

'The right thing, I guess...,' said Harry. 'I'd better go. I've said too much and made this into a long day's work for all of you. You just caught me at a low moment, I'm sorry.' He was ashamed by his show of emotion - out of necessity he'd grown adept at keeping his true feelings under wraps.

'Don't be sorry. Do you have somewhere to stay tonight?' Bex was concerned - it was horrible outside. Though she'd secretly thought this most of the time since her arrival in the UK, this time she was right.

'I didn't, but I suppose I do now. I'll have to go back to Stacey.' The prospect filled him with dread. 'And I'll need to find work, pronto. I need to provide for the baby.' Like his own parents had failed to do, he thought.

'Well, if there's ever anything you need, you're welcome here any time.' Eve touched his hand.

'Thank you. I won't forget it. I would never have come in, only-'

'It's ok. We're glad you did.' Bex smiled a smile that cast a little beam of light into the darkness that sat heavily within Harry's heart. He reached into his pocket for some precious loose change.

'No! Don't even think about it. We often have food leftover at the end of the day and we'd far rather it was used than left to go to waste.'

Harry was embarrassed but relieved. He followed the girls to the kitchen and Bex helped him on with his jacket, Dave's keen eye on him the whole time to make sure he didn't nick anything on his way out. Just as he was about to disappear into the night, Dave thrust a bag laden with food they hadn't used that day into his hand. Harry thanked him, and Dave nodded curtly.

'Still got all your valuables, ladies?' he asked. 'Right, I'm off - you've kept me here long enough with all your bloody do-gooding.'

'Come on, you're as do-gooding as the best of us really – you even gave him your dinner!' Anyone who knew Dave knew what a gesture this was. 'And it's got to be better than do-badding?'

Dave ignored them. After making sure Harry wasn't hiding around the corner ready to pounce, he cycled off confident that the two women would be safe - they were just leaving anyway. It's a pity then, that he didn't see the lone young woman watching from the shadows, her once pretty features hard and her mouth twisted in perpetual scorn.

♥

The following day revealed a welcome sun. Too many days of miserable weather can dampen even the brightest of spirits, so there was a mutual sense of cheer and relief at the brief reprieve. Somehow the chill ceased to matter quite so much once the sun had come out.

Whilst a polarising debate about climate change was in full swing over at the activities table, Bex and Eve were reflecting over the events that had brought Harry to them the previous evening and were wondering what they could do to help.

'Perhaps we could start leaving little food parcels outside after we close up on the off chance he might pass by?'

'For Heaven's sake, Bex, he's not a cat!'

Despite the sunshine, Eve had been in a bad mood all day. It had started when Thom made an unexpected appearance that lunch time - peak hour at The Melbourne - at which point an over-enthusiastic member of Christmas Crafts had accidentally sent a pot of silver glitter flying into someone's pumpkin soup which they'd had to replace. Just after that, the stray grey cat they had been feeding left them a present (a very dead mouse) on the doorstep and Dave had immediately hit the roof and expressed his profound disgust before re-scrubbing the kitchen to within an inch of its life and declaring that from now on felines were definitely not welcome.

In hindsight, Eve should have known something was amiss the moment Thom presented himself at the counter and bid her a good afternoon, bright and cheery as though nothing untoward had ever happened between them and looking at her in the oddest way as though they were both complicit in some little secret she knew nothing about.

He was wearing a navy fleece over paint-splattered dungarees and carrying an assortment of paintbrushes and tins as well as a set of ladders. He winked and said he hoped she still remembered how he liked his tea, then hauled his gear out to the back yard, dealing expertly with the unfortunate mouse on his way out and raising an eyebrow at Dave as though to indicate he couldn't understand what all the fuss was about. Bex was impressed, Eve was confused, and Dave was relieved but stated loudly that he would've dealt with it himself given half a chance.

Just then Eve's mobile phone rang.

'Hello?'

'Evie.'

'Emily? I thought you were supposed to be resting.'

'Resting? There's no rest for the wicked, as you're well aware.'

'Ems, you've got to take it easy, you're almost ready to drop!'

'I know, and I'm not doing too much, trust me. You're all making sure of that. You're just like Mark.'

'Someone's got to slow you down a bit.'

There was silence, then Emily asked, 'So, did anything exciting happen at the café today?'

'Not that I can think of, if you discount the discovery of a dead mouse in the backyard this morning and that we've inadvertently added glitter soup to the menu.'

'Glitter soup? Very festive. Can't go wrong with a bit of bling.'

'Oh, and Thom turned up just before. Said he's going to do sort out the backyard for me. It's very strange, because when I called him last week to ask about it, he refused to help and practically hung up on me.'

There it was, that silence again. *'Emily?* The penny dropped.

'What?'

'What have you done? You must have way too much time on your hands if you still have the time to meddle in other people's love lives.'

'Honest, there's been no meddling - it's for charity, isn't it?'

'So, you're telling me that after his flat refusal, something's suddenly tugged at Thom's heart, and he's decided to help me out after all?'

'Yes... And I may have told him you wanted him to take you out on a date tonight. He's been really looking forward to it.'

Eve almost dropped her phone. 'What? You did WHAT?'

'Braxton Hicks, I'd better go. Have a wonderful time tonight and don't do anything I wouldn't do. Bye.'

'Emily!' But it was too late, she'd hung up.

'When are you planning on bringing that tea out for me?' Thom appeared, a film of perspiration on his brow despite the chill in the air. 'Those yo-yos look nice.'

Eve eyed him warily. 'You know, there's a whole world of beverages out there besides tea with milk and two.'

'It's a shame we can't all be cultured globe-trotters like you. Go on then, enlighten me.' And off he went.

♥

A few minutes later, Eve gave Thom two yo-yo biscuits and a huge mug of creamy pumpkin-spiced latte topped with lacy foam, whipped cream, a chocolate flake, and a dusting of nutmeg and chocolate shavings. She thought it looked very impressive, but he eyed it with derision.

'You can't expect me to drink that – it's for bairns. Look at me!'

Eve looked and her cheeks flushed. He was extremely good looking in a more solid, rugged way than James had been, and no longer the shy kid she had once known. He seemed to have retained a level of the sensitivity she remembered, though the fact he knew her through Emily seemed to help him be less reserved where she was concerned - not to mention the fact that thanks to Emily, he now thought she wanted to date him. Eve realised the memories of James she had clung onto so tightly when she'd first returned to England had become sort of fuzzy, and her recall of his features was no longer quite as sharp.

'Dear me,' she said, exasperated by Thom's dismissal of her efforts, 'you could at least try it – you might like it! There are straight guys out there wearing fake tan and mascara, and you're worried how you might look drinking a cup of coffee? I promise not to tell anyone. Now get back to work, you're doing a grand job.'

He'd already scrubbed one grimy brick wall and had tipped out some charcoal paint ready for the first coat. There was no sign of the little grey cat though - it was probably still smarting from Dave's rejection of its catch.

'You call that simple? Then I'd hate to see one of your complicated beverages. And I've never met a straight guy who wears mascara. Is that how they go about in Oz, is it? No wonder you came back – though having the hots for me can't have helped, haha!'

Eve flounced off back to her customers, but not after peeping through a gap in the kitchen blinds where she watched Thom absolutely demolish his flake, dunking it into the whipped cream before biting off a large chunk then chugging down the hot liquid and licking his lips. She was fairly certain she had just expanded his repertoire.

♥ 16 ♥

Bex looked smug as she peered at Thom from the kitchen window just as Eve herself had done a few hours earlier. He was in the process of packing up his work bag after thoroughly rinsing out his paint brushes under the outside tap. He seemed oblivious to the bitter air, the combination of a strengthening wind and physical activity flushing his cheeks a hearty red that contrasted nicely with his fair hair.

'Enjoy your date. If you don't want him, feel free to send him my way.'

Dave looked mildly envious but said nothing. He was hanging around longer than he usually did after a day's work, the inherent gossip in him afraid to miss a trick. The little grey cat that had been absent since the mouse incident was currently circling Thom's legs, and they watched him lean down and give it a little scratch under the chin before it set itself down at a safe distance away from the splashing tap.

'Vermin,' Dave muttered.

Eve was still smarting that Emily had dropped her in it like this, and on a day where she hadn't washed her hair and was wearing the same old work outfit she'd worn repeatedly over the course of the last few weeks, no less. Her make-up was minimal, but now and then she did like to glam it up a little bit. She'd never gone on a first date in such a poor state of grooming - she couldn't remember when she'd last shaved her legs, not that she planned on needing to worry about that. She looked towards Bex about to ask if she had a lippie or an eyeliner she could borrow, but immediately thought better of it. This was Bex after all, it was doubtful if she even owned a razor.

She snuck into the loo with a pink lipstick she'd been grateful to discover at the bottom of her handbag and quickly smudged some onto her lips, and in the absence of any blusher dabbed some on her cheeks too. She hung up her burlap apron and opened the top buttons of her white shirt. She unpinned her messy bun and allowed her thick hair to cascade just beyond her shoulders – it had grown while she'd been home and was made wavy by the contours of its style. She tousled it with her fingers then appraised herself with large hazel eyes, her full mouth pursed, surprised to find that Thom's good opinion of how she looked mattered. This was the best she could do with the limited tools she had to hand, though she would have given anything at that moment for a decent pair of heels. Bex and Dave whistled.

'Shh,' she warned, her cheeks flaming in case Thom heard it.

'I thought you didn't care what Thom thinks about you,' said Bex.

'I don't. Not at all.'

'I hope you do just a little.' It was Thom. His special skill seemed to be in appearing at the most inopportune time.

'Have fun! I want to hear all about it when you get home.'

'*If* she comes home,' Dave added. 'Though it's been so long her vagazzle's probably closed over.'

Thom laughed just a little too much.

'Thanks for that,' said Eve. 'Don't come knocking for a pay rise any time soon. Bye!' She strode into the navy night with what remained of her dignity, before tripping over the front doorstep in her hurry to get away as the door closed behind her on a burst of laughter.

'Steady on!' Thom grasped her elbow. 'We haven't even got to the ice rink yet - if you can't walk in a pair of flats there's not much hope for you on a set of blades.'

'We're going ice skating?' Oh no. Eve had always been useless on a pair of skates. She felt her last remnants of control over the evening slipping out of her grasp.

Thom had never seen anyone so lovely look so comically uncoordinated, and he hadn't laughed so hard in a long time. He knew that Eve was mortified, which only made her more endearing, and he secretly quite enjoyed the opportunity for close contact that pulling her up repeatedly from the hard ice afforded. It was nice to play the knight in shining armour for once - or the knight in paint-splattered dungarees - but he suspected she didn't regard him in quite the same way. He couldn't help but laugh - she put Bambi to shame.

'When you said you were useless on a pair of skates, you weren't kidding, were you? Emily told me you *loved* ice-skating.'

'Did she now?' Eve spoke through gritted teeth.

It should have been terribly romantic. The ice rink itself appeared every winter and was nestled near a row of bars close to the River Tyne. Colourful lights strung like icicles hung all around, casting their glow upon the bobbled hats of the children and adults beneath, as they soared hand in hand with rosy cheeks, smiling faces, flapping scarves, and cold breath that was carried off on the wind along with the festive tunes from the rink's DJ. Eve, however, clung onto the handrail for dear life, taking uncertain shuffling steps that entertained the teenagers who whizzed confidently by her and irritated the small children who wanted to get past. As she dragged her unwilling feet into a semblance of a glide that resulted in her landing on her soaking bottom one more time, she began dreaming up ways to exact her revenge on Emily.

Humiliated, drenched, and bruised of bottom and of ego, Thom finally suggested they call it a night and get a hot chocolate - just a plain one - none of that fancy stuff she liked to serve. He led her along the subtle curve of Grey Street, a fine example of Georgian architecture that ascended gently towards Monument, where to Eve's delight a Christmas market had sprung. They air smelled of spices - ginger and nutmeg, cinnamon and anise, and a choir made their ears ring and their hearts soar with their carolling. They warmed their hands on thick hot chocolate as they explored the trinkets for sale, and Thom treated her to an intricate glass snowflake she'd had her eye on to adorn the Christmas tree of The Melbourne.

The magic of the evening eventually drew Eve to Thom's side as she tucked her arm through his, joy lighting her eyes as they meandered slowly onwards. To say he was surprised would be an understatement, but he didn't say a word lest he spoil it. There was something intangible about Christmas that drew people together, but he didn't dare to hope for too much.

Eve bought a chewy gingerbread cake as a gift for Bex and Dave, and some for her dad too whose sweet tooth couldn't be forgotten, then they sat huddled together with a glass of mulled cider at a wooden bench amidst the busy throng.

'I think we'll scratch ice-skating off the list for any future dates. Or any type of activity that requires balance and coordination.'

Eve giggled. The chilly air and the hot cider were already getting to her. She felt free. Time for herself had become a rare treat since The Melbourne had opened.

'I think I'll scratch your horrible sister off *my* list. Wait 'til I see her.'

'Now you have an idea of what I had to put up with growing up.'

Eve could just imagine.

'The night hasn't been too horrible for you though, I hope?'

There she went again, hurting his feelings with her big mouth. 'No, not at all,' said Eve sincerely. 'I've had a wonderful evening with you. Though I doubt my bottom will ever be the same again.'

'That's a shame, it's a rather exemplary bottom.'

She blushed. 'You were looking?'

'You can't tell me you haven't had a peep at mine. It's human nature, and I've been told I have a fine bottom. In fact, I think mine might be better than yours.'

'I thought you were sweet and shy?'

'Only around girls with a better bottom than mine.'

Eve laughed. Was she finally ready to move on? She missed male company. Flirting. Having someone to confide in, learn from, and be intimate with. She knew now that she could never go back to Australia, and that James would never come to England to be with her. She used to think he might turn up one day unexpectedly and beg her to start over, that he'd soon realise a life in England with her in it had more meaning than a life in Australia alone. There was a time she couldn't help looking up at each passing plane and wondering if he was on it or hear the café's bell ring with the entry of each new customer, hoping it was him. But it was never going to happen. James had Isabelle, and she had her home, her family, and The Melbourne.

'Are you ok?' Thom asked. 'You've gone very quiet.'

'Have I? I think I've had too much cider, that's all. I'm fine.'

'Tell me about him. James, isn't it?'

Eve was taken aback. 'Yes, but are you sure you don't mind me talking about him to you?'

'Not at all – not if it might help. I promise to not to get too jealous. He must've been some guy. Though why you're here right now and he isn't, I have no idea. On second thoughts he can't be that great - he must be crazy! But I can't complain, otherwise he would be picking you up from the ice and admiring your bottom instead of me.'

'You give me too much credit, and yourself too little. But that was the problem - he didn't want to come over here, and I didn't want to stay over there. I love my home and my family and friends just as much as he loves his.'

Eve told him everything with a dim resignation in her voice, and Thom sat patiently and listened, comforting her with a reassuring squeeze of the shoulder. It felt strange to be talking to a prospective partner, if that's what he was, with such emotion about an old one who it was obvious she still had feelings for. At the same time, it seemed right somehow, as though she were opening the door to them potentially building something together on an honest foundation. When she had finished, they sat together quietly, Thom's strong arm about her shoulders.

'What about you?' she asked after a while. 'You know a lot about me, but I know so little about this Thom - other than how you take your tea, that you're very creative, fantastic at your job, extremely patient, a little bit cheeky, and not so shy or modest after all. Oh, and you have a great bum, or so I'm led to believe. And very little taste in hot drinks.'

'Trust me - it *is* a great bum. You'll see.' It was evident from the glint in his eye that Thom enjoyed this summation of his character immensely. 'Her name was Julia and I loved her very much. We were together for three years and I thought she was the woman I would marry - since I couldn't have you,' he winked. 'We were happy together, but towards the end she became increasingly cold and detached. I kept asking her what was wrong, and how I could make things better, but she said everything was fine and that she still loved me.

'I thought maybe I'd been working too many hours and needed to make more time for us as a couple, so I booked us a week in Santorini as a surprise. She didn't really want to go, and I couldn't understand it - I thought she'd be thrilled. Turns out she just couldn't bear to be parted for so long from the guy she'd been seeing behind my back. She'd been meaning to tell me about him, apparently, but hadn't been able to find the right time.

'Anyway, they're married now - I think she met him through work - and I never did get to go on that holiday. I sold it at a loss. I saw Julia recently in town pushing a baby. She didn't seem as happy as I thought she would, just tired. She looked straight though me as though she hadn't seen me, but I think she did. That was sometime last year.'

'Oh, Thom. I'm so sorry to hear that, how sad.' Eve's heart ached for him. She'd heard snippets from Emily of course, but hadn't taken as much of an interest as she did now. How could Julia string him along like that? She could understand falling out of love with someone – but surely the kindest thing to do would be to let their partner go and find what they were looking for elsewhere?

'We're quite a pair, aren't we?' said Thom. 'Both let down, and both scared to allow ourselves to take another chance.'

Was he afraid too? He certainly didn't show it. 'I don't want to live a life without love,' Eve said. 'I just need more time.'

'You'll get there,' he said, all the while hoping.

♥

They'd both had too much cider to even consider driving home, so without a word Thom organised a taxi to drop Eve off at her door then take him onwards to his place alone. She appreciated this gesture that spoke volumes in terms of his patience with her, respect for her, and the absence of pressure he placed on her, that she couldn't help but place a soft kiss on his mouth as her way of saying thank you. In contrast to the brisk air, his lips felt warm, soft, and inviting, with the scent of spices still lingering on his breath. The kiss felt right, unexpectedly so. She waved him away, and the kiss combined with the intensity of those huge cobalt eyes stayed with her long after the taxi had driven off.

Perhaps love could unfurl, Eve thought, as she pulled up the covers tight about her in bed that night. Perhaps it didn't always need to knock you off your feet like it had done when she'd met James. Just before she relaxed into sleep, heady from a wonderful evening and a budding romance, she whispered aloud into the still darkness, 'James, it's time for me to let you go.'

♥ 17 ♥

It was Christmas Eve, the day of the fundraiser, and the incongruent scent of the barbeque reached into the farthest corners of Victoria Terrace, watering the mouths of many a hungry soul who happened by. The Golden Oldies huddled around the activities bench nursing hot teas, a handful of Avid Gamers dressed in elaborate Cosplay outfits nursed their beers outside whilst enjoying a lively debate on the virtues of the PS5 versus Xbox One in a jargon only they could understand, the Christmas Crafters were basking in the glow of mutual artistic appreciation and one too many pear ciders, and the book club members were discussing the merits of Dickens over mugs of mulled wine.

Tony had made a supportive appearance from the flat upstairs, as had Eve's parents and Thom. Paolo and Gianni had bought tickets too, and Eve was looking forward to seeing them both again, though they were yet to arrive. She wondered if the busty blonde from that night at the restaurant might be accompanying Paolo, though she wasn't sure he was the sort of man who would entertain the idea of a second date.

Though landscaping wasn't strictly Thom's forte, he received many a pat on the back for all he had managed to achieve in the café's back yard with such a limited budget in a short space of time. He'd diligently scrubbed away at what seemed like a century's worth of algae, mould and grime from the surrounding walls, and had turned the neglected concrete and red-brick space into a cosy little nook it was now a pleasure to spend time in.

The ivory paint he'd chosen for the walls opened the space, making it appear a lot larger, and he'd refreshed the cracked old concrete with stencilled tiles. Solid wood benches were fixed along the walls fronted by tables and chairs that had been chosen to match the ones out front. Solar lamps studded above each seat provided a light source for those bleak winter afternoons, and there were outdoor heaters to provide respite from the cold and a canopy overhead to offer some protection should it rain.

Ornate metal trellises awaited the climbing plants that would eventually adorn them, but the most impressive feature was a huge vertical garden that Thom had promised to stuff with herbs and plants at a more clement time of year. Scattered upon each table were colourful pinecones diligently collected and hand-painted festive colours by the members of Christmas Crafts, and hurricane lamps containing flickering candles added to the scene.

What struck Eve most of all was Thom's care and attention to detail. He'd gone so far as to place a water bowl by the kitchen step should the little grey cat pay them a further visit, a touch that hadn't escaped Dave's notice but which he'd chosen to ignore given it came from the sexy handyman he'd been admiring from the window of late, adding an element of titillation to arduous days spent in the kitchen.

Despite the turnout, Eve was stressed - they all were. Mark was too busy taking orders from his heavily pregnant wife to be of much assistance on the barbeque front, Robert was more of a hindrance than a help as his attentions were diverted by the temptations of the cake stand, Carol was too preoccupied with the book club to lend a hand, and Betty was in her element running the 'Roo Raffle and no-one had the heart to disturb her. Bex was flat out on the coffee machine, and Dave was turning out snags like the clappers. Eve was milling about trying to keep everyone well-fed and watered, and Thom was roped in wherever he could be of assistance even though he'd already contributed more than enough. Everyone but Eve seemed to recognise that his real motive was more to please her than anything, but no-one dared say so.

All sixty tickets had sold, raising a sizeable contribution to the local cancer charity that had helped her brother Daniel during his illness. Though nothing changed the fact it was freezing outside; the rain held off, the outdoor heaters were on, and everyone seemed to be having a good time. All they really needed was an extra pair of hands. Eve was just about to take a break when she was interrupted by her dad.

'There's some weirdo at the door claiming to know you,' said Robert in a hushed tone. 'He insists on speaking to you.'

'What?' Eve stopped mid-mouthful of pavlova, the only thing she'd had a chance to eat all day. Though it wasn't strictly Aussie, and she wasn't a meringue fan herself, she'd never been to an Australian Christmas celebration that hadn't involved a massive pav. This one was so heavily topped with fruits, berries, and fresh cream that it had collapsed in the middle, though no-one seemed to mind.

'I didn't invite him in because he hasn't got a ticket.' A dollop of cream had caught on Robert's moustache - Eve obviously wasn't the only one who'd been at the pavlova. 'Besides, he has a better beard than me, so I don't trust him one bit.'

Beard? Eve wracked her brain, but she couldn't think of anyone she knew who had a beard. Maybe Paolo had grown one? For the briefest of moments, she thought it might be James sporting a fresh look and her heart went all jittery, but she quickly dismissed the idea. It couldn't be.

'What does he want, did you ask?'

Robert shrugged. 'Didn't ask.'

Seriously. 'Leave it with me. Now do you think you can lay off the cakes long enough to ensure everyone else gets a piece?'

'Dunno...' He already had his eye on Eve's unfinished slice. It didn't look promising.

♥

Eve cut through the merry throng to the front door. She initially didn't recognise the man standing before her until she caught sight of those familiar clearwater eyes.

'Harry! You look wonderful.'

His hair and beard were neatly trimmed, and he was wearing what appeared to be a set of new clothes. His face had lost that haunted expression, though when he smiled it still didn't quite reach his eyes.

'Eve, I came to thank you for your generosity and to apologise for the state I was in last time you saw me...' He glanced nervously over her shoulder. 'I'm sorry I've caught you at a bad time. I just assumed things might be quieting down here now with it being so close to Christmas.'

'You assumed right. We're technically closed but having a gathering here today to raise money for charity. You must be freezing, please come in! You're quite welcome to stay and grab something to eat - there's plenty to go round. Bex would love to see you! And there's really no need to thank us, we're just glad if we were able to help in some way.'

Harry hesitated - he'd always been nervous in a crowd - but before he had a chance to say so he was ushered into the warmth inside and led through to Bex, who was snowed under with orders at the coffee machine. Abruptly she stopped what she was doing. Unlike Eve, she recognised Harry instantly.

'Harry, wow! Good to see ya, you spunk!' She dashed round the counter and pulled him into a bear hug that flushed his face until it was almost as red as his hair. 'How are things with Stace? All sorted?'

'I suppose... I've moved back in with her, and the baby seems to be healthy, considering...' he trailed off. 'I'm still looking for work, though.'

'It's a pity you can't work here - we could do with an extra pair of hands!' Bex caught Eve's eye. 'Unless-'

Eve was reticent.

'Well, couldn't he? We *do* need someone, especially since I'm going to be moving on soon...'

Harry was crestfallen at this but recovered himself quickly. 'Oh no, I didn't come here looking for handouts or anything. I'm sure I'll find something soon.'

Eve regarded Harry. Could he be trusted? She knew so very little about him, and what she did know of his background wasn't exactly promising. Didn't users sometimes steal to fund their habit, even from those they loved and cared for? What would stop him from doing that to an employer where there was no emotional attachment? And while he claimed to be clean, what if he relapsed? What if everything went smoothly, but his dodgy friend Jamie or someone like him made an appearance?

Harry seemed like a genuine guy – he'd just been through a lot. Eve could see he'd worked extremely hard to make changes in his life, and now he had the responsibility of parenthood to work towards, he'd have a lot to lose if there was ever any trouble. They really did need someone, so why shouldn't it be Harry, who deserved a chance as much as anyone else, and needed it even more? Her parents would think she was mad, but The Melbourne *was* a community café, and it would be hypocritical of Eve to exclude him.

'Do you have any experience?' she asked.

'I worked at a coffee shop once, years ago. I suppose it's a bit like riding a bike?'

Bex smiled.

'Ok, ok... Well, do you think you might want to work here? I can't offer many hours, but if you could do some weekends and a few hours through the week, that'd be a great start, and if you could help us out here today that would be amazing - we can see how you go and take it from there?'

'Actually, I'm starving,' said Bex. 'I could murder a snag and a piece of pav and a sit down, but I've been chained to this bloody machine since I came in this morning. There'll be nothing left at the rate this lot are eating.'

Whilst Harry was sure the offer of work was genuinely meant – and for once he had happened to be in the right place at the right time - he didn't want to feel like a charity project, it was too shaming. Still, with a child to support, Stacey in his ear, and his job options limited by his record he was in no position to be choosy. The café itself had a nice feel to it and he really liked Eve and Bex, though he was wary of that moody chef of theirs and was under no illusions that the feeling wouldn't be mutual.

'Ok, that would be great! Just tell me where to start. And Bex, if you'd like to take a break, I'm sure I'll pick things up again if you run through the coffee machine with me. It might not be anything special to begin with, but I think I can make something drinkable.'

'Oh, I wouldn't worry too much about that. Look around you - most of these people are too tipsy to care.' Bex pointed out one particularly exuberant Cosplayer who was dancing to Santa Baby whilst dressed as a storm trooper as his mates videoed him on their smartphones - no doubt creating something of a social media sensation before morning.

'It's mostly the Oldies wanting a hot drink, and they seem to lean more towards tea than coffee, apart from old Stanley over there who loves his lattes. If you get stuck, just yell.'

And that was that. If Eve had had the measure of a certain Stacey Tate however, she might have made a different decision.

MEET ME AT THE MELBOURNE

♥

The afternoon passed successfully, and it was starting to get dark. Some of their guests moved inside to nurse content bellies when the winter chill outmatched the outdoor heaters, and others had dispersed after the excitement of the Roo Raffle with the main prize having been won by a thrifty Golden Oldie who would have been happy to receive anything for free regardless of what it was.

'Say, "Thraw another shreemp on the baahbie, mite!"' old Stanley nagged Bex in a surprisingly good imitation of her accent, ever eager to remain the centre of attention amongst the Oldies crowd. Bex looked irritated and the Oldies all laughed.

'I'll throw *you* on the barbie, Stanley, if you don't stop that this instant.'

'Now in England, love, that's not what you call good customer service. And there's not enough meat on my old bones to satisfy this lot anyway.'

More laughter.

'Shush Stanley, leave the poor girl alone,' Betty chastised him. She was finally able to put up her aching feet, and had her hands wrapped around a soothing mug of hot tea that Harry had made for her. Betty was a dear old thing, thought Bex. Unlike her husband!

'Who's the new dish then?' Emily whispered when she joined Eve at her table, pointing out Harry who was busy getting to grips with the coffee machine. His brow was knitted in concentration as he took his time over each order, keen to get things just right.

'That's the guy I was telling you about, the one who's been hanging around outside the café.'

Emily was aghast. 'The homeless guy? Working here? Have you completely lost your marbles or is this the hot cider talking? Next, you'll be telling me you're letting him do the cashing up tonight. Honestly, Evie, don't be so naive! Your dad will have kittens.'

Fortunately, Robert and Carol, who were now sharing a table with Emily and Mark, were too caught up in their own conversation to hear them.

'Shh, he'll hear you.' Eve was irritated. 'Besides, he isn't even homeless - he lives with his girlfriend. They're expecting.'

'Oh?'

'What do you mean, oh?'

'It's just... Well, I'm sure I saw him looking over at Bex a few times.'

'Why wouldn't he? She's been showing him the ropes. And she does sort of stand out.'

'No, it was more than that...'

Eve frowned. Emily was right, there did seem to be something between them, and Bex had dated guys with a similar look in the past. He was too pale of skin and wiry of build for Eve's taste, but there was something quirky in his style that made the two of them seem more suited.

'I'm pretty sure I saw her looking at him too.' Emily grinned.

Eve followed her line of sight and sure enough she did catch a couple of stray glances between the pair when each thought the other wasn't looking. 'You don't miss a trick, do you, Emily? No baby brain for you.'

'Ciao, bella! Eve, my darling, you look more beautiful than ever. It's been too long.'

In walked Paolo looking as much like a model as ever - a fact that wasn't lost on the remaining ladies among the throng - followed closely by Gianni who trotted behind him looking a little preoccupied. Oblivious, Paolo grabbed Eve in a tight squeeze and kissed each of her cheeks, his gaze trailing appreciatively downwards from the thick mane of hair she had decided to leave down for once. The exchange between Eve and Paolo didn't go unnoticed by Thom, who was slightly irritated as he hovered in the background.

The fact Eve now spent every day on her feet for a living meant she was trimmer than usual, and the burst of confidence this gave her meant she was wearing an uncharacteristically clingy jersey dress that Emily could no longer fit into, along with a borrowed pair of heeled ankle boots. The dress emphasised her bust and bottom in a way it never could on her naturally slender friend.

'I am sorry we are so late,' Gianni apologised, taking in as he did so all of the changes that had been made on what was once his turf. 'Oh, it looks good. Very good.' He nodded his approval but remained distracted.

'Better late than never,' said Eve. 'It's so good to see you! We've saved you some food, and unless you'd prefer something stronger, our new barista here will make you a coffee to go with it.'

Harry nodded his assent, and Paolo wandered over to grab the plates from Dave, who was about to take a much-needed rest himself. Interestingly, he made a beeline straight for the empty seat beside Tony.

'Everything ok?' Eve asked Gianni conspiratorially when Paolo was out of earshot. 'You seem a little preoccupied.'

The old man sighed wheezily before fixing his molten eyes on hers. He would have been handsome in his time and no doubt a charmer too like his son, though a combination of hard work, a messy divorce, and years of heavy smoking and drinking had left their mark.

'Ees Paolo.' He glanced at his son. 'It's time he grew up - thirty-three years old and still no wife. No babies. I had hoped to become a grandfather someday, but all he cares about is boobies, boobies. He lacks focus and does not see what ees really important. Now he is losing interest in the restaurant too - I feel it! Ees bad for business. And I... Sometimes I feel old. I have worked hard, and now I grow weary. Ees time for Paolo to take over, but why would he want to while he is without roots? A wife would stabilise him. If only...'

He looked at Eve as though he considered her ideal daughter-in-law material, then his voice trailed off and he mumbled a string of what she assumed were Italian expletives.

'Oh dear.' Eve glanced over at Paolo. Perhaps what Paolo needed was to step out his father's shadow and become his own man. She was just about to say something to this effect when a loud yelp from behind cut her off.

'Ouch!' It was Emily, one hand flying to her bump. Everyone turned her way.

Mark was alarmed. 'Not here!'

'Ooo,' Emily moaned.

Across the crowded room, Eve and Thom's eyes met and he smiled. Given how busy the fundraiser had been, there hadn't been a spare moment for them to catch up properly since their impromptu date in the city.

'Oh no...' Emily looked down, embarrassed. Her waters had broken.

'Someone call an ambulance!' Carol yelled as she leapt from her seat. 'The baby is coming!'

And chaos descended on The Melbourne Community Café.

♥ 18 ♥

'No! No ambulance - not yet!' said Emily between breaths. 'Don't need it.' She panted until the grip of another contraction had passed.

'But we've got to get you to the hospital!' Mark paled from the magnitude of the situation.

'Is there anyone here who's still sober?' Eve yelled hopefully.

There was a collective murmur of assent from the Golden Oldies, and a drunken roar of dissent from the Cosplayers who had come in from outside and were relishing all the excitement.

'Someone who is actually in possession of a car as opposed to a free bus pass?'

'I could take her on the back of my bicycle if you think she'd fit,' said Dave. Once his catering duties were done for the day, he'd quickly managed to get himself half-cut, spurred on by his mutual flirtation with the café's dashing salt-and-pepper haired neighbour. Tony nudged him playfully.

'I can drive you both, but I don't exactly have a licence,' said Harry. 'If you don't mind then I don't.'

'Who *are* you anyway?' Robert spluttered. 'And where's your bloody ticket?'

'He's my new barista,' said Eve, making her mind up on the spot. 'He doesn't need a ticket.'

Robert eyed Harry suspiciously. He'd overheard some things about him that afternoon that he didn't like the sound of, and he felt it was far safer for his daughter to keep her distance than to take him under her wing.

'I am?'

'Absolutely. If you want to be.'

'I do.'

Bex beamed and patted him on the back. 'Congratulations, mate!'

Robert was dismayed.

'Sorry to break up this little gathering, people, but I'd just like to remind you that MY BABY IS COMING! Can everyone please just FOCUS ON ME!'

'I knew we shouldn't have bloody gone out so close to your due date,' Mark moaned, 'but you had to insist, didn't you?'

Ordinarily Emily would have risen to the bait, but her only response was another groan of pain.

'Right then,' said Mark, leaping to his feet. 'It's not ideal. but if you're happy to drive my car up to the hospital for us, that would be great. I've had one too many anyway and I'm in no fit state. We'll just have to hope you don't get pulled over, that's the last thing we need.'

'I don't think the police want to deliver this baby any more than you do,' said Eve.

Harry agreed, and he hung back whilst Thom and Mark grabbed Emily's arms and slowly helped pull her up to standing.

'Eve, I'm so scared.' Her eyes were wide. 'Can you come too?'

'Of course I can.' Eve stroked her friend's cropped hair. 'I'd love to be there with you, but I need to lock up here first.'

'I'll do it,' said Bex.

The crowd was dispersing anyway as afternoon crept into evening, and Bex had seen Eve lock up often enough to know what to do. Eve hesitated only briefly. She trusted Bex to be as thorough as she was. 'That would be great, but don't forget to remove the charity funds and whatever's in the till. It's best we don't leave that amount of cash in the building.'

'I won't,' Bex promised.

The small group exited The Melbourne with a pained and panting Emily, to the drunken well-wishes of those left behind. It seemed Emily's spontaneous labour had only added to the enjoyment of the afternoon for their guests, who yelled their thanks as Eve went.

♥

Thankfully, they made it to the city's hospital without any police interference or the arrival of Emily's baby. They were at the same hospital Eve had worked at upon her return from Australia, and she couldn't believe how far those days were behind her now. She didn't miss them one jot and was relieved she was still in a position to make a positive contribution to the local community without the emotional turmoil of constantly dealing with other people's grief and loss. She couldn't imagine doing anything else.

Eve and Thom sat side by side on unforgiving plastic chairs outside the delivery suite. Whilst it would be nice to say they were waiting patiently; in all honesty they were flagging. It had been hours now, and the morning's early start combined with the stress and excitement of the fundraiser and the adrenaline of Emily's labour had left them both drained, though nowhere near as depleted as they knew Emily would be right now.

'So...' said Thom, 'am I always going to have to compete for your affections with exotic strangers?'

Eve grinned. 'Maybe, though Melbourne can hardly be considered exotic!'

'It's across the Tyne, isn't it? And tropical to boot. But I'm referring to that slimy Italian bloke - Pèpe, or whatever his name is.' Thom frowned.

'It's Paolo, not Pèpe, and you've got it all wrong. He fancies anything with boobs, and I refuse to become another notch on his bedpost.'

'I see.' Thom was somewhat placated. 'Do you fancy becoming a notch on mine instead, then? Hehe.'

'Thom! I would like to keep my virtue intact if that's quite alright with you.' She gestured towards the delivery suite. 'I've heard enough moans and groans in here to put me off for life.'

'Haha, well perhaps we just won't have any children then - though I've always fancied four or five.'

'That's because you get the pleasure of putting them there without the pain of bringing them out again.'

'True, true.'

The double doors opened behind them, and a pale-faced Mark appeared looking the worse for wear. 'You may as well go home, guys. It looks like nothing's going to happen here for a while.'

'Are you sure?' Eve had assumed the baby was well on its way.

'After all the excitement at the start, she's not, erm-,' Mark struggled to find the right words, '*dilating* as fast as we'd hoped. But everything's fine.' He looked almost as embarrassed as Thom, and Eve thought how strange it was that people could talk to so openly about intimacy but not about its results.

'Do you think she would mind if we went?' Eve was knackered, but not as knackered. Her heart went out to Emily who was only at the start of her labour. 'If she needs either of us, we'll come straight back - we're just at the end of the phone.'

'She's so spaced out on gas and air that she won't remember either way, so go and get some rest. It's been a big day for all of us. And look, it's almost Christmas Day.' He gestured at the clock - it was getting on for midnight. 'Anyway, where's Harry? I wanted to thank him for getting us all here in one piece.' Mark's relief was obvious.

'He left hours ago - he had to get home to his girlfriend. But don't worry, I'll tell him. Let us know as soon as your precious one arrives.'

Eve got up and hugged Mark. She had the sense that something monumental was about to happen to this couple she loved so dearly.

'Will do. I can't believe I'm going to be a dad! Today there's just two of us, but this time tomorrow our lives will be changed forever. It's hard to even imagine.'

'What a memorable Christmas? And Emily will no doubt seething, because at this rate it looks as though she'll have to eat the hospital's Christmas dinner like she'd feared.'

'I'm the one who'll be getting it in the ear as always.'

'You wouldn't have it any other way though, would you?'

'Not for the world. And soon there'll be two Emily's!' It was as though the concept had just occurred to him for the very first time. 'Send help!'

Eve laughed. 'Good luck! Give my love to Emily and the baby. Can't wait to meet her!' For a moment Eve felt broody, until another moan emanated from the other side of the double doors.

'Good luck, mate.' Thom gave his brother-in-law a reassuring slap on the back, then Mark disappeared back into the abyss between pregnancy and parenthood. There was little hint of Christmas in that bare, sterile corridor, the place where lives began.

♥

Eve and Thom braced themselves against the chill outside the hospital building, but there wasn't an accommodating bus or a taxi in sight. Snow threatened, heralding the possibility of a white Christmas.

'What shall we do now?' Thom asked.

Eve shivered and stifled a yawn. 'What do you mean, what shall we do? Go to sleep like normal people - I've been up since six o'clock this morning! This is fast becoming the least Christmassy Christmas Eve I've ever had. Almost - you can't get much less Christmassy than a hot summer's day in Australia.'

Eve stopped when she registered Thom's disappointment. Since their reacquaintance it seemed she had become a dab-hand, after experiencing so much disappointment herself, at becoming the cause of it in her prospective suitors. What was she hanging onto anyway? A dead dream of a romance that could never be. Her life couldn't stop there though, it had to go on.

She regarded Thom. He was so steadfast, so earnest, so... gorgeous. There hadn't been a spare moment since their date for them to find out where the other was at, not that she was sure she ready to. Right now, her fantasies revolved less around romance than they did around the prospect of collapsing into bed for twelve hours straight then gorging on turkey, fizz, chocolates, and telly before enjoying three full days off work and the chance to give her aching bones a rest.

'It's just, I... Never mind.' Thom faltered. Unlike Eve, he'd appreciated the opportunity for them to spend more time together despite the circumstances. But he noticed there were dark shadows under her eyes and that she was rubbing her lower back.

'What were you going to say?'

Thom looked at Eve thoughtfully, his eyes deep a shade of navy as the wintry night.

'Well, I was going to ask if you fancied going to midnight mass down at the cathedral.' He glanced at his watch. 'I know it's getting late, but we might just make it. It might even make you feel more Christmassy. My parents used to drag me and Emily along every year when we were kids. We liked it because we got to stay up late, then afterwards our mam would make us a hot chocolate and tell us we had to get to sleep quickly otherwise Santa would run out of time to visit before morning.'

'That sounds so lovely.' Christmases with Eve's older brother Daniel had been rather less idyllic. As the older one between them, he'd often teased her for her unwavering belief in Santa, and he once went so far as to tell her what presents their parents had bought her and where they were hidden just to prove his point and spoil the element of surprise. He'd felt bad about it later, and after she'd told her parents he'd gotten into a heap of trouble.

'It was, though on second thoughts it may have just been a clever way for my parents to score a lie-in on Christmas morning. We wouldn't get out of bed until we were sure we'd given Santa enough time to come.'

Eve laughed, and Thom smiled. 'You're so beautiful,' he said.

She thought of all the things he had done for her at the café over the last couple of months, how much he had put himself out for her for little in return, and even now he was still thinking up ways he could please her.

'You know, I think I could find my second wind - for you.' She stifled another yawn and grinned.

'Really?'

'Mmhmm.'

Thom beamed. 'We'll have to hurry then. Listen...'

Somewhere in the distance, the cathedral bells sounded the quarter hour, and Thom grabbed her hand and pulled her into a canter. Luckily, the route was all downhill - Eve didn't fancy spending another night with Thom flat on her backside.

> *'O Holy Night! The Stars are brightly shining*
> *It is the night of the dear Saviour's birth.*

Long lay the world, in sin and error pining
Til he appeared and the Spirit felt its worth.
A thrill of hope, the weary world rejoices
For yonder breaks a new and glorious morn.
Fall on your knees! Oh hear the angel voices!
O night divine, the night when Christ was born;
O night, O holy night, O night divine!
O night, O holy night, O night divine!'

Thom gently pulled back the heavy oak door of the city's cathedral so that their late arrival wouldn't cause a disturbance. It was five minutes to twelve, and the very end of the service. Hand in hand, the pair crept to one of the farthest pews and admired the grand building emblazoned with candles and extravagant boughs of holly and ivy. The air smelled of that ancient smell old churches seem to have - of burning wick, crisp air, cool stone, and ages gone by. The atmosphere was heavy with centuries of hopeful prayer, all of life's agonies and joys caught between the building's solid arched walls.

They sat together, side by side in an old wooden pew. Eve was in awe at the intensity of the choir. Their voices rang with strength and humility as they sang *O Holy Night*. It was as beautiful as it was moving. Emotion welled within her, and a tear slid from her eye drawing an enquiring glance from Thom. She squeezed his hand tightly, and he squeezed back. She was sobbing quietly, her eyes closed as the chorus engulfed her.

'...The King of Kings lay thus lowly manger
In all our trials born to be our friend.
He knows our need, our weakness is no stranger;

Behold your King! Before him lowly bend!
Behold your King! Before him lowly bend!'

Eve felt the coarse fingertips of Thom's hand brushing her cheek, ever so gently just under her eye, catching a tear. She lifted a hand up to his face and cupped it in hers. She felt him move towards her, and she turned her face to his. They were at the very back of the cathedral, unseen and touched only by the shadows of flickering candlelight. She looked up at him, and Thom held her gaze.

'...With all our hearts, we praise His holy name
Christ is the Lord! Then ever, ever praise we;
His power and glory ever more proclaim!
His power and glory ever more proclaim!
O night, O holy night, O night divine!
O night, O holy night, O night divine!'

Slowly, slowly, Thom lowered his lips to hers. He stopped only a moment out of reach, and Eve could feel the heat of his breath upon her mouth. She angled her body towards him and pressed herself close against his chest. He smiled, enveloping her in his arms. Eve tilted her head and brought her mouth the infinitesimal distance between them to meet his.

As the carol came to its bittersweet end and the church bells rang in Christmas Day, Thom and Eve shared their first real kiss. It was a kiss that remained imprinted on their lips and their hearts well beyond sunrise, which incidentally despite how tired they both were, is just how long it took them to find the time to go to sleep.

♥ 19 ♥

It was Christmas, somewhere in that peaceful space between dawn and day, where living room lights cast a hazy glow into still streets that for one morning of the year would remain relatively undisturbed and unusually silent. It was somewhere after the last gifts had been opened and before the bustle and activity of lunch preparations had begun, or the rush of visiting this relative and that with towers of presents in hand. It was then that Thom woke Eve with a squeeze and a kiss, slipping a tray holding a mug of hot coffee and a wedge of toast thick with marmalade under her nose. Sleepily she responded to the kiss, and Thom pulled away.

'If you keep that up, we won't end up with any breakfast at all.'

'Why, are *you* going to eat it?' she asked innocently. 'You should never start what you can't finish, you know.'

'Oh, I can finish it alright.'

Eve peered up at him from her vantage point in his bed. He looked divine with his sandy hair all tousled, his wall of chest defined by solid muscle and a smattering of golden hairs, his cobalt eyes bright with a desire that masked his lack of sleep, and his hands and fingers mildly calloused from the physical work associated with his job. He was comfortable with his nakedness to a degree that mesmerised Eve, who couldn't imagine ever having the confidence to wander around like that in front of anyone. She allowed her eyes to linger upon his impressive physique.

'Right, that's it, I did warn you.' Thom reached over to take the tray from her hands before setting it aside on the bedside table, and after that breakfast was the last thing on their minds for quite some time.

'Have we missed Christmas?' she asked him later - much later. It was the best sleep she'd had in months. She'd forgotten how much more soundly she slept tangled in the strength and warmth of a man.

Thom checked his watch. It was nearly twelve. 'Nope, it's still Christmas. And may I say it's up there as one of my favourites so far.'

'Just one of your favourites?'

He mulled it over a bite of cold toast and a mouthful of lukewarm coffee. 'Well, there's the year I got my first console. I'm sure you'll agree that's not easily beaten.'

Eve feigned disappointment.

'Actually, come to think of it, there is a way to top that Christmas.'

Thom's eyes trailed deliberately slowly from the fronds of hair that grazed Eve's shoulders in one thick, chestnut brush to the gentle rise of creamy décolletage that led to the enticing swell of breasts only just concealed by the sheets she had pulled up around her for extra warmth. He reached out a hand and allowed a frond of her hair to fall through his fingers before tracing his index finger slowly downward.

'Thom, if we don't leave now, my parents will never forgive me - it's my first Christmas at home in years and I'm not even there to celebrate it with them. They'll be wondering where I am and-' She stopped short as he gently cupped her breast with his hand and rubbed the peak through the thin sheath of sheet.

'You'll be amazed at what can be achieved in, hmm, say half an hour, when you set your mind to it.'

And it was not so reluctantly that Eve leaned back and gave herself over to the exquisite pressure of Thom's hands and fingertips.

♥

'Remembered where you live, have you?' Carol chastised her daughter who had just let herself in through the front door looking rather sheepish.

Eve had been hoping not to bump into her parents straight away to give her time to at least change her clothes and make herself look presentable. But Carol was chastened when she clocked Thom coming in behind her and could barely contain her delight.

'Come in, come in, Thom. Merry Christmas!'

Thom had the grace to blush as she pulled him into a hug. Carol was positively beaming.

'You're embarrassing me,' Eve muttered.

'Nonsense, embarrassing you?' She looked from one to the other then glanced pointedly at Eve's crumpled clothes from yesterday. 'I think you've done that already. You should get changed before your dad sees you.'

'It was late when we finished up at the hospital - I didn't want to disturb you in the night.'

'*Sure* you didn't.'

Eve wished the ground would open and swallow her up, but no it was still there, a perfectly solid hardwood floor. Thom laughed and gave a saucy wink. She wasn't sure if this was meant for her or if it was an effort to charm her mother. This had better have become his favourite Christmas.

'I didn't know I was expecting extra guests. Fortunately for you I've got us a turkey so big it could feed a small army. Come through.' Carol led them down the hall.

Obediently they followed her through to the kitchen, their mouths watering at the delicious smell of roasting meat that greeted them there, their appetites fuelled by their antics from the night before. They were ravenous. Robert appeared and shook hands with Thom, giving him the sort of look of resignation that suggested if someone had to spend the night canoodling with his daughter, he'd rather it was him than anyone else.

Bex was on Yorkshire pudding duty and was whisking away diligently, but when she spotted Eve, she stopped what she was doing to smother her in hugs and kisses interspersed with knowing looks and raised eyebrows. She was resplendent in a sequinned jumper and flimsy paper hat, the kind you'd find in a Christmas cracker, paired with black leather trousers and a pair of workman's boots. She'd even dyed her hair a festive silver.

'Has the baby arrived yet?' Carol asked as she made a start on the veg.

'No, no sign yet. Emily must be having quite a time of it.' Eve shivered at the prospect of childbirth that remained some sort of fearful mystery for the uninitiated. 'We're going to head over to the hospital to see her after lunch. I thought it might be nice to bring her some turkey if there's any left over.'

'Did you now? Is there anyone you don't expect me to feed - that big hairy bloke from the café, perhaps?'

Eve rolled her eyes. 'That would be Harry.'

'You can take what you want provided you make yourself useful like your good friend Bex here.' Carol handed her a potato peeler and a sack of potatoes. 'Merry Christmas.'

'Fancy a beer?' Robert asked Thom. 'There's sports on.' This was a mark of approval indeed.

Eve scowled at the unfairness of the situation, and Thom grinned at her, clearly far more comfortable with a pint in his hand than a potato peeler. 'Have fun.'

'Oh, yes - go sit down, you two. You'd only be in the way.'

Eve took to potato peeling with such a frenzy that there was more skin left than potato. Carol tutted and couldn't refrain from remarking that Bex would have done a better job.

♥

'Soo, how was it with the Adonis?' Bex asked later when the pair were finally alone.

They were putting together some treats for Emily, who had at last given birth to a beautiful baby girl late that afternoon. They'd decided to call her Joy Elizabeth, Joy both as a nod to the season and to the happiness she'd brought in making them a little family of three.

'How was what?'

'The sex, of course - it's written all over your face.'

'I don't know what you mean.'

'Don't play the innocent with me when it's clear you've been up all night being quite the opposite!'

'It was...' Eve thought about it and blushed.

'Pretty amazing by the look of you. You haven't looked this happy in months.'

'It was wonderful! It was like - like he really *knew* me.'

'About time too. And he does know you, he's known you since you were kids.'

Eve grimaced.

'So, what's next for the two of you? Are you dating? Do you think you've finally managed to put James behind you?'

'Almost. He certainly seems to have put me behind him. And no, nothing is official between us yet.'

'Well, that's a start, I suppose. And it's best you forget about what James is doing and just concentrate on yourself.'

Eve was keen to move the topic onto safer ground. 'And what about you and love - has anything changed since we last talked?'

Bex fell quiet. 'Me? I don't really have enough time left to fall in love. My work here is almost done. You're finally making coffee like a true Melbournian, *and* you make a mean lamington! You have no further use for me.'

She looked a little sad at the prospect of leaving, and Eve was too. She couldn't imagine running the café without her. Bex was part of its integrity, and the customers loved her, especially Stanley, though you wouldn't guess from the way he always teased her.

'And Harry?'

Bex was uncharacteristically coy, confirming Eve's suspicions.

'Emily said she thought there might be something between you two - a connection. She reckons she saw him looking at you too.'

'She does?' Bex seemed to take the idea and hold it close. 'It's a hopeless situation, isn't it? Like with you and James. Harry's committed to someone else now, and there's a baby on the way. It's best I put him out of my mind and move on, and the sooner the better before there can be any real harm done.'

'I wish you didn't have to go.' Eve had avoided preparing for this reality. She realised now that she'd hoped all along Bex would decide to stay. 'Besides, you've become too fluent at Geordie - you'll have no use for it in Melbourne.'

'I wish I didn't have to go either, but until they start offering visa sponsorship to mere baristas it looks as though I'll have no choice. And like I said, it's probably for the best.'

♥

Though her eyes were shadowed with exhaustion, Emily was beaming. 'Eve, this is Joy. Joy, say hello to your Aunty Evie.'

Reluctantly Mark left the room to grab a refuelling coffee with both sets of ecstatic new grandparents, making space for the visitors to meet their little daughter. Eve had never seen her friend appear either more exhausted or more content. Motherhood suited her - it softened her edges, or perhaps it was the labour drugs, only time would tell.

Emily slipped the precious pink bundle into Eve's arms and ever so gently, Eve cradled her close and studied her perfect sleeping form. She hadn't anticipated the swell of affection she would feel, or the pride in her dear friend who had been more like a sister to her throughout their lives. Thom had already had a cuddle with his new niece, holding her tenderly with an endearing combination of anxiety and awe. It had brought a tear to his eye, and to hers too. Men never looked so vulnerable as they did when holding a baby.

'She's perfect, isn't she?' said Emily dreamily, gazing across at Joy, primed to respond to her every need.

'With your genes how could she be anything else?' Eve looked down as she felt the baby begin to stir and let out a little moue of displeasure.

'Pass her to me, she needs fed. Or at least I think she does – I have no idea what I'm doing.'

Eve handed Joy over, and Emily put her to the breast as naturally as if it was something she'd been doing all her life.

'She has her mother's pout,' Eve remarked.

'Yes, she has my mouth - but her eyes and her nose are all Mark's.'

'Poor kid.' Thom grinned.

'How was the labour?' Curiosity had gotten the better of Bex.

Emily's face twisted with horror. 'Horrible. Just horrible. I've got stitches in places it would make your eyes water to think of, and it feels like no part of me will ever be the same again. I'm terrified of ever going to the toilet again...'

Thom's face paled.

'But it was worth it.'

'We've brought you some Christmas dinner if you're feeling up to it.' Eve deftly changed the subject.

'Thank goodness for that! Mark's parents have been too much on tenterhooks to cook, and you know *my* mam can't cook to save her life – which must be where I get it from. I'm ravenous, feed me! And give me all the gossip while you're at it.'

Thom coughed. 'I could murder a cuppa.' He'd been waiting to make his exit ever since his sister had taken her breast out, not to mention what she'd said about her stitches. Emily didn't miss the look that passed between her brother and her best friend on his way out.

'*You* are the gossip - going into labour like that right in the middle of my café!'

Eve handed Emily her plate after popping out to ask an over-worked hospital employee to warm it up for her. Emily placed a content and sleeping Joy into her crib then tucked in as though she hadn't eaten for days.

'Mmm, it might be lukewarm, but it tastes bloody amazing. Now come on, out with it. I know there must be some gossip because you seem to be deflecting. I'll prise it out of you sooner or later so you may as well just tell me. As a boring mother I'll be counting on other people's dramas to subsist on from now on.'

'Well,' said Bex, 'Eve didn't come home last night. And when she did, this afternoon no less, your brother was with her. You should've seen the look on her parents' faces, haha!'

'Is that so?' Emily eyed Eve shrewdly. 'I can't say I'm surprised. What is surprising is how long it took the two of you to get it on in the first place - my soon-to-be sister-in-law.'

'Hold on, one step at a time, please - I haven't completely forgotten about James. And anyway, Bex has been fawning over our dashing new barista!'

Bex' reddened cheeks betrayed her.

'It seems I have missed a lot in the last twenty-four hours.'

'But at least you didn't miss out on your Christmas dinner,' said Eve. 'And you've got a beautiful new baby.'

'How long will you be in hospital for?' Bex asked.

'I'm going to stay here as long as I can. You know what men are like - I'll get more help from the nurses than I will from Mark, so I may as well take full advantage of it while it lasts.'

There was a knock at the door as Mark, Thom, and both sets of grandparents made an eager reappearance.

'We'd better go,' said Eve. 'Try to get some rest. You've just created a miracle, after all.'

'Yes, the miracle of pushing something bigger than a pumpkin out of a very, very small space.'

Eve hugged her friend and planted a kiss on the baby's head. 'Congratulations, she's perfect.'

Thom stayed behind to spend some time with this little new addition to their family, slipping Mark a celebratory cigar when his sister wasn't looking. As Eve passed him on her way out, he discreetly brushed his fingertips against hers, a small gesture of affection that would have to sustain them both until they could be together again. Naturally, it wasn't lost on Emily.

♥ 20 ♥

It was the day after Boxing Day, and Eve couldn't have felt less like leaving the cocooning warmth of her bed. Several days off had reminded her of the less hectic pace she had known pre-café, and as much as she loved The Melbourne, she loved a pyjama day too.

It was with some indignance that she tapped silent her piercing alarm clock, then with a resigned sigh heaved back the covers, her toes recoiling as they met the cold wooden floor. She felt as anyone might feel who had spent their days gorging on sweet-mince pies, hot roast dinners, sparkling wine, and Quality Street - satisfied, sluggish, and a tad guilty. She was beaten to the bathroom by a static-haired Bex, who looked pretty much how Eve felt.

'You go in first.'

'No, you go.'

Eve grinned. 'Really, the only place either of us wants to go is back to bed.'

'Speak for yourself. I'm a terribly enthusiastic employee, at least that's what you've got to say on my reference when I move on from here. Anyway, you're the boss - go on through and I'll put us some toast on.'

'No need - Dave said he was going to make us breakfast this morning to soften the blow of our return to the coalface.'

Bex made a lunge for the bathroom door. 'Well in that case, I was here first.'

'It's *my* house!'

Bex shrugged her shoulders and sauntered on through.

MEET ME AT THE MELBOURNE

♥

'Wow, I never would have thought back when I was sunbaking back in Melbourne - sunbathing, sorry - that one day I'd get so cold my breath would frost up. I feel like an extra in a Dickensian novel, or an ice-encrusted Jack from Titanic.'

As though to emphasise her point, she rubbed her hands together and hunched her shoulders, her head sinking further into the woolly snood that had been a welcome gift from Eve's parents. It was still dark as night outside and the air was as cold as stone.

'We reserve only the best weather for our international visitors.'

'No kidding. I won't take the Aussie heat for granted in future, that's for sure - I'd take a stinking hot Christmas back home over this any day!'

Prompted by a seasonal bout of homesickness, Bex had booked her flight back to Melbourne a little earlier than intended, flying via Asia where she planned to spend a couple of months travelling. That meant she would be leaving them soon and Eve was gutted. She didn't know what she'd do without her, let alone how they'd manage at the café, but it wouldn't be fair of her to let that show. She knew all too well what it was like to be painfully homesick.

'Are you looking forward to going home?'

'Yes, and no. You Geordies have grown on me - even old Stanley. Sometimes. And how will I live without stottie and pease pudding?'

Eve laughed. 'And let's not forget Harry... He's working today, you know.'

Bex simply stared at the road ahead. 'Hey, do you hear that?'

'What?' They were listening to Wham's *Last Christmas* - not the cheeriest of hits but a classic all the same. Eve turned the radio down as Bex searched for the culprit. 'I think that's your phone vibrating.'

'Again? At this time?' Eve's hands had been too full of freshly baked lamingtons to answer when it had rung earlier.

Bex frowned. 'It must be important if someone's prepared to keep calling you at six in the morning. Shall I answer?'

'Nah, I wouldn't worry - it's most likely Dave wanting to tell us off for running late. It'll take more than Christmas to bring out the cheer in him.'

'I think a certain salt-and-pepper haired gent from upstairs might manage it though, don't you?'

'They did look pretty cosy together pre-Emily's waters breaking, didn't they?'

Eve parked up then got out of the car and ran to Bex' side to take the cumbersome box of lamingtons off her hands.

'It's bloody freezing,' Bex moaned, as with some reluctance she set foot outside. 'And it's dark all the time. How can you people live like this? I feel like I'm trapped in Narnia.'

As they rounded the corner of the frosty lane, arms linked so as not to slip, they paused to glance up at The Melbourne Community Café. As they approached, it was with plummeting hearts that it suddenly became clear Dave hadn't been calling to tell them off at all, nor to whet their appetite with the promise of a chef-cooked breakfast on a dreary December morning after all the Christmas excitement had passed. It was much worse than that.

'What the-?'

Though it was still dark, the closer the two women got to the café the clearer it became that both of The Melbourne's bay windows had been smashed right through, with shards of the remaining glass sticking out at jaunty angles. Sprayed across the front of the building in large lettering were the words 'MERRY CHRISTMAS' – though it seemed there was a lack of genuine sentiment to the greeting. A pair of dog-walkers had stopped to gawp, their faces mirroring the shock that Eve felt, and she wished all the onlookers would hurry up and move on - the last thing she needed right now was another witness to her humiliation.

Dave appeared, gesticulating wildly towards the sorry mess that was left of Eve's livelihood. 'Where have you been? Why didn't you answer your phone? I tried to tell you!'

Tony followed. 'I'm so sorry,' he said.

Eve watched their approach as if in slow-motion, unable to get her head around the bleak reality she was now faced with. She let out a groan of anguish that turned into an angry, exasperated cry.

'Arghhh!'

Bex folded Eve into her arms as she cried with neither self-consciousness nor grace and allowed herself to be led into the bones of her café. A breeze blew icy air through the broken windows and fragments of glass crackled underfoot, as shattered as Eve's dreams. Unseen, Stacey smirked with satisfaction then turned her back and was on her way.

♥

'Right, that's us done. We've fingerprinted and photographed the whole scene. Looks like whoever's responsible for this had an axe to grind - can you think of anyone who might have had a motive? A dissatisfied customer? Perhaps you undercooked their bacon or over-roasted their coffee beans, haha!'

Sergeant Wilson allowed himself a laugh at his own little joke. Hours had passed, and behind him Eve could see that the team were just leaving. She was confused. Something didn't add up, but her mind was too foggy to figure out what. She certainly couldn't think of anyone she'd offended enough to deserve this.

'It'll be that bloody rascal, Harry! You never should have-'

'Dad...'

'If I ever get my hands on him, I'll-'

'Dad, just stop it, would you? Harry would never do something like this.'

'How do you know? You barely know him! What were you thinking of, taking on someone like that? With a history as long as your arm.'

It was true that Eve hadn't quite realised the extent of Harry's record. She didn't want to doubt him, but it didn't look good.

'Stop it, Robert, you aren't helping matters,' Carol admonished him as she handed her daughter a steaming cup of tea with two sugars to help counteract the shock of the morning's events. 'There you are, darling.'

Dave and Tony pottered about in the background, salvaging what they could now they were permitted to do so once the police had left.

'Sabotage. That's what this is - bloody sabotage!'

'*Robert*. Shush!'

'Now, before we move on is there anything else missing, or anything else you think we should know?' When no-one replied, Sergeant Wilson cleared his throat, prompting a response.

'No, there's nothing else missing,' said Eve. 'Just the little that was left in the till.' She couldn't understand why anyone would wreak such devastation for so little reward. She'd always been meticulous in ensuring that very little cash, if any, remained on the premises overnight.

'Ooh...' Bex paled. The sergeant assessed her, sensing a lead.

'What?' Eve regarded her friend with a sense of dread. *'What?'*

'Oh no, you're going to hate me...'

'What is it? Out with it.' Sergeant Wilson had taken out his notepad, pen poised to add more to his notes.

Bex looked pained. 'It's the money we raised at the Christmas barbeque - I totally forgot to take it out when I locked up that night. I'm so sorry, there was just so much going on. I had the cash in my hand ready to go, but I got distracted right as I was walking out of the door.'

Eve nodded. There was no point in getting angry, it was an honest mistake. Accidents happened, and what was done couldn't be undone.

'Yes...?' The sergeant was keen to maintain their focus on the task at hand. Emotions were a distraction in his opinion.

'You see, a good friend of ours went into labour at the barbeque. And there were people everywhere. It was a celebration - a fundraising event.'

'I see. And how much money was raised?'

'Close to one and a half thousand pounds.'

'And do you remember where you left it?'

Bex tried to recall her steps. 'Over there - just behind the counter. I put it down momentarily then I obviously forgot to pick it back up again. It was inside a container that one of our groups had turned into a sort of post-box. It's very distinctive – pillar-box red with cotton wool snow on top.'

'Was there anyone else here when you were locking up that night?'

'No. There was just me, Dave, and a couple of others who were helping out with the clean-up. As we were leaving, a woman approached to ask if there was any work going. That's when I put the box down. She couldn't have taken it though - she was with me the whole time. I would have noticed.'

'And where was this Harry chap?'

'He wasn't here.' Bex was defensive. 'He's the one who drove our friend to the hospital.'

'Was he now?' The sergeant referred to his notes. 'Driving without a licence,' he spoke aloud as he jotted into his notepad. He remembered Harry and his misdeeds from back when he was a youngster.

Bex paled, feeling that she'd betrayed him. 'It was a special circumstance - we were desperate! We couldn't have managed without him.'

Robert's face was fire. 'But where the hell is he now, eh? That's what I'd like to know. You said he was expected in for work today and he hasn't shown up - interesting that, isn't it?'

Carol shushed her husband. Again.

Eve had tried calling Harry several times, but his phone had gone straight through to voicemail. She'd left a couple of messages urging him to get in touch, but if he had any inkling of what had gone on at The Melbourne, it looked increasingly doubtful he would return any of her calls.

'We've had officers around his place this morning, but he wasn't there. His girlfriend was in though, and she said Harry didn't come home last night. Poor soul. Pregnant too. The house was freezing, not enough money to warm it apparently, and she looked as though she'd had a sleepless night.' Sergeant Wilson stroked his chin. 'Now there's a possible motive.'

Eve was defensive. 'While Harry's personal challenges might explain why he'd be tempted to take the cash, it doesn't exactly explain the state of the place, does it?'

She was still reluctant to accept that Harry could have had anything to do with it. He might be any number of things, but vindictive and cruel were not traits she had learned to associate with him in the brief time she'd known him. Then again, with his background it was obvious that he'd hurt people in the past, so what would prevent him from doing so again if circumstance necessitated it?

'Here's my card. We'll continue looking into it for you, Miss Winters. In the meantime, if you remember anything else, no matter how trivial, please don't hesitate to call.'

'So, you're looking for this Harry bloke then?' Robert was hopeful.

'We're looking for him,' the sergeant confirmed. 'From what I know of Harry, he's the most appropriate focal point to this investigation.'

Robert shook his hand, his relief palpable.

'Just one more thing.' Sergeant Wilson gingerly avoided tripping over a broken table-leg. 'Perhaps you should consider police-checking your employees in future, ideally *before* they start working for you.'

♥

'Eve - I'm so sorry. I'm such a mole! I can't believe I was stupid enough to leave all that cash behind. I know I got distracted, but I couldn't have imagined anyone would be cruel enough to do something like this - at Christmastime, too.'

Eve brushed Bex' words aside. 'Please can you put the Closed sign up on the door?' She was grateful for Tony and Dave's efforts to make the place somewhat secure until the necessary repairs could take place - there'd already been enough questions from the curious customers they'd had to turn away that day.

'I think anyone with eyes can see you're closed today!' Robert was exasperated by the day's events. 'I don't think there's much call for spending the afternoon in a smashed-up dump, even if grunge is all the rage in Melbourne.'

'That's enough Robert.' Carol was swiftly losing her patience with her husband, but she understood it was out of sheer concern and anger on their daughter's behalf that he was behaving like this.

Eve didn't have the energy to respond, she sat nursing her cup of tea and wondered why she had ever bothered coming home to England if it turned out it'd all been for nothing. Somehow, she'd managed to lose James, her savings, and her livelihood in a matter of months - not to mention the money the people of their local community had donated in good faith.

It seemed she would have been better off staying in Melbourne after all, just as James had wanted her to. Maybe life *was* better in Australia - everyone seemed to think so, and hardly anyone outside of her immediate circle could understand why she'd chosen to come back. Most of her customers thought she was mad to have given up a life over there to return to the wet, miserable England she loved so dearly and had missed so much.

Perhaps what had happened was a sign she should return to Melbourne with Bex and start again all over again. But by then, James would already have moved on, and she couldn't bear to live in such close proximity to him, only to be forced to keep her distance. She had no idea what to do. 'Do you really think Harry could have done it?'

'Pah! Who else?' Robert was exasperated. It was obvious to him.

'You really aren't helping matters,' said Carol. 'Come on, we're going to head off out for a bit - it's probably for the best.' She didn't want to leave her daughter in the midst of all this chaos, but she didn't want their presence at the café to make things worse for her either.

'Who else *could* be responsible?' said Tony. 'Harry knew about the fundraising event, and he's been obviously short of cash with a baby on the way and a demanding girlfriend. From what Dave tells me he hasn't known either of you long enough to feel any sense of obligation towards you.'

'In a street of terraced houses, you'd think someone would have seen or heard something. Anything!' Holes were being picked in Bex' defences, and she didn't know Harry well enough fill them in.

'I was over at Dave's place last night.' Tony was sheepish. 'Otherwise, I might have heard something. The police have already done their rounds and it seems half the street were either out for the night or away for the holidays.'

Dave returned from the kitchen, tripping over an upturned chair on his way in as he was distracted by the screen of his smartphone. 'You're not going to believe this,' he said with a grin, 'but one of our customers has started a Save The Melbourne page. By the sounds of it, a small army are on their way over here right now to help clean up this mess. With all these hands on deck, it shouldn't take too long - with a bit of elbow grease we can be open again in no time!'

For a moment Eve's heart soared with hope. The prospect of losing the café felt something akin to losing a limb, and though she had insurance, her excess was scandalous, and she knew they'd probably find some sort of loophole given she had agreed that cash wouldn't be kept on the premises after hours. If what Dave said was true, then the people of the northeast regarded The Melbourne as their very own community café, just as she'd always hoped.

'Maybe,' she said, 'but whoever did this is still at large. What's to say we don't put in all this hard work only for them to come over again one night and ruin it? The people of this community have done enough for us already, and I won't take advantage of their good nature by asking for anything more. I think it's best we just finish up here altogether. Tell them thank you, but we're closing down.'

'Closing down? Not on my watch!' Dave realised how much he had enjoyed being part of The Melbourne – getting it off the ground, preparing great food for the locals to enjoy, meeting Tony... Despite his distinctly uncompetitive salary, he couldn't imagine doing anything else. Eve might be feeling defeated right now, but there was enough fight in him left to do all he could to save this place he had grown so fond of. It was more than just a workplace - it was a home from home.

'Look,' he said to Bex, 'why don't you take Eve out somewhere for the day – as far away from here as possible – and we'll stay here and see what can be done.'

Bex nodded and Eve required no prompting to leave. She couldn't bear to stay at the café as it was now a moment longer.

She could scarcely believe that all the collective hard work, time and effort it had taken to bring her dream to life had been ruined in one single night through a senseless act of betrayal, not to mention the loss of the donations her customers had kindly made to charity in Daniel's memory. She'd have to find some way of paying them all back, but without a café she was without an income, and she still had wages, bills and rent to pay in addition to the cost of the repairs. Whatever would her landlord say? The implications were dizzying.

As Eve turned her back upon The Melbourne, she felt as though she'd not only let herself down, but she'd also let down her parents, her colleagues, her customers, and now Daniel, too. If James could see her right now, she bet he would be saying, 'I told you so.'

♥ 21 ♥

When Eve got home, she hid in her bedroom. She wanted to be alone. She had half a dozen missed calls on her mobile phone, most of which were from Thom, but she couldn't face talking to anyone yet, least of all him - it was just too complicated to think about right now. She set her phone aside and curled up on her bed. Her phone rang again and eventually she leaned over to pick it up after a brief glance at the screen. It was an unknown number. She hesitated, but before she could answer the ringing stopped. No sooner had it stopped however, than it started up again in earnest. Maybe it was the police? She diverted the call to voicemail. A moment later, a notification popped up that she had a message, and with some reluctance she dialled through to listen.

'Miss Winters, Sergeant Wilson here. We've located Harry, but he's in a bad way at the hospital – overdose, apparently. Please give me a call as soon as you get this message.'

Eve felt winded. Her first thoughts were of concern for Harry's welfare and horror at what he must have gone through, marred by the possibility he might have somehow been responsible for all this. Regardless, she leapt out of bed, threw on her coat, and ran to Bex' room. Whatever had happened, they both wanted to be there to support him and were determined to find out the truth once and for all.

♥

For someone who had worked most of her adult life within hospital boundaries, Eve now found any return to such an environment oppressive. It couldn't be avoided, as Bex needed someone to be there for her when she saw Harry for the first time. With that in mind she linked her arm, gave it a little squeeze, and together they made their way down the stark corridor to the HDU.

'How is he?' Bex asked the first nurse who crossed their path.

'Are you relatives?' The nurse's manner was abrupt.

'No, we're friends.'

'His *friends?*' She looked sceptical.

'He works with us,' Eve supplied.

'Well,' the nurse relented, 'since you're the only visitors he's had so far, I'll let you see him, but only briefly – it's not quite visiting hour. Maybe you could shed some light on his situation for me - do you know who his next of kin is?'

'We know he has a partner - her name's Stacey. But we don't have a number for her.'

The nurse frowned. 'You'd think she'd have paid him a visit by now - she almost lost him!'

The two women exchanged puzzled looks. The police would surely have told Stacey that Harry had been located. If not, then maybe they should be the ones to do it. It might be easier for her to take the news from people who knew him and cared.

'I'll take you through.'

She led them to Harry's bed, one of four, each of which were occupied by patients caught in webs of wires and machinery and lost in that mysterious space somewhere between life and death. Bex shuddered when she saw him - his expression blank, his face pale, cheeks sunken, and his body at the mercy of contraptions she didn't understand.

'He was found just in time. He's stable but unconscious. We're hopeful there'll be no permanent damage, but at this stage we'll just have to wait and see. From what I've heard he could be facing charges for stealing from his employer - but you would know more about all that than I do. All being well, perhaps he'll see that it's time he got some help - we can make the necessary referrals, if he's willing. You two can help him see sense, otherwise he might not be so lucky next time.'

This nurse was old school, but Bex barely heard a word she said for her sole focus was on Harry. She pulled a chair up close to his bedside and gripped his hand, murmuring to him softly. Eve thought she saw his eyes flicker beneath their lids but dismissed it as fancy. Her heart went out to them both and she sent up a prayer for his swift recovery, knowing that even if Stacey didn't need him, their baby certainly did.

♥

They'd promised the nurse it wouldn't be a long visit, and as anxious loved ones of the other patients arrived, she looked pointedly at the clock. Laid out on Harry's bedside drawers were a neatly folded pair of trousers and the jumper he must have been wearing when he'd been found. The nurses had obviously forgotten to put them away, or perhaps they'd been left out for the police to look over. As Bex leaned over to whisper goodbye, she knocked into the drawers, causing everything upon them to tumble and drawing a few stern glances from the other visitors who had gotten a shock at the sudden clatter amidst the unnatural silence of the ward.

A bifold leather wallet must have fallen out of a pocket as the clothing fell. It dropped, open and face down onto the floor. As Bex leaned over to pick it up, her wayward eyebrows furrowed.

'Bex?' Eve was concerned. 'What is it? Are you alright?'

'Oh my gosh!'

'What?'

Bex held the open wallet out towards her. 'Look,' she said, her eyes widening as her face paled. 'Look who it is!'

Tucked inside was a small photograph, an image of a fair-skinned and sharp-featured young woman with straight, auburn hair. Her face was contorted into what better resembled a snarl than a smile.

'Stacey?' Eve assumed it must be Harry's girlfriend, though she couldn't see what was so remarkable about that. Eve placed a hand on her arm. 'Oh Bex, I'm sure it must be hard for you to finally see her in person. Hearing about her and actually seeing her when you feel the way you do about Harry must be two very different things.'

'It's not that.' Bex paced back and forth, wallet in hand, staring at the picture. 'Well, it's not quite like that... You see I *have* seen her - I just didn't know who she was until now. She looks younger on here but it's definitely the same girl.'

'What do you mean, you've seen her before?'

'She was at the café on the night of the barbeque.'

Eve frowned. 'There's no reason why she wouldn't be, is there, given Harry works with us now? Maybe she needed to talk to him about something in person?'

'No, it can't be that. If she'd only come looking for Harry, she would have said so. But she didn't - she said she'd come looking for work. She didn't identify herself or mention Harry at all.'

'That does seem strange, but what does it mean?'

'I don't know. Why would someone suddenly start looking for work partway through their pregnancy when their partner's just gotten a job? It seems a bit odd to me.'

Eve thought of Emily, who'd practically had to be physically restrained from working throughout hers. 'It's hardly a crime though, is it? And they could probably use the extra cash.'

'No,' Bex conceded, 'it isn't a crime. But robbery is. Criminal damage is!'

'You mean...?'

Bex stared right at Eve, nodding slowly.

'Surely not.'

'If something doesn't feel right, chances are-'

'It isn't,' Eve finished.

They met one another's eyes then glanced towards Harry's lifeless form. Eve felt sick. She knew what Bex was thinking. If Stacey was somehow involved in what had happened at her café, could she not also be involved in what had happened to Harry? He'd hinted that all was not well in their relationship - the baby seemed to be about the only thing holding them together - but were things between them really this bad? Stealing charity money and smashing up Eve's café was one thing, but putting another person's life at risk was something altogether more sinister. If only Harry would pull through and shed some light on everything.

Bex, having convinced herself of Stacey's guilt, was now furious on Harry's behalf. Eve, however, was relieved. When the break-in had first happened, her gut had told her there was no way he could have done this, and now she felt reassured that her instincts were correct, and her judgment wasn't so misguided after all. The question was, if Harry pulled through, with all the evidence pointing to his guilt, how could they prove his innocence?

She pulled Bex into a hug and soothed her, willing Harry to get well again as she tried to work out what to do. The more she thought about it the more convinced she became that whatever had gone on that night, Stacey must have had something to do with it. If they were to prove Harry's innocence and seek justice for him as he lay helpless in his hospital bed, they decided to start their investigations with her.

♥

Hacks Court, a nod to Lord Hacks to whom the land was built upon had once belonged, was more colloquially known as 'Axe Court' in reference to its notoriety for the acts of violence that were rumoured to have occurred there. The venerable Lord Hacks would have turned in his grave had he known his stately grounds would be so diminished thanks to the antics of his wayward and self-entitled descendants' penchants for drink, gambling, and visiting houses of ill repute. Even Bex looked ruffled as they stood by the metal railings that encircled the high-rise like a prison - and she'd grown up in Melbourne's dodgy end. They'd parked the car a few blocks away just to be on the safe side, but now they wondered if it could have been put to better use in making a quick getaway.

'On second thoughts, is this really such a good idea?' said Eve, as a stumbling older man reeking of booze leered at them on his way past. They shrank back as he bared what remained of his rotten set of gnashers.

'Think about it. If *we* don't do this, who will?'

'I don't know, the police? At least they have batons and pepper spray. What are we going to do, throw lamingtons at her?'

'*Capsicum* spray. Look, we both know the police have got it in for Harry, and I very much doubt Sergeant Wilson will trouble himself over someone like him. He's an easy target unfortunately, and it ticks a job off their to-do list.'

'But he's not like that anymore. He's changed.'

'I know, but how do we convince them of that? We've *got* to do this.'

Goosebumps dotted Eve's forearms and she felt a strange tingling at the back of her neck. She really didn't want to do this. 'Why are you always right?'

In contrast to the cool brightness of the day, from the top of its twenty-five stories to the crudely paved entranceway at the bottom, Hacks Court seemed to be shrouded in deprivation. With great reluctance, Eve allowed herself to be led into the very bowels of its concrete gloom and along uniform corridors that were strip-lit ineffectually every few yards with harsh light.

The lift bore the stench of stale urine, and the girls held their breath as it cranked its way up to the seventeenth floor.

They exited to their right, startling at the rough bark of a dog here, the slamming of a door there - a yell, a clatter, a cry. The hallway was part-obstructed by an odd mix of old bike frames, shopping trolleys and pushchairs, and littered with empty wrappers, bottles, and cans. They gingerly avoided a syringe.

When they reached flat one-seven-eight, they hesitated before knocking. It took so long to get an answer they assumed no-one was home, and were just about to turn back, when they heard a muffled sound from within.

'Who is it?'

The woman who answered the door was bedraggled, with greasy auburn hair, a bloated face, menacing eyes, and a fitted cotton shirt straining over her growing belly. Aside from her now obvious baby bump, her frame was otherwise what would best be described as scrawny. Her teeth were yellowed, and her face marked with the lines of perpetual scorn.

Sensing their intimidation as a dog senses fear, Stacey drew deeply from her cigarette and exhaled the smoke into Eve's face, who grimaced and wafted it away. Her inner nurse recoiled at the thought of what all those chemicals would be doing to this woman's unborn child.

Bex stepped out from the gloom of the corridor that was lit inadequately by a small window at one end. As she had hoped, a flicker of recognition discomforted Stacey who glanced around her and pulled the door in close, blocking any glimpse of what lay inside. If it was possible, her scowl intensified.

'*You*,' she spat, her eyes on Bex.

212

♥ 22 ♥

Eve and Bex were startled by the venom emanating from the petite young woman before them, who stood, hands on her hips, blocking the doorway.

'Well, are you just gonna stand there gawping, or are you gonna tell me what you're doing here? If you're some sort of charity, social worker, or selling something, you're not welcome. And if you're looking for Harry, I haven't seen him.'

'We know he's not here,' said Bex, whose need to protect Harry from this cretin overcame any fear she might have had in confronting her. 'We thought you might like to know that your partner, the father of your child, is currently unconscious in the High Dependency Unit of City Hospital.'

'So?' Stacey was unruffled. 'Serves him right for robbing the café he's worked at for five minutes to fund his filthy habit while leaving me here to fend for myself and our baby.' She rubbed her stomach insincerely and exhaled another plume of smoke into their faces. 'Always was a selfish git. Anyway, you should know - it's your café he's screwed over.'

'Actually, it's mine,' Eve corrected her as she steadily met Stacey's gaze. 'And we don't believe it was *him* who screwed it over. And it's not just us who've suffered because of it, but all those in the community who go there. That money we'd raised was for charity.'

'Don't care whose fucking café it is, and I don't give a toss about no community or no charity. What's anyone ever done for me, eh? Of course it was Harry - who else could it have been? Serves you right for being daft enough to trust someone like him. Didn't they teach you anything at university?'

'Stace?' It was a male voice. 'What's going on? Tell whoever it is to bugger off, then come back to bed.'

Stacey flushed. 'I told you to keep your trap shut, Jamie!'

'You don't sound very alone to me,' said Bex, her eyebrows arched.

'That's none of your business. Jame's been looking out for me and the baby since there ain't no-one else to do it.'

'Why did you come looking for work at the café a few days ago?' Bex persisted. 'Seems a bit odd to me, given what's just happened. And now suddenly Harry's in the hospital and you're shacked up with that lowlife...'

Uh-oh, thought Eve, shooting Bex a warning look. She'd encountered enough challenging patients in her nursing days to know that if they didn't tread more carefully, things could get out of control quickly, and the seventeenth floor wasn't the easiest place from which to make their escape. She fingered her phone in her pocket, trying to remember which button to press to make an emergency call. In a ward situation she'd have a security team to rely on, but here they had only their wits to defend them.

'Hear what these two bitches are saying about you, Jame?' Stacey deflected. 'I'd hot trot it right out of here if you don't want to lose the ability to make coffee for good - he has one heck of a temper.'

'Sounds like a real keeper,' said Bex. 'Like you! Good luck to you both. When Harry wakes up, we'll find out the truth. And when we do, we'll send Sergeant Wilson your way.'

'What do you think they're gonna do to someone in my condition? Not a lot, I can tell you. Anyway, I was home all night - I've got witnesses. I might've known the new, reformed Harry wouldn't last long. He always had a problem with resisting temptation.' Stacey looked at Bex through narrowed eyes, and suddenly the inspiration behind her café's destruction made sense - it seemed the green-eyed monster had paid her a visit. 'You're welcome to him, you tramp.'

Bex came as perilously close as she ever would do in life to lamping someone, and Eve shuddered as the sound of heavy footsteps made their way towards the front door.

'What the fuck is going on?'

Eve caught a sight of a hairy hand clutching a can, and a whiff of stale alcohol emanated from behind the front door. She didn't intend on sticking around to see the face of the person to whom the hand and stinky breath belonged to.

Stacey grinned. 'I think that's your cue to get out of here, don't you?'

Bex was about to argue, but Eve grabbed her by the arm and tugged her along the corridor towards the stairwell – there wasn't enough time to wait for the lift. They were sneered at by some equally frightening spectators who'd been lured to their doors to watch yet another drama unfold, glad that for once that it didn't involve them.

There was a fearsome bellow followed by a great many expletives and pounding footsteps that seemed to be gaining on them as they took the stairs two at a time down the stairwell, out of the main entrance, through the gate and railings, and down the street. Not once did they stop to look back, and when Bex tripped on the gravel path, Eve heaved her back up to standing as quickly as she could. When at last they reached the car, they stood gasping great gulps of air before jumping in, locking the automatic doors, and looking anxiously behind them as though the infamous Jamie might appear at any moment ready to do who knew what to them.

'That didn't exactly go according to plan,' Eve wheezed, as the tires of her dad's Golf screeched on their way out of the estate. 'She has a way with words, that girl.'

'If she wasn't pregnant, I would have quite happily have thrown a whole bloody tray of lamingtons at her. How did Harry ever put up with her?'

'Don't worry, we won't give up. We just need to take a different approach next time.'

Though neither of them said it aloud, they didn't hold much hope. Things weren't looking good for Harry. Not good at all.

♥

The Melbourne was the last thing on Eve's mind. It hurt too much to think about it, so instead she channelled all her thoughts and energies into figuring out how to help Harry.

Bex was back at the hospital, incensed by Stacey's total disregard for his welfare, and Eve and her parents were at home. She'd given them an account of all that had occurred that day, and her dad had hit the roof at the idea of two young women going to Hacks Court alone - in his car, no less. When he'd finally calmed down, after a cream cake or two, he was able to acknowledge that there was something fishy about Stacey's behaviour but remained reluctant to let go of the idea that Harry must have at least had a part to play in the whole debacle. Incidentally, so did Sergeant Wilson, to whom she had also regaled the entire tale. Whilst he took what she said on board, he was like a dog with a bone and still thought Harry must have had something to do with it.

Until Harry awoke and could speak for himself, his fate remained uncertain. Eve prayed for just that, and after much persuasion, Sergeant Wilson agreed to look into matters a little more vigorously, starting with Jamie whom he described as a nasty piece of work he knew from way back.

Eve was exhausted from what had been an emotional roller-coaster of a day. She wanted to catnap, but her thoughts were circling the day's events. She opened a book but closed it again after the first chapter. She just couldn't get into it. She sighed, tossing and turning whilst staring out of her window at a darkening sky. The doorbell rang and she heard muffled voices downstairs. It was probably her Aunt Sam, who was due Up North for her usual Christmas visit.

Eve thought nothing of the gentle tapping at her door. Presumably, her aunt had come up to wish her a Merry Christmas. She assumed a mask of false cheer and braced herself for the inevitable inquisition - Aunt Sam had always had a lot to say.

'Come in.'

The door opened slowly, almost uncertainly, and Eve glanced up. There was nothing hesitant about Aunt Sam. The first body part of her mystery guest to enter the room was a strong, hairy arm. Definitely not Aunt Sam - unless Aunt Sam had become Uncle Sam since the previous

Christmas, which was entirely possible nowadays. She peered more closely. Yes, there were the tell-tale paint splatters, and Eve grinned despite herself before leaping off the bed and flinging open the door.

'Whoa! Don't you ever check your phone?' Thom scolded. 'I've been worried sick about you ever since I heard what happened!'

'Thom, thank goodness you're here.' Eve threw herself into his arms and wept the tears she'd been holding back. He led her to her bed and lay down by her side, rocking her gently as her shoulders heaved, stroking her hair and murmuring words of comfort.

Eve looked up into his earnest eyes, their unique shade of blue deepening from a combination of concern and desire, and she reached out a hand to stroke the fair stubble of his jaw. She pressed the tip of her thumb gently to his lips and he kissed it lightly in response. She leant forward and brought her lips to his, kissing him deeply as she ran her hand along the taut muscle of his back and sides. He groaned, and for a little while Eve forgot about everything that had happened and concentrated only on the delicious sensations of Thom's hands and mouth, the heat of him beneath her fingers, and the feel of his body against hers.

'I've missed you,' he murmured later as they cuddled into one another. He ran his fingers through her hair, and she could feel the tension leaving her body.

'I've missed you too.'

'I'm sorry about your café, and for what's happened to Harry.' He'd been suitably regaled, and he too had cracked it at the thought of her and Bex going to Hacks Court alone. 'What are you going to do?'

Eve sighed. 'I honestly don't know. Close down and go back into nursing?'

'What? Emily said you hated nursing!'

'I did. Not the job, but the emotion of it all, and what it makes me remember...'

Thom had known her older brother Daniel. Not very well because he'd been a few years above him in high school, but they'd played footy at the same club and his death had touched the local community of youths who had known of him.

'The café is salvageable, Eve. You don't need to go back into nursing. We can help you get The Melbourne back up and running - we *want* to help; you just need to let us. You're the only place for miles around that does decent coffee, apparently. Can't stand the stuff myself - it tastes like dirty dishwater.'

'No.' Eve was resolute. 'You've all done enough for me already! It's too late. If something is meant to be it will be, and if it isn't then there's no point in trying to force it.'

'That's not true. I had to work so hard to establish my business. It takes time, patience, and risk. It was a long time before I established a reputation and reached the point where my income exceeded what I was investing so that I could afford to pay myself a living wage. If I'd looked at things the same way you do, I'd have given up ages ago, and potentially be doing a job I hate right now because of it.'

'But what if what happened was a sign that I wasn't supposed to come back here after all? That I should've stayed in Australia where things were working out.'

'That's not true!' Thom sat. 'You might've been having a great time in some ways, but you were in a job that made you unhappy and with a man who wasn't able to make the sacrifice he needed to be with you, and you weren't able to do the same for him. That doesn't exactly sound to me like things were working out.'

'Maybe I should go back there?' Now she'd said it aloud, it suddenly felt real, and the prospect made Eve anxious. 'Bex flies out next month, maybe I could travel with her?'

'What! What about us?'

'Us?' Eve hadn't really begun to think of them as an 'us.' Too much had happened too fast, and there hadn't been enough time for thinking in between.

'Yes, *us.*' Thom was angry and hurt. He got up from the bed and started yanking on his clothes, stubbing his toe on the bed frame in the process. 'Gaah.'

'I'm sorry, Thom, but I just can't think about us right now.'

'Because you're too busy thinking about *him*, aren't you, and how you can get him back? Why don't you just admit it!'

Eve didn't know what to say, and Thom interpreted her silence as assent.

'I can't believe this. I've been a total idiot! All this time you've been using me to get over James and to get your jobs done at your café. As soon as things have gotten a little bit tough, you're ready to run back to a guy who wouldn't make any changes in his life to be with you, whereas I would have done anything to keep you! The Eve I knew - the one who travelled the world and started a successful café in a short space of time - wouldn't have quit at the first hurdle.'

Thom's eyes were glossy, and Eve looked away, unable to bear the disapproval from him of all people. She was confused. Whilst she did have feelings for Thom, they were muddled, and with everything else that was going on in her life she didn't have the space in her mind to unravel it all just yet. Still, the last thing she wanted to do was hurt him. 'Thom, that's not how it is. I'm sorry if I've made you feel that way.'

His face was hard. He'd never looked at her that way before. 'No, I'm the one who's sorry. I thought you'd moved on, but I was wrong. My mistake. I won't waste any more of my time chasing someone who wants someone else. Good luck in Australia, Eve, I only hope he makes you happy.'

He turned his back and was gone. It wasn't until after he'd left that Eve realised she didn't want him to go. She jumped off the bed and ran to the door. 'Thom!' she yelled. But it was too late. The front door slammed, and her parents peered up at her from the bottom of the stairs. She heard the engine of his van trundling off into the distance.

'Everything ok, love?' Carol asked.

Eve was about to reply when her phone rang, she made a dash for it, hoping it might be Thom so she could ask him to come back and give her a chance to explain.

'Eve!' It was Bex. 'Harry's awake! Can you believe it? Come quickly.'

♥

Bex' eyes shone with relief as she gripped Harry's hand tightly in hers. He was going to be alright, and she could hope for nothing more beyond that. She didn't tear her eyes away from him until she heard footsteps coming towards his bed. Eve beamed at her, before redirecting her attention back towards the patient, their friend.

'Harry, it's so good to see you're awake! How are you feeling?' Eve unloaded fruit and a selection of books and toiletries she'd picked up for him on her way over to the hospital.

Harry flinched beneath the weight of his guilt as he came face to face with his employer. 'Please, let me explain...'

'Shh,' she soothed. 'It's alright, I didn't come here to harass you with questions. I'm not upset with you at all - just worried. All you need to concern yourself with right now is getting better.'

'It's just that I... I know how it must seem. But I need you to know that I didn't, would never, do something like that to you - to anyone! I know you took a chance on me.' Harry was desperate for her to believe him, no matter how damning it all looked.

Eve smiled, pulling up a chair beside Bex. 'I know.'

In that moment, she *did* know. Whatever his past, Harry had had nothing to do with what happened at her café. For better or worse, people can and do change. Given what he'd been through – the loss and rejection, addiction, exploitation and homelessness - it was remarkable and a testament to his resilience what a thoroughly decent man he was determined to become.

He looked so tired and forlorn, still trying to process his presence at the hospital and all the events leading up to it. 'But it's still my fault.'

The two women were quick to reassure him otherwise.

'Really. It *is* my fault. For having people like Stace and Jamie in my life - the sort of people who could do such a terrible thing. The sort of thing that at one time, if I'm honest, I probably would have done myself. I hate myself for it.' His turmoil was written into his every feature.

'Oh Harry, you mustn't blame yourself,' said Eve. 'Whatever you might have done in the past when you were young and trapped under the thumb of those two, rather than in the care of people who should have loved and nurtured you, the only people at fault here are those who are directly responsible for what happened. You mustn't trouble yourself like this, it will only delay your recovery.'

'Is that why you took the... stuff?' Bex whispered.

Harry shook his head, wincing as he did so, and heaved himself up. He couldn't begin to even think of his recovery until he'd made everything clear.

♥ 23 ♥

Harry cleared his throat. 'It started somewhere between Emily going into labour, and me getting home to discover Stace and Jamie drunk together and in a compromising position on our sofa.'

'No way!' Bex cupped her hand over her mouth when the surrounding patients remained eerily silent.

Harry winced. 'I was angry. So bloody angry. I told Stacey it was looking likely that this baby of ours was actually a baby of *theirs*. They denied it, but I knew... Jamie said I have no proof that anything has ever happened between them in the time we've been together. He told me to face my responsibilities and stop looking for excuses to get out of it, and that what I'd just witnessed was a moment of comfort between old friends that had gotten out of hand. Stacey said that if I'd been at home supporting her instead of hankering after some girl at your café, none of this would ever have happened.

'She said that if it wasn't for her, I'd still be on the streets. I said it's because of how crap things were between us that I was on the streets in the first place, and the fact I'd gotten back with her and found a job was because I was facing up to my responsibilities. I said I'd always been prepared to take the baby on as my own because between the three of us, it would have at least one person in its life it could depend on. Stacey insisted that the baby *is* mine, and I said we'd find out for sure from a paternity test.'

'You do realise,' Eve ventured, 'that if it isn't your baby then it's not your responsibility. There are people out there whose job it is to protect it and keep it safe if you think it could come to any serious harm. If you intervene yourself, you'll never be free of her. Of either of them!'

Eve was convinced that what Harry needed to have the best chance of rebuilding his life without relapse was complete separation from these people. Having met Stacey and Jamie for herself, it was obvious no good would ever come from his continued involvement with them. As they'd already demonstrated, they were the sort of people who would think nothing of exploiting his better nature if they thought they could get something from it.

Harry sighed. He wasn't ready to relinquish the sense of responsibility he felt towards Stacey's child. He knew what it was being born into, and that scared him to death. No-one knew what these two were capable of like he did, and he'd experienced first-hand what the involvement of child protection services was like, and his experience had not been a promising one. That said, unlike him, Stacey had a nice family she inexplicably wanted nothing to do with, even though they'd pursued contact with her for years. Her head had been turned by Jamie at such a vulnerable age and he'd seen that and corrupted her, yet she remained blind to the fact just as he had done for so long.

Eve and Bex could see the emotions playing across his face but weren't privy to what they meant.

'Anyway,' Harry continued, 'at first, they were angry and defensive, then they tried to placate me. They said they were onto something they could let me in on that would be of benefit to all of us. They knew about the barbecue and the fundraising event because I'd mentioned it to Stacey. She said she'd already been over to the café to scope it out and that she'd actually spoken to you.' He glanced apologetically at Bex.

'I was furious. I said I was trying to give myself a fresh start and that Stacey needs to do the same if she wants her baby to stand a chance. She argued that the money from the café would set things up nicely for us, and we'd be able to afford everything we needed to care for the baby, though in hindsight I doubt she had any intention of using the money to that effect. Then she asked me why I cared so much about the café, and if it was anything to do with *that* girl, I hadn't been able to stop talking about lately.'

He paused to look at Bex and his face flushed. Having had the displeasure of meeting Stacey, it wasn't lost on the two women that she would have jumped on his visible reaction and interpreted it in whatever way suited her.

'I told her my interests in the café were as I'd already explained - an honest start for us as a family. That I was fortunate enough to have met you both and you'd been kind enough to give me a chance, despite everything. Jamie said not quite *everything*, and that you might be interested in knowing the true extent of my background then you'd regret having taken a chance on someone like me.'

He looked at the two women imploringly. 'I can't tell you how ashamed I am that I didn't get everything out in the open with you straight away. I did a lot of stuff when I was younger, half of it while out of my mind on one thing or another and none of it that I'm proud of. I planned to tell you if anything longer-term was to come out of the opportunity you had given me. It was just so unexpected that I didn't quite know how to handle the situation. Between that and dealing with my housing and financial issues and getting my head around Stacey's pregnancy-'

'It doesn't matter now,' said Eve. 'I employed you for the person you are today, not for who you were in the past. We've all done things we're not proud of, but this version of you is the only you that Bex and I have ever known, and we're proud to call you, our friend.'

Harry looked down. 'They said it didn't matter if I was in on what they had planned, that I would be blamed regardless and the first person the police would look for - and they were right. I said I'd stop them - get to them before they had a chance to follow through with any of it. Jamie reckoned I'd never report the mother of my child. I said again, the child isn't mine. I moved over to the front door, determined to stop them. Just as I reached for the handle, I felt Jamie's breath on the back of my neck followed by a sharp pain in my arm. It was a syringe with who-knows-what in it.

'I shrugged from his grasp and ran from the flat. As I was leaving, I heard Stacey shout, "No-one's gonna take you seriously now!" and they both cracked up laughing. I was heading towards the café, but on the way, I started feeling really weird. I couldn't focus on what I was doing or remember why I was doing it. Then my heart started racing and body sort of gave up on me. That's the last thing I remember before being here. I'm just sorry I didn't get there in time to warn you, though who in their right mind would've believed me in the state I was in? They were right about that.'

It was clear that the adrenaline fuelling Harry's need to explain what had happened had worn off, and he sank down into his pillow. Just then, a nurse appeared and said she needed a private word with him. Harry said there was nothing that couldn't be said in front of his friends.

'Very well. Now that you're feeling better, you'll be transferring to the ward and are likely to be discharged within a couple of days.'

'That's great!' Bex beamed.

The nurse coughed. 'And I'm sorry to have to tell you this, but the police will be meeting you there later today. There are things they need to discuss with you. They asked to be informed as soon as you woke up - I held off for a little while, but I couldn't any longer. I hope you understand.'

Despite her demeanour, the woman seemed to have a soft spot for Harry, and Eve wondered what had happened in her life to inspire it in her.

Harry nodded.

'Oh, Harry,' Bex breathed, tears clouding her eyes. If only she could protect him from whatever might happen next.

♥

It was New Year's Eve, and Bex and Eve were at a travel agency in Newcastle's city centre. It was quiet inside, the booking of holidays not usually at the forefront of anyone's mind or budget at this time of year. The occasion to Eve was more often a cause for anxiety about the milestones she wasn't meeting than a celebration of those she had, and in light of recent events, this year was no different. Judging by the ominous grey clouds overhead, the weather seemed to share her view.

'Are you sure you want to do this?' Bex asked for what must have been the hundredth time that day. 'It seems a bit hasty.'

'Yes, I'm sure.'

'Stop sooking!'

'I'm not sooking, I'm sulking.'

'You only correct my Australian when you're being a sook.'

Eve didn't know what was more annoying - being called a sook, or the idea that Bex might be right.

'Will you be paying by Mastercard or Visa, Madam?'

'Visa.'

'I really think you should rethink-'

But Eve handed over the card with only a moment's hesitation.

'That's all done, Madam. Here's a copy of your itinerary. Enjoy your trip!'

Having paid a not insubstantial fee to swap over their details, Eve would be returning to Melbourne next month on Bex' ticket, and Bex would be remaining in England indefinitely to stay close to a certain someone.

Eve didn't know where to start – she still had all her family and friends to tell, loose ends to tie up at the café, savings to salvage to help secure her an apartment back in Melbourne, and her old nursing job to approach with her tail between her legs. She supposed that if things got desperate, she could always become a barista - she was bound to have better luck with that than last time. Once she arrived in Australia, she would simply go through the motions until she felt as though she was living again. She'd done it before, and she could do it again.

'Do I look old enough to be a madam to you?' she asked, wrestling with her brolly against a determined wind as they marched down Northumberland Street together.

'Only when you're sooking, and to anyone in their late teens, then yes, I suppose you do. We're not spring chickens anymore, unfortunately.'

'I promise to stop sooking if you stop questioning my decisions and try to look a little less loved up in my presence – as happy as I am for you and Harry, it's making me nauseous!'

Bex' face glowed as though she was lit up from the inside. It was a transformation Eve had never seen in her from previous relationships, and little wonder.

After a hungry pursuit from Sergeant Wilson, who had relished pressing charges against Harry for the café's robbery the moment he was well enough to be discharged from hospital, he was now in the clear thanks only to the sheer stupidity of his old friend Jamie, who'd been in a car crash after driving erratically in a stolen vehicle through the Scottish Borders in the dead of night.

It turned out he was drunk, with a worse-for-wear Stacey beside him clutching a wad of cash. Fearful that Harry or the girls might dob them in, they'd planned to move to Scotland, leaving a string of debts in their wake, but they'd started fighting on the way and things had gotten out of hand pretty quickly. With tensions and emotions running high, they'd each incriminated the other, and it hadn't taken long for police to join the dots. Jamie was facing a string of charges and was looking at a stint in prison, but Stacey was being granted leniency because she wasn't personally involved in the café's robbery or criminal damage. What had happened at the café was only part of the legacy they had left behind them in the northeast.

Eve and Bex were thoroughly relieved for Harry's sake, though it was tragic that Stacey had lost the baby she was carrying as a result of the impact. Still, they couldn't help but wonder what sort of life the child would have had - Harry's involvement would have been its only saving grace.

'You could be as happy as Harry and I are too, you know,' said Bex. 'And for what it's worth, I don't think you'll find that sort of happiness in Melbourne – you've already looked there, remember? Anyway, what do you think Thom's going to have to say about all this - have you taken his feelings into consideration at all?'

Eve looked down and her heavy fringe veiled her eyes. 'Thom has appeared in my life at the wrong time. It's kinder on him if I let him go. I'm not ready to give him what he needs right now and I'm not sure I ever will be. I'm only messing him around otherwise.'

'Sometimes the right things happen to people at the wrong time. Look at me and Harry – I don't have a long-term visa to stay here, he has a crazy ex-girlfriend who could wreak revenge on us at any point, and his ex-best mate can't be best pleased at facing jail for what he did either. This is far from perfect timing or the best circumstances in which to start a relationship, and yet we're making it work. You'll always find barriers if you look for them, but sometimes it's worth putting these things aside to pursue something much greater together.'

Eve listened but said nothing. She'd become a sook again.

♥

It was the moment she'd been dreading, and it had come much sooner than she'd bargained for. No sooner had Eve put her key in her parents' front door than she clocked from the corner of her eye the nose of Thom's white van drawing up behind her. It was the worst possible timing.

She jumped at the slamming of the driver's-side door and the tapping of footsteps upon her parents' cobbled driveway. He was dressed in fitted jeans with a jumper over his shirt, a look that softened but still accentuated the lines of muscle in his arms and chest. He looked so different out of his work clothes. For once there wasn't a speck of paint on his hair or hands and his face was clean shaven, his eyes warm and bright.

'You look like a deer caught in headlights, Madam,' Bex grinned. 'Have fun!' and she disappeared into the relative safety inside.

If only she could follow suit, thought Eve, but it would only delay the inevitable. She could see the apology on Thom's face before he'd even spoken it, when it was her who should be apologising to him. If he'd happened into her life a little later, not so soon after she'd left James, things might have turned out very differently between them. She pushed the notion aside - it wouldn't help them now.

Thom was coming towards her with his arms outstretched as though ready to pull her into a tight hug. Why did he have to be so gorgeous? Why did he always want to give her so much more than she deserved?

He reached out to take her in his arms and she stiffened. There was a look of confusion and hurt as he dropped his arms to his side and pressed his lips together, his mouth firmly set. Something inside Eve ached, but he'd soon be free of her, and she would no longer have to be the cause of his pain.

'I came to see if you wanted to watch the New Year's Eve fireworks with me in town tonight,' he said, 'but in the space of just a few days it seems the prospect of an evening alone with me has become somehow distasteful to you.'

Eve flinched. She took a deep breath, her fingers absentmindedly drawn to the one-way flight itinerary sitting in her handbag. 'There's something I need to tell you - I'm going back to Australia next month. I've just booked my flight, or rather I've bought Bex' flight from her – she'll be staying on here with Harry.'

She could kick herself for adding that last bit. It only emphasised the fact that she wasn't prepared to make the same sort of sacrifice for Thom.

'You're going back to *him*?'

'I'm not going back to James.'

'Running away, then?'

'That's what Bex thinks.'

'That's what everyone will think.'

'Maybe I don't care what people think any more.'

'But aren't you - running away? Throwing away everything you've worked for and leaving behind all the people who love you, and for what?'

'I'm not throwing anything away,' said Eve. 'It's not my fault my café was taken from me! It's just not meant to be, and *we* obviously aren't meant to be either, otherwise it wouldn't be this hard.' Tears sprung to her eyes, and she shook her head as though to shake them away.

'It isn't hard, Eve, you just make it hard. I don't know why, but you seem bloody intent on it.' Thom sighed. 'You can walk away from me, but if you walk away from what was fast becoming a successful business and the beginning of a future here at home where you belong, then you're a fool. Happy New Year.'

He stalked to his van, threw himself into it, slamming the door hard enough to make the windows rattle. He reversed off the driveway with a squeal of tires upon cold tarmac, and as Eve watched until the van become a little white speck in the distance, she couldn't help thinking what a thoroughly dreadful Christmas and New Year this was turning out to be. The sooner she got on that plane back to Australia the better.

♥ 24 ♥

Eve had been planning on accompanying Bex to Emily's place to see in the New Year with a small group of her friends and family - as a new mother it would be Emily's tamest NYE since she and Eve were teens, stealing alcohol and cigarettes at their parents' house parties growing up.

Eve wasn't in the mood for celebrating, and her spirits had dropped even lower when Emily called to tell her not to bother coming over because Thom would be there, and things might get awkward between them and spoil the night. There was a frost to her tone, and Eve groaned at the possibility of a lifelong friendship damaged.

Aside from her issues with Thom, Emily had been peeved that she hadn't been the first to know of Eve's plans to return to Australia, which had gone down like a ton of bricks with the very few people she had shared them with so far. Eve wondered how many more people she was going to annoy this year. That was one of the benefits of living on the other side of the world – there was less opportunity to hurt those closest to you, and the time and space available to repair things with those she had.

To make matters worse, now that she was excluded from Emily's gathering, she had little choice but to show her face at her parents' one instead. As much as she liked her parents' friends, many of whom had known her since she was knee-high, she didn't feel up to putting a brave face on things and being sociable, but she was unfortunately a bit beyond holing herself up in her bedroom like a huffy teenager. Stuff it. She'd just have to doll herself up, paint a smile on her face, and get down there and mingle. It might even take her mind off things - if not. then her mam's potent mulled wine surely would. She would wallow in self-pity later.

After making her way downstairs, she was embraced by more than a dozen family members and friends. Many of them knew what had happened to her café and were either too embarrassed to risk upsetting her by asking about it or were so curious about the drama that had unfolded they couldn't help but ask her awkward, probing questions. Her marital status and the state of her aging ovaries was another area of interest to them that Eve would rather not discuss. She diverted these questions best she could and redirected the focus onto them.

'Make yourself useful and serve the wine, would you?' Carol whispered. 'Might stop you from moping.'

'I'm not moping.'

'It's over on the breakfast bar.'

'Carol, how lovely to see you! Gosh, hasn't Eve grown into a beauty!'

Eve rolled her eyes and made a hasty getaway. No-one ever wanted to get stuck with that particular family friend. She'd gotten drunk at one of her parents' parties a few years ago and made a bit of a fool of herself over her dad. Marital problems had inspired the lapse in judgment apparently, and one too many snowballs which had been all the rage back then. Her husband was one of her dad's closest friends, so she had been forgiven and politely tolerated ever after. Eve suspected however, that the flame hadn't quite burned out.

Eve alternately simmered or ladled out wine, almost dizzy from the steady inhalation of steamed cinnamon and cloves that tickled her nose and caught at the back of her throat. Her face was beaming, and she felt hot and damp. She blew air up under her fringe and loosened her ponytail, wafting her hair to cool the back of her neck. She felt strangely detached from the cheery gathering, content to just watch and avoid the small talk as far as possible. Fortunately, the guests were now more than a little bit merry and barely noticed her, not least her father, whose deep belly laugh reached all the way into the kitchen, he and their guests' inhibitions steadily lowering as the night wore on. Her parents' friends could be a raucous lot beneath their lower-middle-class façade - they were Geordies born and bred.

'There's a tall and handsome someone at the door asking for you, Eve. It's a wonder I heard him knocking amidst all this racket - never did quite get your mother's taste in music.' It was the scarlet woman herself. 'It's not polite to keep a gentleman waiting.'

Eve made for the front door. Outside stood Thom, tapping his foot nervously upon the doorstep, his shoulders hunched for warmth.

'Thom?' Eve frowned. 'I thought you'd be over at Emily's place tonight.'

Her thick brush of hair now free of its usual ponytail shone lustrous in the soft light of the hallway. Her hazel eyes were emphasised by a shadow of silvery-grey, and her lips were plump and tinted with a becoming shade of rose. She wore a simple jade-green dress that wrapped at her waist, cinching her in and drawing Thom's eye to the inviting spread of her hips. A necklace nestled at the top of her generous cleavage. He longed to kiss her, a notion that he quickly pushed to one side. He was in no mood for another rejection tonight. He cleared his throat and when he finally spoke, he was abrupt.

'Don't worry, this isn't a friendly visit.' He looked about as merry as she felt. 'Get in the van.'

Eve baulked at his tone. It brooked no argument. She was mystified as to what he was doing there. Whatever the reason, it was clearly under sufferance, and she hesitated for a moment before doing as he asked.

Whenever his leg happened to brush against hers as he drove, the denim of his jeans stretching taut over muscular thighs, he flinched as though scalded and promptly drew himself away. Eve felt hot all over, whether from the over-powering heat of the van's air-conditioner or his mere physical presence she couldn't tell. Her breath caught at his nearness, yet there was a chasm between them that she didn't know how to breach.

'Warm enough?' he asked.

There was no sincerity in the question. Judging by how high he'd turned up the van's heating, he wanted to make her feel as uncomfortable as possible. Sweat was beading in her cleavage and her breathing was ragged. She glanced over at the clock on the dashboard. It was nearing a quarter to midnight, and the start of the new year. Whatever the reason and in whatever capacity, Thom had chosen to spend it with her instead of celebrating it with his family where she was certain he would have been in far better spirits. She opened her window and gulped in the cool air rushing past her.

They soon reached Chillingham Road, and just a few streets away was Eve's café. On their approach her body stiffened. She didn't want to face it yet, she wasn't ready. Why was Thom doing this to her?

She felt close to tears but wouldn't give him the satisfaction of seeing her cry. Instead, she remained dutifully meek and compliant. As though sensing her change in spirits, he automatically went to place a reassuring hand on her knee before thinking better of it at the last moment and snatching his hand away. He snarled. Eve had never seen him like this before. He didn't turn into Victoria Terrace as she'd expected, instead he parked close by on Chilli' Road.

'Out,' he said.

She was immediately assaulted by icy fingers of freezing air that chilled the sheen of sweat upon her body until it was almost like sitting in a cool bath. She shivered.

He stalked forwards and she followed reluctantly behind. It must be almost midnight by now. As they reached the corner there was an unexpected roar followed by a squeal and an explosion, and the inky darkness was pierced with a burst of fluorescent green. Another roar, another squeal, and another explosion was soon followed by another, and each time came a shower of rainbow fire. Eve paused to watch, nibbling her lip with her lower teeth. It was spectacular, and it seemed to be coming from Victoria Terrace. Was it the New Year already?

A moment later, a group of young revellers rounded the corner and staggered past them in high spirits and incredibly pleased with the world and everybody in it. Some of their faces were familiar because they'd utilised The Melbourne as a place to meet and study. That all seemed so very long ago to Eve now.

'Happy New Year!' they yelled, slapping Thom on the shoulder, and catching Eve up in a little jig.

Awkwardly, the pair returned their well-wishes, but the group were too caught up in their own cheer to register the icy dynamic between them. Thom grabbed Eve by the hand. His fingers were as cold as her own. 'Hurry,' he said.

They turned left onto Victoria Terrace and Eve closed her eyes, submitting herself to his stern grip. When she next opened them, she knew she would see her café – the first red-brick terrace on the left - the source upon which she had pinned her dreams of a new and fulfilling future here in England at home with her loved ones. A week had passed already in which so much had happened Eve would rather not think about, all of it seemingly propelling her back to a life in Australia that she'd thought she had left behind. She didn't want to open her eyes. She didn't want to see.

'Happy New Year! Happy New Year! Happy New Year!'

There was a chorus of voices. Her eyes startled open and there they all were, standing beneath the sign of her café, a handmade banner that said, 'Welcome Back!' thrown haphazardly across it, a café that looked impossibly close to what it had when she'd left it on the night of the Christmas barbeque.

There was Emily looking as glamourous as ever and not at all like someone who had just given birth a mere week ago, cradling baby Joy in her arms who had somehow managed to sleep through the din. And then there was Mark, Bex and Dave, Eve's parents and a small group of their friends who were just exiting a taxi, old Stanley and Betty - even Gianni! Then Tony appeared from the alleyway brandishing a firelighter and a smile – the source of their impromptu fireworks display. Eve froze in disbelief, but from the corner of her eye she could still make out Thom's disapproving snarl.

♥

It wasn't the first time that Eve had wished the ground would open up and swallow her whole. Maybe in doing so, she'd find herself plummeting through a secret tunnel linking Heaton with Australia - or perhaps that was just wishful thinking.

Despite the chill, her cheeks flamed with shame at the scene before her, and all at once Thom's attitude towards her that evening made perfect sense. It was Christmas time, a time to be shared with family and loved ones and for overindulging on food, wine, and telly. It wasn't the time for a small army to gather and in a matter of days fix up a broken café for the benefit of a failed former friend, employer and hostess. And despite all the effort they'd obviously gone to, Eve was about to leave for Australia, throwing all their undeserved commitment and hard work back in their faces.

'Well?' Thom nudged her, his smile more of a sneer.

'I don't know what to say.'

'I *bet* you don't.'

'What are you waiting for?' Yelled a ruddy Dave. 'I'm freezing my bollocks off out here - it's Baltic! Come on, bacon butties all round!'

He turned and the crowd followed eagerly behind him, jostling Eve to the front, each as keen to get out of the cold and wrap their lips around a bacon sandwich as they were to see her reaction to the result of all their hard work.

It had been a team effort - one they were all proud to have been a part of. In one way or another, the café held a special place in the hearts of all those who had contributed, and they couldn't bear to see it go. In a vast world so preoccupied with wealth, image, and success it could be hard to find a place to fit, and yet here in the outskirts of Newcastle was a place of community, of belonging - Harry himself was evidence of that. Not to mention that it sold the best coffee for miles around.

Inside, everything was just as it should have been that awful Boxing Day morning. The Melbourne was restored almost exactly, and in some ways, it was even better. In the main room, the cracked and dusty old fireplace had been carefully uncovered and preserved, and once restored it would make a wonderful central feature. Then Eve caught sight of a brand-new retro coffee machine that took pride of place on the counter, replacing the bulky old thing she'd been leasing before.

The smell of sawdust and fresh paint mingled with the scent of coffee beans that still lingered despite the viciousness of the attack upon her hopes and livelihood. But despite all of that, what caught Eve's attention most of all were the dozens of colourful post-it notes pinned up on the chalkboard where the community program's timetable was usually displayed. She wandered over to get a closer look, blinking away tears.

To all at The Melbourne Community Café, it is thanks to your community program that I have settled in and made some great, like-minded new friends here after moving up to Newcastle to study. Thank you :)

Dear Eve, thank you for replacing a wonderful restaurant with a wonderful café. Here's to a Happy New Year, love from all of us at Victoria Terrace.

To the canny gang at The Melbourne - your coffee from The Hatch gives me the motivation I need to get up for work every morning. Cheers!

To the chef at The Melbourne (Dave?) - thank you for curing my Sunday morning hangovers with your fantastic breakfasts. Keep them coming!

Dear Eve, Bex and Dave - thank you for taking a chance on me when no-one else would - I don't know what I would have done without you. From your dear friend, Harry x

Dear Eve, we are so proud of you we have bought you a shiny new coffee machine to show you just how much. All our love, Mam and Dad xxx

Dear Eve, many thanks to you and the community at The Melbourne for your generous donation to our charity in memory of your brother, Daniel :o)

Dear Eve, as you can see you are needed more here than you are in Melbourne. Please stay. Love, Thom x

It was the notes that finally made Eve's mind up for her, or rather unmade it. In truth her decision to return to Australia had been far too hasty and borne from a sense of shame that at the ripe age of thirty she felt she had managed to fail not just once, but twice. She'd buried her head in the sand, too afraid to pull herself together and do for herself what this wonderful group of individuals had ended up doing for her. How ungrateful they must find her! But judging by all they had done, that didn't seem to be the case at all.

If she could've torn up her flight ticket right there and then she would have done so gladly, but in this digital age she would have to be content with simply pulling out her mobile phone and deleting her e-ticket instead. There were cheers, and the next thing she knew a tall glass of wine and a bacon butty with lashings of brown sauce were being pushed into her hand as glasses clinked against hers, sloshing liquid amber everywhere. The whole café was suddenly uplifted with music, and in the background, Eve could hear fireworks popping from all directions. Through the haze of smiling faces, the one that mattered most to her was Thom's.

He stood a little removed from the throng, his arms crossed defensively and his gorgeous face aloof. She took a deep breath and walked towards him. She pulled him into her arms, luxuriating in the sensation of his solid warmth against her body, all at once realising how natural it felt to be there and just how much she had missed it. He didn't turn her away and she kissed him boldly, deeply, and within the kiss tried to convey every feeling she had for him that she couldn't put into words. How sorry she was, how grateful she was, and how thankful she was that he had come into her world, shook it up, and filled her heart.

He was restrained at first. Uncertain. But as was so characteristically Thom, there was nothing unforgiving in the kiss he soon returned her to a cacophony of wolf whistles and celebration that drowned out the sound of the music and the fireworks until there was nothing left but the two of them and their togetherness.

♥ 25 ♥

Over at The Melbourne Community Café, Eve was wiping down tables in preparation for the lunchtime rush. It was a Wednesday afternoon in early February, 'hump day' for those whom the weekend couldn't come fast enough. Unfortunately, it wasn't hump day for Eve and her little staff of three, but she wouldn't have it any other way. How lucky she was to be doing what she loved, she thought, and not for the first time.

The Melbourne had been saved thanks to the combined efforts and sheer goodwill of the small community it had managed to foster within a remarkably short period of time, and it was to that community Eve felt unutterably grateful and indebted. She could scarcely believe her café seemed to matter to others almost as much as it did to her, and the knowledge was both comfort and reward that made the highs and lows of the whole venture worthwhile.

She ran her fingers across the shiny new coffee machine that had been gifted by her father as a mark of acceptance for the new direction she had chosen to take with her life, which was a big step away from the traditional career path he had tread throughout his own. To Eve it was a token of his belief in her, something even adults still needed from their parents at times. With the café restored, she could finally put down roots and look to the future with hope rather than with the uncertainty of before. She felt due a reprieve from drama for a while, and she fully intended to enjoy life's peaks while they lasted.

Eve looked around the café and all was as it should be. Dave was busy cooking up a storm in the kitchen, Harry was on the floor serving - fully recovered and looking remarkably healthy and well, Bex had been badgering her all morning to practice her coffee art – the next stage in her barista journey - and Tony was sipping an espresso as he perused the afternoon papers on a rare day's leave. There were business lunchers lunching, dog-walkers resting weary legs, and old friends nattering over hot drinks and wedges of cake. The students were studying, the crafters were crafting, Harry and Bex had the spring of love in their steps, and if Eve was completely honest - so did she!

She admired Thom's lean form as he painted the recesses of the original fireplace he'd uncovered while restoring her café to its former glory. It was going to look fantastic when it was finished and would form a central feature between the two rooms, hopefully throwing out enough heat for both next winter. Thom caught her look and smiled a smile that warmed her insides and melted her heart.

'Stanley! Betty!' Eve greeted when the bell above the front door signalled the entrance of the old couple who had become so dear to them. 'Welcome back! The crafts group has been lost without you, Betty - you're back just in time to help them prepare for Valentine's Day.' She led them to their favourite window-seat that had only just been vacated. 'How was your cruise?'

The pair were positively glowing - literally as far as Stanley was concerned whose pale, freckled face was ignited by sunburn. They looked younger somehow - more relaxed and carefree. Refreshed. Their eyes were brighter and their movements sprightly, their joints having been nicely lubricated by a month of heat and activity.

'It was hotter than it is here, I can tell you! Brr!' Stanley grumbled. 'That man of yours had better get a move on with that fireplace - my old bones can't take much more of this miserable weather.'

'Uh oh,' said Bex, who was already making them a steaming pot of tea, 'looks like someone forgot to Slip Slop Slap like I warned!' Stanley glanced back at her sheepishly.

'I kept reminding him,' said Betty, 'but he thinks he's invincible.'

'I am. Inside, I'm still sweet sixteen.'

'Maybe so, but outside you're a hundred and sixteen!'

'What were the highlights?' Eve allowed her thoughts to linger briefly on her own memories of Melbourne - of summer barbecues, street-side breakfasts, languid picnics, laneway lunches, and amazing coffee... It really was wonderful, and how lucky she was to have had the opportunity to experience it all. Even with the pain of losing James, she'd never regret those experiences and opportunities for a moment - they had helped carve her path and shaped her into who she was now.

'Snorkelling the Great Barrier Reef,' Betty answered without hesitation. 'It was incredible!'

'Bloody fish everywhere – thought I might get eaten by a shark or stung by a box jellyfish! No, thank you - the grub on the ship was the *real* highlight.'

'The grub on the ship? What about Sydney Harbour Bridge? Uluru? The Opera House?'

Stanley patted the paunch of his belly - it seemed there was rather less give in his trousers than there had been before. 'Everyone knows the best thing about a cruise is the grub. Wouldn't have gone otherwise. Australia wasn't too bad either, though I'd rather stay put here.'

'I'm so pleased you enjoyed it.'

'Aye. Six courses there were!' said Stanley. 'Every night! And it was great sitting up on deck catching the rays.'

'Evidently.' Bex frowned.

'Anything exciting happened around here, then?' asked Betty as she regarded Bex' dyed grey hair with some scepticism. 'Apart from that.'

'Grey's all the rage these days.'

'Well, I wish someone had told me before I got my highlights put in.'

'Bex has gotten herself a boyfriend!' said Eve, unable to help herself.

Stanley was affronted. 'You mean you didn't save yourself for me?'

'Congratulations,' said Betty. 'Anyone we know?'

Bex gestured towards Harry with pride. He was looking particularly smart in his red checked shirt and black skinny jeans and was deeply engrossed in conversation with a member of their debate group.

'By, he's a handsome chap. Always did like a redhead - Stanley was a redhead once, believe it or not. And what about you, Eve, do I need to buy myself a new hat yet?'

Eve glanced at Thom who was still hard at work on the fireplace, characteristically unable to sit still for more than five minutes at a time. His skin held the sheen of exertion, and the sleeves of his t-shirt had crept up revealing the muscle and sinew of his arms. He felt her eyes on his back then turned to give her a slow smile that made her heart contract and her insides fizz.

'About time!' Betty grinned. 'Oh, I've just remembered.' She fished into the depths of her oversized tartan handbag and pulled out a packet of Tim Tams. 'These are for you girls to share - there was another pack, but *someone* ate them.'

'Don't look at me!' said Stanley. ''Try not to eat them all at once.'

Unable to resist a taste of home, Bex tore open the packet and grabbed a couple of the delicious chocolate biscuits. 'Now, I know it's not quite the QE2, but what can we get you?'

♥

As soon as he set foot outside of Newcastle Airport, his ears and nose clawed at unforgivingly by a biting wind and his cheeks assaulted by tiny balls of ice that flung at him most unnaturally in hard, horizontal whips, James realised his outfit was a mistake. He'd left Melbourne in a great hurry on the hottest month of the year, buoyant with anticipation and driven to act before his courage deserted him.

Now he found himself thoroughly unprepared for whatever lay ahead - would Eve still feel the same way about him as he did her, or had she moved on? If by some miracle she loved him still, would she be prepared to reinstate their engagement and make as though these dreadful months of separation had never happened? He shuddered. In the harsh light of day over thirty hours later, feeling sluggish and sleep deprived, this didn't seem to be quite as good an idea as he'd originally thought over a contemplative schooner. But there would be no turning back now - he only hoped he wasn't too late.

A grey sky fat with storm clouds hung ominously above, below the ground was sodden with mounds of hail banking up at its edges, and opposite beyond the airport's car park there was nothing but the bare sticks of lifeless looking trees James was convinced it would take more than the coming of spring to replenish. He suddenly craved the heat and comfort of home and felt a belated pang of sympathy for Eve who'd had to get used to the contrary for several years whilst struggling with an ever-nagging homesickness. He also empathised with the thoroughly miserable looking taxi driver however, who hurled his suitcase into the back of his waiting cab, about as much of an advert for the country as the weather.

It was hard to comprehend why Eve had deserted him in favour of returning to this bleak, barren land that robbed you of comfort and where nothing seemed to grow. Still, James was prepared to live wherever she wanted. He had come to realise that a life with her in it was by far better than one without - it was just a shame he hadn't figured it out sooner and that where she wanted to be wasn't a little more clement.

The orange-haired taxi driver, who looked as though his spirits had encountered one too many days like these, mumbled something in a Geordie accent so strong it was barely coherent.

'To The Melbourne!' James replied, hopeful this was the correct response to the question, as the icy water from the roadside puddle he'd accidentally stepped in when getting into the cab soaked its way through the fabric of his right shoe and saturated his sock, eventually causing him to lose all sensation in his toes, something he'd never before had cause to experience. England in winter he realised, as he ineffectually blew warm breath into his cupped hands, was even worse than he'd imagined. He now understood firsthand what it was that made the poms whinge. But he would put on a stiff upper lip. He was in Britain and that's what Britons do. It was where the woman who held his heart belonged, and he was sure that over time he would learn to love it too.

♥

As soon as he set foot outside of Newcastle Airport where he was heartily assailed by wind and hail, Paolo felt invigorated and purposeful. He breathed deeply of the icy air and pulled his scarf tighter about his neck, digging his free gloved hand deep into his pocket as the other wheeled his suitcase along behind him.

Yes, there was no doubt about it, the whiff of spring was in the air. Snowdrops and primroses, crocuses, and daffodils he knew by now would be risking a peep above their warm blankets of earth to see if it was yet safe enough for them to come out (spoiler - it never was). The nights were getting lighter and the days slowly longer. Birds that had spent the long winter in warmer climes would soon begin their migration home, welcoming in each new day with their sweet song. It was good to be back, thought Paolo cheerfully, and even better now he knew for what felt like the first time in his life exactly what it was he had to do.

'Paolo, mio figlio. My son.' Gianni kissed him on each cheek and patted his back in greeting. 'How is your mother?'

'Bene, padre, bene. And how is the restaurant?'

'Good, ees good.' Gianni nodded. 'We have new chef from Sicily. He is ok - not as good as me. I... Well, I have grown tired. I prefer to be front of house now. My hands are no longer what they used to be, and my lungs are not either.' Gianni took another draw of his cigarette then coughed noisily, blowing a plume of smoke in Paolo's direction. 'And since my son is determined to return to Italy, I am forced to look elsewhere.'

'I'm sorry, father, but I must chase my own destiny. You know you are welcome to return at any time to run my seafood restaurant with me.' Paolo had reopened Vista restaurant on his mother's property to rave reviews, and it felt good to make his home profitable again like it had been in the old days before his parents' separation. Though his mother had done all she could, she now benefited from the extra pair of hands and fresh vision and natural culinary talent of her son.

'No, no. We are a family of chefs, my father and his before me. I am happy you will continue in the family business even if it is back in Italy, and ees good for you to be close to your mother again. I will take holiday and visit you soon - I am in need of a holiday, and you are in need of my help in the kitchen.'

'And *you* need to quit smoking!' Paolo grasped his father's cigarette and stamped it out on the pavement. 'You love it here, don't you?'

Gianni considered. 'I have grown to love it here. Italy ees too hot, but I may return there some day - I miss the food. These English - they know nothing about flavour. Now,' he swiftly changed the subject as they made their way to the car, 'will you be dining with us tonight?'

'No. There is something I must do. Someone... I must see.'

Gianni regarded the determined set of his son's handsome jaw and hoped. Eve, he knew, would do his son good, but whether he would do her any good that he could not answer - it would take a strong woman to tame Paolo. He had never before seen Paolo so taken with one woman, especially not one who had initially refused him. Perhaps that was part of the appeal? Paolo reminded Gianni of himself when he was young, eagerly pursuing a path that led only to hurt, heartache, and divorce. Hopefully, he had learned from his papà's mistakes and would not be so stupid. Yes, it was high time Paolo settled down, and Eve was a lovely girl.

♥

'Divven't kna where The Melbourne is unfortunately, mate!' said the taxi driver, somewhat belatedly given they'd left the airport ten minutes prior. 'You sure it's not back in Oz where you left it? Haha.'

He really was a bit of a character. Customer service obviously wasn't his strong point, and judging from the way he was cutting in and out of traffic, it seemed that driving wasn't either. James hung onto his seat and regarded the ticking meter. He hoped he wasn't being ripped off - he'd heard all about the Geordies, or was it the Scots? He'd made the assumption that, being a local, the taxi driver would have heard of Eve's café. He couldn't check the details on his phone because the battery had gone flat, and he wasn't about to ask the driver to do it for him - it was safer if he maintained his focus on the road ahead. Never mind, he'd find it himself.

'All I know is that it's in the centre of somewhere called, erm, Heaton. Have you heard of it?'

Eve had never mentioned Heaton to James during their previous visits to her home, so he was surprised she'd chosen to set up her café there - surprised she'd set up a café at all, come to that. He knew that nursing had always gotten to her - it brought back memories of the loss of her older brother - but she'd had to do it to secure the visa that had allowed her to remain in Australia. It seemed she had finally found her niche, and James was as happy for her as he was proud.

'Aye mate, everyone's heard of Heaton. It's where all the rowdy students live who just happen to be the bane of my life. Central, you say?'

'Yes.'

'Well then I'll drop you on Chilli' Road, the main road that runs through there - you're bound to find what you're looking for. If not, use your tongue and someone should be able to direct you. Though what you've wasted your time coming all the way awa here for, in winter no less, I'll never know.' It was obvious he thought James was mad. 'It's summer awa there noo, isn't it?'

'Correct.'

'Always fancied gannin' te Oz me'sel! They say it's a better life.'

Eve didn't seem to think so.

The taxi driver's tone was wistful. 'Hear there's a demand for drivers awa there, but the wife's too frightened - all those spiders, sharks and snakes... Jellyfish and what have you!'

James rolled his eyes, bracing himself for the inevitable. He hadn't spent much time abroad, but most of the discussions he'd had with people from overseas were confined to the thornier end of Australian wildlife, a demand to hear about encounters he might have had with killer spiders or snakes, and the frequency with which he rubbed shoulders with the cast of Home and Away or Neighbours. Outside of this rather limited box they took little interest in his experience of what it had actually been like to grow up and live in Australia, preferring instead to bore him with tales of people he might know who had moved over there, or like the taxi driver, to expound their own dreams of a life in sunnier climes. Eve was about the only Brit he'd ever met who wasn't trying to escape this miserable isle.

'Here we are, then.'

The cab stopped abruptly at the very top of a long street with two-storey red brick terraced homes on either side interspersed haphazardly with shops, restaurants, and cafés.

It looked like the right place from the one picture of the café's facade that James had seen on social media.

'I don't fancy heading any farther down than this if that's ok - traffic's a nightmare 'roond here.'

The taxi driver had obviously never driven up Hoddle Street in peak hour, thought James, to whom the streets appeared positively barren. 'No worries, thanks.' He slipped the driver a twenty then braced himself as much for what he was about to do as for the chill he would encounter the moment he left the relative comfort of the cab.

♥ 26 ♥

During a brief lull, Eve brought Thom a cup of builder's tea heaped with sugar just the way she knew he liked it and encouraged him to take a break from his hard work on the fireplace. Reluctantly he agreed, giving Eve the opportunity to rest her aching feet and Thom the opportunity to rest a warm hand on her leg as they sat together in companionable silence.

She glanced over at Bex and Harry who were standing behind the counter sharing a giggle, Bex brushing his arm affectionately. Harry planted a little kiss on her shoulder when he thought no one was looking and she beamed. It was wonderful to see Bex so happy at last, and Eve was selfishly relieved that she no longer had any imminent plans to return home. She savoured the sensation of Thom's lean frame pressing against her right side and thought there was nowhere else in the world she would rather be at that moment.

'What are you thinking?' he asked.

'Nothing!' Eve tucked herself closer into his side.

Thom raised his eyebrows. 'If there's one thing I've learned about women, it's that you're always thinking of something.'

'Which is where we differ from men, who never think of anything!'

'That's not strictly true, we definitely think about *some* things.' Thom moved his hand a little higher up her thigh. Just then the doorbell rang as a pair of new customers walked in, and so as not to disturb Bex and Harry, Eve swatted Thom's hand away and leapt to her feet to greet them.

'I'm not exactly sure that qualifies as thinking,' she giggled. 'Besides, we have work to do - that fireplace isn't going to reveal itself, you know.'

'No, but I wish *you* would.'

'Later,' she promised. She could hardly wait for the afternoon to pass so that she could spend an entire evening with Thom. She picked up his empty teacup before seating her customers and offering them each a menu.

♥

There was a metro due at two-thirty. Paolo ditched his suitcase then indulged in a couple of stiff drinks with his father for liquid courage, all the while watching the clock and itching to get on with what it was he'd come back here to do. He'd gotten part way down the road before having to scurry home to borrow change for a ticket, forgetting in his befuddled haze that he had only Euro with him in his wallet.

'Good luck. *In bocca al lupo!*' Gianni yelled as Paolo dashed out the door for the second time.

He picked up his pace, tutting loudly when he realised that two of the station's three ticket machines were out of order, and an elderly lady with arthritic hands was at the other holding a purse laden with small change that she spent a considerable amount of time counting out then inputting slowly into the machine. Paolo tapped his foot. He'd have offered to do it for her to save them both time, but he didn't want her to think him a thief. He glanced up at the screens which indicated that his train would be arriving in exactly two minutes.

Just when he'd given up, a ticket emerged, and the old lady made a fumble for it before slowly wandering off. Paolo slammed a few pound coins into the machine, two of which were promptly spat back out again. He swore and stamped his foot, shoving them back in until they were finally accepted, and a beeping noise signalled the arrival of his printed ticket. He grabbed it before dashing through the barriers and making straight for the escalator.

He could already hear the screeching of the train as it barrelled into the station. To his dismay, the same elderly lady was standing directly in the centre of one of the escalator steps about halfway down, blocking his path with her bulk and bags. He made for the stairs, but just as he did so the train's passengers disembarked and a rush of bodies emerged stomping purposefully towards him, seemingly blind to his presence in their senseless clamour to get out of the station.

As Paolo forged his way through, bopped on the arm by one person then on the shoulder by another, he made it to the bottom of the staircase just in time to see the back of the lady's white head bobbing onto the train.

'Stand clear of the doors, please!' trilled the announcement as a warning tone sounded.

Paolo leapt for the doors, shoving a hand in to part them, but it was too late. He yanked his arm free before it got jammed and the doors closed gracelessly in his face. The last thing he saw as the train pulled away was a fuzz of white hair easing into a remaining seat. The next train was not for another fifteen minutes, which to an ardent Paolo seemed like a lifetime.

'Merda! Bastardo!' He kicked his foot upon the tiled floor to the mild interest of those on the platform opposite, then threw himself into a swinging yellow plastic seat to wait, his eyebrows knotted.

♥

How strange it was for James to find himself back in England again, amidst both the familiar and the unknown all at the same time. He had spent the past fifteen minutes moving from one indistinguishable terraced street to another. His teeth chattered, and he was convinced he had the onset of frostbite in his right toes. His suitcase was damp, and its load felt increasingly heavy for a man who'd had so little sleep and hadn't eaten a decent meal for a couple of days.

The thin sweatpants and hoody he'd donned in Melbourne for the purpose of passing a comfortable flight were ill-suited to the bitter cold. He sought shelter at a bus stop for long enough to root around in his suitcase, but nothing more suitable was forthcoming. From head to toe his clothing felt damp and cool to the touch, and he was chilled to the bone. But one thing he knew for certain was that he couldn't check into his hotel without first telling Eve how he felt. The thought sustained him as he walked from street to street, each one seemingly identical to the last. He swallowed his pride and determined he would ask the next person he saw for directions to The Melbourne, and hope they'd heard of it. Providence came in the form of a group of cheerful youths clutching leather satchels stuffed with laptops and textbooks.

'G'day,' he said. 'Can either of you tell me how to get to The Melbourne? It's a café somewhere round here.'

'Aye!' said the smallest member of the group. 'It's just roond the corner on Victoria Terrace. The easiest way is to go back the way you came - left onto Chilli' Road, straight ahead, third left, and then you'll see it.'

Which would pretty much bring James back to where he'd started – it must've been right under his nose all along.

'You'll love it, they do great coffee!' the lanky one enthused.

James, who'd been thoroughly disappointed with all of his coffee experiences outside of Australia, doubted that very much.

'We go to their study group,' the lanky one continued. 'There's free Wi-Fi and they don't seem to mind us hanging around.'

There was a murmur of assent.

'We're glad it didn't close down after the burglary,' said the small one. 'There's a rumour they even employ a thief, but he's actually really cute - if you're into beards...'

'He wasn't a thief - he was an addict,' the petite blonde corrected.

'He was homeless too apparently, but I heard he's sorted things out now.'

What kind of café *was* this? James wondered as he retraced his steps. Was Eve providing some sort of community service program to the northeast's young bogans?

He was so deep in thought that he almost careered into a purposeful-looking bloke with dark curly hair who sauntered along the pavement as though he'd just stepped out of an aftershave advertisement and was cruising the Champs Elysées in mid-summer rather than some remote outpost of Newcastle in mid-winter. He attracted more than a few admiring glances from the women nearby, and James envied him both his warm scarf and his good looks, then hurried his pace. *Tosser,* he thought, to coin an English term - sometimes 'drongo' didn't quite cut it.

In no time at all, he was opposite The Melbourne Community Café, a haven of warmth amidst the bleak, uniform terraces that had started giving him a headache. He hoped to get a brief glance at Eve from outside, but the bay windows were steamed with condensation providing only an indecipherable silhouette of those indoors.

A young couple pulled up in a flashy people-carrier, the male clutching a car-seat in which a tiny baby dressed from head to toe in pink nestled, fussed over by its mother. *Hang on, was that?* Yes, there was no doubt about it, it was Emily - Eve's best friend and staunchest defender. Paolo shuddered. When they'd visited for her wedding a couple of years ago, she'd had it out with James about his intentions towards Eve and his refusal to at least consider moving to the UK with her. Well, better late than never.

He waited. A couple of minutes later a smartly dressed and neatly coiffed middle-aged woman clutching a pile of books wandered into the café, deep in conversation with a gaggle of other ladies. There was something familiar about her. *Wait - was that?* No, it couldn't be. It was Eve's mother

- the last thing he'd wanted was an audience. His courage deserted him as he paced the street outside deliberating his next move. One thing was for certain, he couldn't tolerate the cold for much longer.

♥ 27 ♥

Paolo thought it was just typical that The Melbourne Community Café happened to be located at the absolute opposite end of Chillingham Road to the metro station. The proximity of his father's old restaurant to the metro station had never been an issue for him before, but still at least he had made it and now he was getting closer and closer to his beloved.

He picked up his pace, almost careering into a tall, athletic male dragging a cumbersome suitcase who had rounded the corner in such a hurry that he wasn't watching where he was going. *Bastardo!* Paolo muttered, and not for the first time. The man was handsome in a craggy, weather-beaten sort of way, and judging from the admiring glances of the women nearby he obviously wasn't the only one who'd noticed - though from his ridiculous outfit he was clearly ill-equipped to handle the British winter. It was a wonder he hadn't frozen to death!

The man apologised - *obviously not from round here,* thought Paolo when he heard his accent – *must be a New Zealander.* To their mutual irritation, it seemed they were headed in the same direction, and the Kiwi actually turned onto Victoria Terrace before him. Paolo was just about to do the same when a florist's shop on the corner caught his eye offering a welcome splash of colour amidst the dull winter whites and greys. He turned on his heel and made for the shop, recalling how much Eve had appreciated the rosemary he had given her from his hometown. This wouldn't be quite as exotic, but it would have to do.

♥

'Joy!' said Eve. She rushed over to the front door to fuss at the tiny bundle, who, sensing all the excitement around her had opened her eyes and let out a little moue. She was still such a delicate little thing at only a few weeks old.

'Joy? What about *me*? She gets all the attention these days.' Emily shook her head at the injustice. She looked tired but radiant as she smiled indulgently at her baby, in awe of the perfection she and Mark had created between them.

Eve hugged the pair and showed them to a table. It was wonderful to see them - she knew they'd had their hands full for the past few weeks looking after Joy. 'How have you both been?'

'Knackered,' said Mark.

'Shattered,' said Emily. 'This is the first time I've felt up to venturing out since we had her, and I've been going stir-crazy at home.'

'Totally worth it though,' said Mark.

'That's because you're not the one doing the night feeds.'

'I don't have breasts!'

'A poor excuse.' Emily took a seat then camouflaged her baby beneath a thin scarf to feed her. 'You and your bloody useless nipples.' From the relevant safety of the fireplace, Thom waved over at his sister and brother-in-law.

'You'll have to join our parents and bubs group next week - that'll get you out and about. You'd get to meet some other mums. I'm after someone to take the lead on that activity, actually, if you're interested?'

'Get back to me when I'm feeling human again.'

The doorbell rang again. 'Mam!' She glanced at the clock. It was bang on three - book club time. They were onto the Brontë's now. She hugged her mother then dashed behind the counter to help prepare the drinks for its participants, and Harry wandered over to take their orders.

'That's fine work you're doing over there for my daughter, Thom.' Carol gestured her approval at the fireplace. She had embraced Thom in a way she'd never quite managed to with James - but James could potentially have taken her daughter overseas for good whereas Thom didn't pose such a threat.

Carol fussed over baby Joy then settled down with the other women over at the activities bench. Clearing her throat, she brandished her copy of Wuthering Heights in the air, commanding attention. 'Bring me a slice of banana bread, will you?'

Eve was already plating it up.

'Strewth, it's been hectic today, hasn't it?' Bex had just begun to make a dent in the washing up.

'Certainly has,' Eve agreed. 'I'm so pleased you're staying on with us at the café. I couldn't do this without you.'

'Me too.' Bex smiled, and Harry grinned at her from the opposite side of the room. They were inseparable, and Bex couldn't imagine leaving him to go overseas for a minute, not quite yet anyway. 'Now, what have I told you to do whenever you get the chance? Practice makes perfect!'

Bex had been haranguing Eve to practice her coffee art for the past couple of weeks. She'd mastered a heart so far, but her leaf pattern still let her down. It was far easier to just get out the chocolate sauce and write a cheery message or draw a picture freehand on the foam, but that was the cheat's way out apparently, and didn't demonstrate any real skill. The doorbell rang yet again, and Eve groaned.

'Now's your chance!'

Only it wasn't another customer - it was Paolo, looking dapper as ever in his striped scarf and thick woollen overcoat, the collar turned up at the corners. Eve hadn't seen him since he'd gone back to Italy. Grateful of the opportunity to put off any further coffee art practice - Paolo drank his neat - she went over to say hi. Eve quickly realised he wasn't quite his usual self. He was clutching a bouquet of winter roses, and as she neared him, she noticed that his breath smelled of spirits, and he was slightly unsteady on his feet.

'Paolo, what a lovely surprise... Are you ok?' she asked, concerned.

'Eve!' Paolo drawled, fixing her with those chocolate eyes. 'Bella, *bella* Eve.' He shook back his damp black curls then reached out to clasp her hand in his after first proffering her the roses. Her customers paused to witness this spectacle in mild amusement and Emily tittered behind her hand.

Eve shifted uncomfortably from foot to foot as Paolo suddenly dropped to bended knee. 'I have come... to ask for your hand in marriage.'

The café fell silent, and Emily clasped a hand over her mouth. Thom almost dropped his paintbrush and crouched there in the nook of the fireplace with his mouth agape. Eve looked at Paolo in alarm - surely this was some kind of joke? But no, it seemed he was quite serious.

♥

Whoops, thought Paolo. His eyes widened as he regarded his curvaceous, hazel-eyed beloved. He was just as surprised at himself as everyone else was. He hadn't intended to ask Eve to marry him, and yet in the moment it had felt like just the right thing to do. He'd always thought getting married would mean the end of fun and freedom, but with the right woman, perhaps it was just the beginning? The concept was a novel one.

It seemed he was finally ready to settle down, and who better to settle down with than Eve? She understood him like no other woman ever had, and there'd been plenty. But *she* was different, it was as though she could see into his very soul! If it weren't for her, he would never have had the confidence to branch off from his father and forge his own path in life, realising his dream of opening a seafood restaurant back in his hometown in Italy. Most importantly, Eve was wholesome and loyal, reliable and considerate, not to mention gorgeous... Even his father recognised those qualities in her and had given Paolo his blessing. His mother would love her – she'd been pestering him to settle down for ages now.

Yes, Paolo surmised, Eve would make a fine wife. He was certain she was attracted to him too, and he respected her for not giving into his charms as easily as others had done before her. And she was sure to be over that drip of an Australian chap she'd been mooning over for months.

There was only one thing niggling at him. Whilst managing her own café would have given Eve a level of insight into Paolo's business that he would find greatly beneficial to their union, she seemed to love the little place so much he wasn't sure she would be willing to part with it. Still, she could always come over to visit regularly before their children came along, and her staff could probably run the place with their eyes closed anyway. The profits could even help Paolo develop *his* restaurant - he had grand plans for it, after all.

And if that wasn't enough, he was sure she would be seduced by the prospect of living in his family's sprawling, whitewashed farmhouse overlooking the Mediterranean Sea, with citrus trees and olive groves trailing the eyes down the hillside towards the steep cliffs below. Hot, languid days and long, sensuous nights. Fine wines and delicious food. She was sure to appreciate all that, who wouldn't?

Suitably reassured, Paolo fixed Eve with his most dazzling smile and awaited her response.

♥

Right, thought James, *if I stay out here any longer people will begin to think I'm an ice sculpture.* He was numb in places he'd never been numb before, a most disconcerting sensation.

A short time earlier, when he'd finally summoned the courage to go inside The Melbourne, the model-looking bloke he'd almost careered into earlier had turned the corner onto Victoria Terrace and wandered into the café, his sculpted face near-concealed by the flouncy bunch of flowers he held before him. An early Valentine's gift perhaps, no doubt for some equally stunning young lady. James had originally considered turning up on Valentine's Day too, but once the idea was in his head, he simply couldn't put it off any longer - it was now or never. And it sure would be a relief to get in out of the cold. Brr! He took a deep breath, his lungs instantly afflicted by the icy air, and entered The Melbourne Community Café.

♥

Eve peered down at Paolo where he rested awkwardly on bended knee awaiting an answer. Her palms grew damp in the warmth of his hands and her cheeks were aflame. It seemed to be getting awfully hot. She took a deep breath and looked about her hopefully, as though the answer of what best to say or do lay somewhere within the café's walls. Unfortunately, nothing was forthcoming. There was nothing else for it - she didn't want to hurt Paolo's feelings, but she didn't have a choice.

'Paolo, I...' she trailed off, the right words evading her.

Stanley coughed. 'I thought your new bloke was that one awa there!' He pointed at Thom, who was intrigued and mildly amused by the whole situation.

'What? The *builder?*' Paolo eyed Thom with a combination of shock and disdain.

He said it as though the very idea was inconceivable. Eve had been so caught up in the Australian guy when he'd last seen her that he hadn't anticipated the possibility of her meeting someone new in the meantime. He wasn't accustomed to being cast aside. He was normally the one doing the casting, and he didn't enjoy being on the receiving end one little bit. He studied his competition through narrowed eyes, but fortunately determined it to be in his favour.

The doorbell rang and in walked James, with his thin, damp hoodie clinging to his chest, emphasising his athletic physique. Eve's mouth hung open. Carol gasped. Paolo looked from Eve to Thom to the Kiwi and back again.

'Bloody Nora, how many men have yi got on the go, you dark horse?' Stanley was clearly enjoying all the drama. 'Is this a café or a knocking shop?'

'Stanley!' Betty shushed him. 'I'm trying to listen.'

Even Dave had made an appearance, conscious of the absolute silence that had descended beyond the door of his domain. Personally, he was vouching for the sexy Italian.

For Eve in that moment, everything and everyone else melted away until there was just her and James. It was a scene she'd played out in her daydreams a thousand times since she'd left him that Melbourne winter's day at the airport. With every knock of the door and every ring of the bell, this was what she had dreamed of. But he'd never come, and gradually she had lost hope then finally learned to accept what could never be.

Months had passed since that desolate afternoon at the airport had drawn them apart, and yet everything she had ever felt - all the love that had once burned within her for James – resurfaced as if it had never left. He was standing right before her just as she'd always hoped, and he'd come all the way to her home to find her, crossing the very last hurdle she'd so firmly believed would have led to their happiness.

'James!' she cried.

It was more an exhalation than a word - an exhalation that carried the full tumult of her emotions and Thom was sure he hadn't missed a single one of them. Suddenly things stopped being funny. He put down his paint brush and walked out of the café, the bell trilling frantically upon his exit as the door slammed shut behind him. Emily passed baby Joy over to Mark then ran outside. Eve was so caught up in James that she didn't even notice them go.

Paolo blinked in recognition. 'The Kiwi?' he spat, but James didn't seem to hear him.

'Uh-oh, she's blown it now,' said Stanley.

Betty sighed. In their forty-six years of marriage, they'd rarely agreed, but she couldn't help agreeing with him now.

♥ 28 ♥

James was acutely aware of what felt like a hundred pairs of eyes coming at him from all directions. He looked from Eve to Paolo, Paolo to Eve, and suddenly it all made sense. The handsome European on bended knee, the hastily purchased and extravagant bunch of flowers, the romantic proposal and public declaration of his love, the rosy flush that had seemed to warm Eve's cheeks with joy until *he'd* walked in - now she was simply staring at him open-mouthed.

The cosy picture the pair presented almost winded him, but unfortunately the penny had dropped far too late and now here he was, surrounded by at least a dozen witnesses to his folly and wishing himself safe in his bed back in Melbourne, which is precisely where he would have been had he not made the ridiculous decision to come here. He was a fool, he realised. He'd left it too late.

As he stood there feeling like a prize idiot and unsure of his next move, drips of water from his thawing tracksuit pants pooled at his feet. Until he heard her say his name, the faintest of whispers into the stunned silence that now enveloped them, he couldn't summon the courage to even look at Eve. But when at last he did, what he saw in her eyes gave him hope.

♥

Paolo gasped, then dropped Eve's hands and stood, sizing himself up against the sodden Kiwi who'd had the audacity to interrupt this most auspicious of moments. He was convinced that before they'd been rudely interrupted, she'd been about to say yes to his proposal - she was simply overcome with the romance of it all. He couldn't wait to tell his grandchildren all about it! But the Kiwi's unexpected appearance had disconcerted him, as had the old man's revelation that Eve had been bonking the builder too - though fortunately *he*'d had the sense to do a runner as soon as he'd realised she'd been playing him.

Paolo's mamma, the wisest woman he knew, had always said the quiet ones were the ones to watch out for. He'd never had Eve down as a scarlet woman, but now there was a ring of truth to his mother's warning. It seemed Eve was not quite as wholesome as she'd led him to believe, and when considered in this new light he was no longer sure he liked what he saw. Still, he was prepared to give her the benefit of the doubt just this once. Judging by the way he'd seen her looking at the Kiwi, he doubted he stood much of a chance, and was there any wonder given the competition? Paolo felt sorry for him. Almost. He eyed the puddles of water at James' feet with disdain and waited for his beloved to explain herself.

♥

'What... What are you doing here?' Eve asked James.

'Yes, what *are* you doing here?' Paolo spat, as he madly waved the bunch of flowers Eve had discarded, causing loose petals to flutter to the floor. 'Can't you see we're in the middle of something?' But James didn't seem to hear him. In fact, he and Eve hadn't broken their gaze once since he'd arrived.

Had it really been so long since he'd looked into those hazel eyes, ran his fingers through the silken strands of her hair, cupped her cheek and kissed those soft, full lips? She was even more beautiful in person than she'd been in his memories of her that had both comforted and tormented him these past months. He noticed there was a lean firmness to her figure that hadn't been there before, presumably as a result of all those hours spent on her feet. It suited her. And whilst her skin had lost its summer glow, she now seemed to glow from somewhere within.

He'd been a fool to let her go. He should have stopped her. He should have come with her! What had he been thinking? How he longed to cover the distance between them and hold her in his arms once again, but would she turn him away? He didn't think he could stand it if she did.

'Eve...' he cleared his throat. 'I haven't stopped thinking about you since we parted. When you left, you left a massive hole in my heart that nothing has been able to fill. I thought I'd be able to move on - we both knew it was hopeless. But we were wrong, Eve. *I* was wrong to let you go. It's taken time for me to realise that and all I can do is apologise. We Aussies can be a bit slow on the uptake sometimes,' he gave her a wry smile, 'but I realise it now, and I'm prepared to do anything it takes to prove that to you. I'll serve coffees, wait on tables, heck, I'll even live in England!' He shivered involuntarily at the prospect. 'Whatever it takes to spend the rest of my life with you. Because a life without you, Eve, is no life at all. So, I guess what I'm trying to say is,' it was now or never, 'would you consider reinstating our engagement, and spending the rest of your life with me?'

Ooh! Eve coloured.

There was a stirring about her as this piece of news sunk in - Eve and James had been engaged? Bex, who had found the whole thing rather entertaining until James' arrival, tucked her face into the crook of Harry's arm. She couldn't bear to look. Carol kept a tight grip on her husband to prevent him from creating a scene. Well, a bigger scene. Betty was on the edge of her seat, thrilled.

'What?' Paolo was dumbfounded. Ahh, so he was the Australian - not a Kiwi, after all. Now it made sense. Well, he wasn't about to let himself be thrown aside for that *idiota*. He took a deep breath before fixing his gaze upon the imposter. 'First of all, you break her heart. Second of all, you ignore her for months on end. Third of all, you have the gall to march in here looking like a drowned cat-'

'A drowned rat,' corrected Stanley from his favourite perch in the bay window.

'What?'

'The saying is, "like a drowned *rat*", not, "like a drowned *cat*!"'

There were a few muffled giggles.

'Shush, Stanley!' Betty flushed.

'If they're ganna live in our country and steal our lasses they should bloody well learn to speak our language.'

'You can barely speak it yourself.'

'Like a drowned *rat*,' Paolo continued. 'You really think she is gonna marry you now, huh, after all that? A man who took months on end to realise that he even wants her in his life? This is how they show love in *Austraylia,* is it? Pah!'

'He does have a point,' said Betty.

'This,' Paolo wrapped one arm around the small of Eve's back and clutched her opposite shoulder with his free hand, forcing her body close to his. 'This is how we do it where I come from...'

And he dipped Eve into a low back bend until her hair almost brushed the floor, then leaned in above her face fixing ardent, intent eyes upon her mouth before pressing his lips against hers. Loose rose petals fluttered to the floor around them. Paolo had been waiting for this moment since they'd met, and it worth the wait. His kiss was passionate, and Eve's eyes sprung open in surprise.

'Ooh!' said Betty. 'Get me a one-way ticket to Italy, pronto.'

'I could do that,' said Stanley, 'if my back didn't give me so much gip.'

So much had happened so quickly that afternoon that Eve was stunned, and she knew she needed to take control of the situation - letting it run its course had not proven too effective a strategy so far. She hadn't wanted to hurt Paolo's feelings, but it seemed she was going to have to, then maybe she could begin to get her head around what on earth James was doing at her café. When at last she recovered her strength, she pushed Paolo hard with the palm of her hand. He took a couple of steps backwards and looked at her, his anger rising.

'What? You mean to say you would pick this, this *rat* over me?' He pointed a mocking finger at James then wiped the back of his hand over his lips as though to wipe away the taste of her. 'An Aussie who is scared of the cold?'

'I may be an Aussie, but I am not scared of the cold. I'm merely unprepared.'

Both men looked at Eve expectantly. She took a deep breath. 'Paolo,' she began, 'I really am terribly flattered, if not completely astounded, by your proposal. Not only have you never struck me as the erm... the *marrying* type, but I never for a moment suspected you might have taken anything more than a fleeting fancy to me. I have no doubt there are women lining up to become the subject of your affections, but I'm afraid I am not one of them.'

Paolo was as unaccustomed to rejection as he was to competition. 'But I - I don't understand. I am offering you a chance to become my wife. To live with me in my beautiful hometown by the ocean. To run my new seafood restaurant with me back in Italy! My mother and father have certain expectations...'

'Like I said, I'm very flattered. But my feelings towards you are,' Eve struggled to put them into words, 'of friendship only. Marriage is such a big commitment you need to make sure you're doing it for you and not because it's what your parents expect of you. And I'm certain we could never make each other happy.'

Paolo's shoulders slumped. He supposed there was some truth in what she had said – though Eve would indeed make him a wonderful wife, he knew he couldn't be the sort of husband she deserved. He wasn't ready to settle down yet, and if he did, he would be doing it for the wrong reasons.

'I suppose you are right,' he countered. 'I am sorry for this. I will return to Italy, alone, and I suppose you will take this Australian. I very much hope this does not affect our friendship.' As he left, he proffered what was left of his flowers to James and patted him on a damp shoulder. 'Good luck, mite,' he mimicked his accent. 'Be good to her – you're a very lucky man. *Ciao!'*

It was his ego more than his heart that was bruised, and though Paolo didn't know it yet, at approximately eleven-PM that evening in the arms of a busty brunette he would meet on his train ride home, he would find himself overcome with blessed relief that this close encounter with commitment had passed him by. Gianni, despairing, would drown his sorrows in a bottle of port and pray for his son to settle down and make him a grandfather one day, preferably whilst he still had full use of all his faculties.

♥

'Oh, James!' said Eve, when Paolo was gone.

It was as though there was no one left in the world except her and him. No longer able to help herself and not caring who could see she covered the short distance between them and threw herself into his arms, closing her eyes and breathing deeply of his scent. There was such comfort in the familiarity of this man she had loved so well, it was almost as though they'd never been apart. She traced a wandering finger across his stubbled jaw. She could scarcely believe he was here beside her. Their time apart had etched a strain into his features that hadn't been there before, but he was still her James.

'I longed for you to come.'

Emily, who had reluctantly given up on her search for her brother, had returned to the café to find Eve and James mid-embrace. Askance, she gestured over at her husband, who, with a nod of understanding, eased their sleeping baby into her capsule and walked out.

'So did I,' said James, accidentally betraying a hint of the impasse that had separated them, 'but I'm here now.' He did *not* want to ruin this moment. 'I'm only sorry it took me so long.' He shivered again.

'You're freezing!'

He laughed. 'It was over thirty degrees when I left Melbourne, and choosing a suitable outfit was the last thing on my mind. It was now or never!'

Eve smiled. 'But I thought you'd started seeing someone else. I saw something online – it was a while ago now.'

James frowned, trying to recall what or who she might be referring to. 'Oh that,' he said. 'I was set up by some of the guys at work who were getting fed up with me moping over you. I did date a little after your left,' he didn't want to lie, 'but there was nothing serious. I couldn't help comparing everything to what I'd had with you, and nothing even came close.'

Eve nodded; her own experiences having proven similar. 'And you would really consider living here with me?' she prompted. 'In England?'

'Of course.' Though he didn't seem entirely certain.

The café was silent aside from the hushed breath and soft murmurs of her customers. Eve studied his face, wanting to believe him. If it had been six months or so earlier, she wouldn't have hesitated, but now things were different. She thought of Thom, and suddenly she knew what it was she had to do.

'Thank you,' she said sincerely, 'but I can't accept. I *know* you, and I know that living here could never make you happy any more than staying in Australia could have made me. I care too much about you to do that to you, to us, and I don't doubt that over time you'd resent me for it.' She paused. 'My life is here now. It's in the very walls of this café and it's all the people in it. I could never leave.'

'I wouldn't expect you to.'

'I know you wouldn't, but I'm pretty sure you'd be hoping that one day I might. I know I did!'

James knew she was right. For one thing, he hadn't stopped thinking about home since he'd left. Australia felt so far away right now it was almost unnerving - how had she managed to live abroad for so long? But then Eve liked travel and adventure, it was one of the things he'd admired about her, but it didn't mean he had to be that way too. He was content just as he was. Time apart hadn't changed anything, he realised, neither how he felt about her, nor the hopelessness of their circumstances.

'Six months or so ago I would have leapt at this chance for us to be together! I wanted it so bad I would have been prepared to throw aside the consequences and be selfish, kidding myself that this is what you wanted. But eventually it would have been the ruin of us. What we shared together was incredible and it will always be precious to me. We ended things at a time when we could still wish each other well and that's what has made it so hard for us to let one another go. But we need to, James, we need to free each other. We have to let go.'

'Yes.' he said simply. 'I'm sorry for coming here - for making it even harder on us both.'

'No... It means a lot that you would do this for me. Thank you - I know what it cost you to even consider it.' She shifted uncomfortably from foot to foot, unsure of where to go from here. There was nothing left for them to do or say. 'Stay for coffee?'

James became aware of his surroundings for the first time since he'd arrived at Eve's café. 'Hi Carol. Hello Robert,' he greeted her parents.

'Hi,' they responded awkwardly from the corner. Carol was beaming. It seemed there was still a chance that Thom might become her son-in-law after all - for a moment she'd been worried.

'Erm, thanks, but I think I'd better be going. I'm exhausted, and I'm pretty sure there's a flight back to Oz first thing tomorrow morning. I guess I'd better get some rest in the meantime.' That wasn't strictly true, he had no idea when the next flight was, but he sure as heck wasn't going to stick around any longer looking like a dill. The sooner he got home the better.

'I can give you a lift if you like?' said Eve. 'The others can cover for me.' There were polite nods from her staff.

'No need, no need.' If they spent any longer in one another's company, James knew he could never let her go. 'Me and the cabby are like this.' He knotted two of his fingers together.

'Good luck,' Eve whispered, hugging James close and kissing his cheek, her eyes glistening with unshed tears.

'Good luck to you too.' His voice caught. He squeezed her shoulder, smiled, then turned and walked away. All that was left to reflect his presence were two little pools of water on the floor where he'd been standing.

James didn't know it yet, but many hours later, warm and well rested back in Melbourne, he would find himself returning the calls he had missed from his colleague Isabelle with a renewed sense of vigour and interest that had been denied him whilst he'd still held Eve so close to his heart. Fortunately for him, Isabelle was as understanding as she was patient, and before he knew it James discovered that whilst nothing could ever match what he and Eve had had together, something altogether different could one day become just as precious.

'This is better than a night at the pictures!' Stanley grinned when James had gone. 'What else have we missed while we've been away?'

Eve released a breath then looked over to the fireplace expecting to find Thom, but there was no-one there. Puzzled, her eyes darted about looking first for Thom and then for Emily. Even Mark and baby Joy had gone.

'Where did they go?' she was frantic.

'They left, love,' said Carol.

Eve tore off her apron. She wasn't sure where to begin looking, but she knew she had to find Thom, and fast.

♥ 29 ♥

Eve hung up her mobile phone in frustration. She didn't know what to do. Thom wasn't returning her calls, and now it looked like Emily wasn't either. What an absolute mess she'd managed to make of everything.

She replayed the afternoon's events to try to see how it might have looked from Thom's point of view and flushed with embarrassment. She'd never told anyone about her brief engagement to James, so she was clearly going to have some explaining to do there, and her customers were probably left wondering if there was anyone in town she wasn't bonking, which, given the incident over Christmas could turn out to be either good or bad for business – only time would tell. It seemed The Melbourne had inadvertently become something akin to a real-life Rover's Return - no wonder they were always so busy!

What had happened that afternoon had been entirely unexpected, and it had all happened so fast, Eve had barely been able to process it at the time but could only react. Clearly, she'd reacted wrongly, and in doing so had given a terrible impression to those who meant most to her. She felt dreadfully guilty when she thought of how it must have all come across to Thom, and it shamed her to admit that she hadn't even noticed him leave.

James' arrival had been so confusing, and momentarily, everything she'd ever felt for him had resurfaced. It was a scenario she had dreamed of for months after their separation. She'd replayed it in her head countless times -

285

how she would act, what she would wear, what she would say... How James would declare his undying love and his willingness to drop everything to move to England to be with her. Then after a snowy white wedding, they'd live happily ever after in a large old house with period features something like Emily's and make lots of beautiful babies! When he'd turned up out of the blue prepared to offer her all those things, it had understandably caught her off guard.

Surely her reaction was a normal response to the unexpected reappearance of the man she had loved so deeply for so long, the same man she had once imagined spending the rest of her life with? And in the moment, she'd had the feelings of both Paolo and James to consider - it was in her nature to protect others from pain rather than to be the cause of it. She was sure Paolo would recover quickly - it was his pride and not his heart she had wounded. But James, well, all she could hope for was that he would soon find someone closer to home to love. She and James had exhausted the path they had tread together and they both needed to find their own ways to go - alone.

Eve continued pacing the uniformly terraced streets of Heaton without destination. The pavement shone from the morning's blanket of melted hail, and she suddenly found herself longing for spring and for a reprieve from this long, arduous winter. Her cheeks were red from exertion, high winds tugged her hair across her face, and her constant battle against the elements gave the illusion that she was making some headway into resolving this mess, even though the infuriatingly blank screen of her mobile phone showed otherwise.

It was one of life's many ironies that it took the loss of something precious to make you appreciate its value. Being faced with the prospect of losing Thom had crystallised just what he had come to mean to her, what she had been denying in still being hung up on James and thinking that the loss of him represented the end as far as she was concerned. She'd been wrong. She had to find Thom and tell him how she felt. She turned abruptly and made for the car. This time, she wasn't prepared to let him go.

Emily was haughty. 'What are *you* doing here?' She blocked the doorway to her magnificent home with her body. She was holding baby Joy in her arms, who gave a little howl of displeasure as much from exposure to the cool air outside as from her mother's tone.

'Please let me in,' Eve pleaded, 'I'd like to explain.'

'From where I was sitting there doesn't seem to be much to explain.'

'Whatever you might be thinking - you're wrong.'

Emily sniffed, bouncing Joy gently in efforts to soothe her. She was on the verge of relenting.

'You can come in, but I might as well warn you that he isn't here.'

'He isn't?' Eve's disappointment was obvious. 'I've been trying to call him, but he doesn't want to talk to me.'

'I wonder why.' The tone was dry, but Emily opened the door anyway and moved aside to let Eve in.

'Do you have any idea where he might be?' she asked when they were finally seated. 'I went over to his place first, but he wasn't there.'

'How about you explain, then I'll decide whether I should tell you where he is or not.'

Eve shifted in her seat. It seemed Emily had ushered her into one of the hardest, most uncomfortable chairs she owned – a classic case of style over substance. Mark ducked in to relieve them of the baby, scooting right out of there after throwing Eve a polite smile. Meanwhile, Emily looked daggers at her and waited for her to begin. Eve spared a thought for any employees of hers who might have had the misfortune to find themselves on the receiving end of her wrath.

'Marrying James after all then, are we? How could you? After leading my poor brother on for months and all the while it seems you were just using him to get your café into shape. And what on earth was that ghastly scene with Paolo - have you been seeing him too without telling me?'

Eve was aghast. 'Of course not, is that what you think?'

'Well, if my best friend can't even tell me she was engaged to be married, why would she bother telling me if she's been shagging the waiter?'

Now Eve was defensive. 'I can assure you that nothing has been going on between me and Paolo - what happened at the café came as much of a surprise to me as it did anyone else. I don't know what on earth came over him - one too many whiskies judging by the smell of him. I want more than a fling, which is all Paolo can offer.'

'Yes, you want more. With James.'

'No. With Thom.' This time Eve knew it for an absolute certainty.

'But what about your engagement?'

'There *is* no engagement - James is a part of my past. In a few hours he'll be at the airport catching a flight home to Melbourne, and this time he will not be coming back. It's over between us. Finito.'

Emily still wasn't convinced.

'I didn't tell anyone about the engagement because it didn't feel like an engagement. From the moment James gave me the ring everything felt wrong somehow, and I knew it wasn't meant to be. An engagement is supposed to be feel right. But it didn't feel like the beginning of something wonderful - it felt like the end.'

'So that's the real reason you came home.' It was more of a statement than a question.

'Yes.'

'I wish you'd been able to talk to me about it sooner - I would have understood.'

'I know. I just needed time. Until James proposed, even though we'd had our disagreements over where we wanted to live, I always thought we'd work things out and it would all turn out ok. Until then, it hadn't crossed my mind on any serious level that it might not. And to come back home and start all over again, in my thirties no less, made me feel like a disappointment. You did everything the right way - career, house, marriage, babies... I stuffed it all up. Then, when I did get back here, things got so busy with the café... It turned out to be the perfect distraction, and I have you to thank for that.

If you hadn't been so encouraging, I would have missed out on the opportunity to create this career that I love.'

'Yes, and if it wasn't for me finding the perfect premises you would never have met sexy Paolo and would never have received two marriage proposals in one day,' Emily laughed. 'If my own brother wasn't involved, I would have been eaten up with jealousy!'

Eve giggled, relieved that they seemed to be on firmer ground again.

'So where does all this leave things with Thom?'

'I honestly don't know. I know I haven't been very fair to him. Since we've met again as adults, it's as though I've kept a piece of my heart locked away out of his reach. But James' appearance at the café today undid all that - it cemented that I made the right decision when I left that relationship behind me. And while I'll never again experience what I had with James, I know now I can have something altogether different but equally as special - more so, in fact, because it will be based on a foundation that works for us both. We won't have the odds stacked up against us that James and I had.'

'Hang on,' Emily shrank back from her. 'Are you saying you want to be with Thom for convenience's sake?'

'Of course not! I want to be with Thom because over time I've come to love the person he is. I know I've messed him around - drawn him in closer then pushed him away - and I'm so very sorry for that.' Eve was sincere. 'But it wouldn't have been fair of me to pursue him if I wasn't completely sure I was invested, and I am. Completely. Even though Thom can't recognise a good coffee when he tastes one, I can live with that because he is the sum of so many wonderful things and I love him for all of them. He's the sort of person who makes me want to be better and do better, and I can't imagine living my life without him.' Eve's eyes filled with tears. 'I just can't believe I've gone and stuffed it all up, right when things were finally moving forwards between us.'

'I'm sure there's still a chance for the two of you,' Emily reassured her. 'You know what they're like when their pride has been wounded.'

'You think so?' Eve was too scared to hope.

'I *know* so. Give him some space and wait for him to come to you.' Emily glanced at the clock on the living room wall, and as if on cue a wail emanated from the kitchen. 'Now I hate to rush you out of here, but it looks as though it's time for me to start Joy's bedtime routine.'

Eve dabbed at her eyes. 'Then I'll leave you three in peace. Thanks Emily, and I'm so sorry if I hurt you. You know I love you like a sister.'

'Likewise. I'm sure everything will look more hopeful tomorrow. If I see Thom, I'll let him know you were here.'

It was the run-up to Valentine's Day, and Eve wasn't feeling very hopeful, but she took the hint, hugged her friend goodbye, then made the drive back to her parents' house in anxious spirits.

When the door had closed behind her, Emily sighed. She'd felt awful bustling Eve out like that and lying to her about Thom.

'Has she gone?' Thom asked as he stepped out of the kitchen looking wretched. He'd been too angry to face Eve in person and hadn't known what else to do when she'd suddenly presented at Emily's house other than to hide in the kitchen where he'd inadvertently managed to overhear their entire conversation.

'She's gone. But if *that* won't make you go after her then I don't know what will.'

'I've gone after that woman one too many times now,' said Thom darkly.

♥

'Everything all right, love?' Carol asked.

Eve had made a huge effort to pull herself together before she got out of the car, but the smudges of black mascara beneath her eyes betrayed her. She felt a stab of guilt for having put her parents through the mill since her return home from Melbourne.

'An eventful afternoon, that was, eh?' Robert whistled before pulling Eve into a hug. She squeezed him back. 'I think we should start selling tickets to your café.'

'It certainly was,' said Eve. 'Is Bex home yet?' She was keen to find out how the rest of the afternoon had gone after she'd left - she was worried that with any more displays like today's, she might start scaring her customers away.

'She locked up not long after you left,' said Carol. 'Something about going to view a flat with Harry.'

'Oh yes, I'd forgotten about that.'

They'd asked to close-up a little early that afternoon and Eve had been happy for them. It meant that Bex had decided to stick around in Newcastle indefinitely, or for as long as her visa allowed. Eve supposed it was high time she thought about moving out too. However dire her intimate life was, things were going so well with the café, there was no excuse for her to continue impinging on her parents' generosity. It was time they had their house back to themselves and stopped getting first-hand exposure to their thirty-year-old daughter's antics. And as for love, she would just have to wait and see where life took her.

♥ 30 ♥

It was Valentine's Day. If you were lucky, it was a day for lovers. If you were unlucky, you might argue it was a day to stay indoors and hope for better times ahead. This year Eve fell into the latter camp. Still, she'd hate to do her customers a disservice, so she'd painstakingly overseen the fitting-out of The Melbourne to lend a dutifully romantic theme to the day.

The tables were adorned with pink and white roses, heart-shaped bunting was strung across the ceiling, and candles glowed romantically in the bay windows. Betty and the crafts group were responsible for many of the creative little touches here and there – primarily in the form of a riot of hearts and flowers made from every conceivable material, and their wares were selling almost as fast as the heart-shaped treats Bex had coaxed Eve into baking the previous evening. Dean Martin's crooning filled the air, and the dim light of a short and misty winter's day made one long for little more from their fellow man than comfort and warm cuddles.

Some bloody Valentine's Day thought Eve, who had been uncharacteristically grouchy all morning. She'd had her fill of romance for one lifetime, and if she had to serve even just one more doe-eyed young couple in love, she'd throw up her breakfast, which would be a shame since Dave had made a particularly nice one that morning in efforts to cheer her up. It hadn't worked. She let out a long sigh.

'Oh puh-lease,' said Bex. 'Go and take a break, would you? You're depressing me. I can't take any more of your mournful sighs.'

'What mournful sighs?'

'The ones you've been making every five minutes since you got here this morning. If you don't stop it, you'll put people off their food, which isn't a good business strategy.'

Eve sighed. 'Ok, ok. You're right...'

'Course I'm right – I'm Aussie. Now scoot and try coming back with a little more enthusiasm.'

'We're so busy - I can't leave!'

'I hate to say it, but you've been more of a hindrance than a help since you got here - dragging that skinny butt of yours around as if it weighs a hundred pounds.'

There was a nod of agreement from Harry, who'd caught a little of what had passed between the two women.

'It does weigh a hundred pounds, actually,' said Eve. 'Heartbreak does that to you, not that you and Harry would understand.'

Bex played an invisible violin. 'My *head* weighs more than you do. And as you know, it hasn't exactly been plain sailing for us either.'

They were interrupted by a doe-eyed young couple in love, and the female of the partnership was pointing enthusiastically into The Melbourne's display cabinet.

'Wow, look at those cute heart-shaped lamingtons!' she said. 'We must have one.'

'Ooo,' said the guy. '*You* have one. I can't - it'll ruin my diet.'

'But it's Valentine's Day!'

'I know, but...'

'Perhaps you could order one to share,' said Bex, 'and I'll bring you over an extra fork. See how you go. There's plenty more if you still have room.'

'You could even feed it to each other,' said Eve, but the sarcasm was lost on them. 'It'd be *terribly* romantic.'

'Great idea!' Hand-clasped, the pair disappeared off to their table.

Eve cut through the kitchen and made straight for the back yard which they hadn't planned on using over winter, but on special occasions like this one they tended to get so busy there was no choice. Dave, who was usually something of a grouch, was humming to himself as he worked. He was expertly flipping pancakes and throwing in a few well-timed hip wiggles for good measure. He stopped guiltily when he saw Eve, who gave him a look that would turn Medusa to stone. He was about to say something, then clearly thought the better of it, and his mouth formed something between a smile and a grimace until he was out of her line of sight.

Eve had walked in on him only that morning telling Bex and Harry his good news – that after a passionate, whirlwind romance, he and Tony were moving in together! Dave had never made such a big commitment before, and he was so excited he could burst. He just hoped they weren't going to have to walk on eggshells around Eve for too much longer - she'd been something of a party pooper of late.

Everywhere Eve looked there were couples, rosy cheeked from the heat of the outdoor heaters. She forced a smile at some of her regulars then cut through the gate leading out onto to the cobbled lane where she gasped in some air. She couldn't afford to cry - it'd be obvious and would ruin her make-up. *Breathe*, she told herself.

She was lost in her thoughts when she heard a curious 'meaow.' She looked down, and sure enough, there was the anonymous little grey cat that often hung about the café meandering towards her - she still hadn't figured out who he belonged to. Eve was relieved to see it, and she hunkered down on her knees and reached out a hand to stroke its soft fur. The cat meaowed in response, rubbing its cheek against her as it circled her legs.

'You always know just when to come along and make me feel better, don't you?'

He purred in response, turning his face up to invite a scratch of his chin. He was almost like a big brother in feline form, looking out for her just when she needed it most. Eve pushed the crazy notion away.

After a while, she could feel the tension in her neck and shoulders begin to disperse. She knew she'd been a miserable cow of late and that she needed to cheer up and make more of an effort to be nice to her staff and customers. Everyone had been walking on eggshells around her, and it wasn't fair and had to stop. There were lots of people like her she knew, who didn't have much to celebrate on Valentine's Day, it was just that unlike her they probably had the option of staying home. Eve had had her fair share of being among the lucky ones, and now it was her turn to be left in the shadows, but it wouldn't be this way forever - she was bound to find someone else. Eventually. And what was the point of the whole day anyway?

She tried to picture it, but man of her future's face was blank. She simply couldn't imagine herself with anyone other than Thom, who loved her and had done everything in his power to demonstrate that to her. He'd been a listening ear in the early stages of her break-up from James and had dropped everything several times to lend his skills at her café just because he cared about her so much. Steadfast, faithful Thom, who had left her in no doubt of how he felt about her through his repeated acts of kindness and generosity, all the while waiting patiently for her to come to him. And when she was finally ready, when she'd finally realised that she loved him too, it was too late.

Idiot! She was getting upset again, and the little cat peered up at her, sensing it.

'Meaow.'

'Oh, I'm sorry,' Eve sniffed, stroking him gently and soothed by the softness of his fur. 'You really are such a beautiful little thing.'

'You're not bad yourself.'

She stopped. She knew that voice. She stood and turned slowly, scared that if she sprung up as fast as she wanted to, the mirage would simply disappear. The cat scampered.

'Thom?' She opened her eyes - had barely realised she'd closed them - and there he was standing before her, a welcome figure emerging from the mist. Sandy hair, blue eyes, and as paint splattered as ever.

'Eve.' He smiled, wielding a paint brush. 'I think it's high time I finished off that fireplace of yours.'

'Thom!' She threw herself into his arms, and he sought her mouth and kissed her deeply.

'Forgive me,' he said, between kisses.

'Forgive *you*?'

'Yes! When I saw you with James, I didn't like it. I was jealous. I knew how you'd felt about him, and I was certain that would be the end of things between us. I'd waited for you for so long and tried so hard to be patient, but that day it looked like it had all been for nothing. I thought you'd never come back to me.'

Eve looked earnestly into Thom's eyes. 'When I left James behind in Australia, I left him for good. As much as it hurt, I knew in my heart it was the right thing to do. I wouldn't have opened The Melbourne if I wasn't committed to my decision to stay in England. I think James came over here because he hadn't resolved all that for himself yet.'

'I see that now,' said Thom, 'and I suppose I can't blame him for coming to you. *I* would - it just wouldn't have taken me so long.'

'You would?'

'I'm here now, aren't I?'

'Yes.' She reached out and touched his face. 'I love you, Thom.'

'I love you too. I think I've always loved you, ever since you were a freckled little thing with frizzy hair. My sister's sexy best friend.'

Eve pressed her lips to his, savouring the warmth of his mouth against hers. 'Well, now we've cleared that up,' she said, 'what are you doing out here slacking when there's so much work to be done inside? And I did *not* have frizzy hair!'

'Is this how you're treating your staff these days? You've spent way too much time with my sister - she's inside with Mark and the baby, by the way. And you had the frizziest hair!'

'She is?' Eve ignored him. After all, she wasn't the one who'd wet the bed at Emily's sleepover back when they were kids, though she was sure he wouldn't thank her for reminding him - she'd save that particular jibe for a rainy day.

'Yep. Said she's been going mad stuck indoors all the time and is looking for a new child-friendly project to set her teeth into while I hold the fort with her business.'

'Motherhood isn't proving a big enough project for her?' Typical Emily.

'She wants to run your parents' group.'

'That's fantastic!' The community program, Eve had discovered, was always more successful when there was someone to take the lead on any given activity. 'I should go in and talk to her about it.'

'I think you should.' Thom draped his arm about her to create their own cosy haven of warmth and protection against the elements and off they went.

♥

Eve was beaming when she re-entered her café, and Dave gave a little hip wiggle of approval as she and Thom cut through his domain.

'It might be a bit early for me to say this,' he ventured, 'but I know of a great flat that's going for rent around here.' He pointed up at the ceiling.

'Oh, yes!' said Eve, 'I didn't think of that.'

It was high time she moved out of her parents' place, and since Tony was moving in with Dave soon, the upstairs flat would be vacant. She and Bex could be housemates - the place she'd gone to view with Harry the previous week had been too expensive apparently, but Tony's flat was affordable, and they'd be so close to the café she had already calculated how much of a lie-in they'd get each morning.

'Well,' said Thom, squeezing her waist, 'there's no time like the present.'

Eve's eyes widened with surprise. 'You mean?' She hardly dared to speculate.

He nodded. 'I think we've waited long enough to be together, don't you?'

'It's only a two-bed, but the rooms are a decent size,' said Dave. 'At a pinch there should be just enough space for the four of you.'

'Just wait until we tell Bex and Harry!'

Dave grinned, relieved that the time for walking on eggshells was finally over.

'Well,' said Bex looking from one to the other, 'who knew that a breath of fresh air could work such wonders? Though you might want to reapply your lipstick, pet.' She borrowed a Geordie term of endearment, which had he heard it, would have impressed old Stanley.

Thom resumed his post at the fireplace. 'I'd like a cup of builder's tea, please,' he instructed. 'Extra hot, just like me.'

'Coming up!' Eve singlehandedly worked on a couple of other orders too since she'd finally mastered the art of making successive hot beverages at once.

There was the welcome hiss of frothing milk followed by the rich, comforting aroma of roasted coffee. Whilst the espresso was brewing, she threw a teabag for Thom into a mug with a couple of sugar lumps – she'd given up trying to convert him to the finer things in life, there would be plenty of time for all of that. Around them, the café hummed with the conversation and laughter of friends and lovers. Right now, Eve thought there was nowhere she would rather be and nothing she'd rather be doing than this. When she thought about the changes she had made in her life over the past few months, she had no regrets whatsoever.

After handing out a pair of lattes to her customers and taking a steaming mug of tea over to Thom, Eve suddenly found herself enveloped in Emily's arms, and even Mark tore his gaze away from baby Joy for just long enough to smile at her in greeting.

'If we're going to be sisters, this time you two had better make it work - especially since you're both going to be godparents to our baby girl!'

Eve flushed with delight at the news and hugged her dear friend. 'Oh, we will,' she reassured her. 'This time.' She smiled over at Thom, her face aglow with love for this beautiful man she was so proud to at last be able to call her own, and to belong to him in return. This time there would be no letting go.

'So,' said Betty to her husband from their usual perch by the bay window, 'looks like it's all's well that ends well.'

'Aye,' Stanley replied, relieved that everything seemed to have worked out for this exceptional group of young people they had become so fond of, even Bex! 'Now then, love,' he licked his lips, 'how about sharing one of those lamingtons?'

Outside and noticed by no-one, the little grey cat who had looked upon the afternoon's events with a keen eye from the vantage point of the bay window, seemingly satisfied, dipped his head then leapt gracefully from his narrow perch before disappearing into the winter mist that now enveloped The Melbourne Community Café.

The End.

Acknowledgements

Dear Reader,

Thank you for reading *Meet Me at The Melbourne*. Having lived overseas in Australia for the past fifteen years, it was a pleasure to revisit my home through the telling of Eve's story. MMATM was largely written over a latte in a selection of my favourite cafés between each of the two countries, and the creative process helped me adjust to this new life abroad. I am now lucky enough to call both cities home, and fortunate that here in Melbourne, the best coffee is never more than a block away.

I would like to thank my husband, Steven, for reading through endless drafts and revisions of MMATM, though romantic women's fiction is not exactly his genre; my parents, Janice and Jeff, for all their encouragement despite my mam's unshakeable belief that the only way to write a good story is to kill off the main characters; and my Aunty Sharon, who has been a constant source of support throughout this journey. I would also like to thank some of my earliest readers including Skye, Jenny A, Jenny P, Rachel, and Louise for motivating me to keep on going. Thank you to Roz Wyllie, author of *Everything You Ever Wanted*, for mentoring me as a young adult who hoped to become a writer one day. Thanks also to Spencer J for bringing *The Melbourne* to life through his beautiful cover art.

Most of all, thank you for taking the time to read Eve's story - it was such a pleasure to write. Your feedback is valued and you're always welcome to connect with me via my website, Instagram, or Facebook. A review is one of most helpful ways to support an emerging author and would be gratefully received and much appreciated.

As you might imagine, it was hard to leave Eve and Thom and their community behind, so the next part of their story can be found in *Marry Me at The Melbourne,* where wedding bells chime against the stunning backdrop of Paolo's coastal hometown in Italy.

Very best wishes,

Gemma Frances

www.gemmafrances.com

@gemma_frances

About the author...

Gemma Frances is a married mum from Newcastle upon Tyne, UK currently living in Melbourne, Australia. She qualified as a Social Worker and has worked with children and families ever since. Her dream of travelling the world as cabin crew was never quite realised, as her interview was cancelled during the Global Financial Crisis, and she was left with an approved career break but nothing to do (which is probably for the best, as she now has a fear of flying!). Armed with a round-the-world flight and a suitcase (never a backpack), she travelled to Australia on a gap year, fell in love with her husband, and the rest is history.

Meet Me at The Melbourne is the winner of Dick and Angel Strawbridge of the TV show *Escape to the Chateau's* Literature Competition in 2020 and was originally published through The Chateau Publishing Limited in 2021.

Ask the author...

How long did it take to write MMATM?

A whopping 2.5 years. Having wanted to write a book since I was a child, my thirtieth birthday was the catalyst I needed to finally put pen to paper and persevere through writer's block.

What was the inspiration behind Eve's story?

One of the things I enjoyed most about moving to Melbourne was catchups with friends that would often revolve around delicious brunches and great coffee at cafés bursting with character, quirk, and charm. Before I left the UK, coffee culture wasn't as established as it has since become. The flavours here were fresh and exciting - especially for someone who has always loved their food. Those factors combined with feeling at a crossroads around a future either in Australia or a return home to the UK led to the idea for Eve's story.

What message do you hope your readers will take away from MMATM?

Eve's story is of community and inclusion, and the message I hope readers take away is of the importance of making room for others. Melbourne is a diverse city, and there is something very special in being able to come together with all our differences, creating new opportunities for connection and growth.

What's been the best part of the writing process for you?

For me, characters I'd never envisaged writing themselves into the story was the most enjoyable part of the process, aside from the relief of seeing a project all the way through from beginning to end for the first time, and proving to myself that I could do it (which has made it a lot easier to do it again). Paolo and Gianni emerged from nowhere and entwined themselves into Eve's story, adding a new dimension that doesn't detract from the original idea but complements it. It was a joy getting to know Paolo and Gianni in this way.

Do you have any advice for aspiring authors?

It's a tough business and rejection is all part of it. Don't get discouraged, and don't stop writing. Like any skill, the more you write the stronger your writing will become and the more insight you'll gain into what works and what doesn't – the most important thing is to keep that forward momentum going. If this project doesn't lead to the outcome you hoped for, it's still a steppingstone in the right direction, and in that respect it's of enormous value.

How do you take your coffee?

This changes periodically, but it's currently a decaf cappuccino with almond milk, always ordered with an apology to the poor barista who ends up making it. A 'large' coffee that isn't actually large is surely a crime against coffee and quite likely to ruin my morning, so I tend to choose my cafés carefully. In this respect, bigger is always better!

Book Club Questions...

- How did MMATM make you feel?

- Which MMATM character did you connect with most?

- Eve moved back to England when she was at a crossroads. What would you have done in her position?

- Eve feels pressure to have her life 'together' by 30. Is this fair? Discuss.

- Three men pursued Eve; did she make the right choice?

- Do you think Thom should have waited for Eve?

- Do you think Bex and Eve were right to take a chance on Harry?

- Do you think Harry was right to support Stacey despite all that had happened between them?

- How well did The Melbourne Community Café meet its aims?

- What was the role of the cat in Eve's story?

Also by Gemma Frances

The Melbourne Community Cafe
Meet Me at The Melbourne

Worthington Manor
The Debutante

Standalone
Fractured

Watch for more at www.gemmafrances.com.

www.ingramcontent.com/pod-product-compliance
Lightning Source LLC
Chambersburg PA
CBHW020225260626
47156CB00002B/534